The Strife of Riley

a novel

De-ann Black

Toffee Apple Publishing

Text copyright © 2010 by De-ann Black

All rights reserved.
No part of this book may be used or reproduced in any manner whatsoever without the written consent of the publisher.

This is a work of fiction. Names, characters, places, and incidents are either products of the author's imagination or are used fictitiously. Any resemblance to actual persons, living or dead, businesses, companies, events, or locales is entirely coincidental.

Published by Toffee Apple Publishing

The Strife of Riley

First edition 2010

ISBN-13: 978-1-908072-09-2

Toffee Apple Publishing

To my father, Joe Black

Fortis Fortuna Adiuvat

Fortune Favours the Brave

By Strength and Guile is the motto of the Special Boat Service (SBS). The SBS is a highly secretive British Special Forces unit. Comparable to the SAS, they are the Royal Navy's elite, although nowadays men are selected from various UK military services, not just the Royal Marines.

The SBS are specialists on both land and water, though excel in amphibious operations, and are skilled Swimmer Canoeists. Their physical abilities, intelligence and skills to survive hostile situations are incredible.

This elite fighting force are sometimes known as the Invisible Raiders, and combine an extraordinary level of secrecy, stealth and guile.

Contents

Introduction		1
1	The Record Keeper	3
2	Imagery Intelligence	19
3	A Hunter's Game	35
4	Fortune Favours the Brave	47
5	Luck of the Devil	63
6	No Rest for the Wicked	78
7	Beyond This There Be Dragons	90
8	HMS Excalibur	112
9	Dark Matter	124
10	The Edge of Nowhere	143
11	Cape Wrath	159
12	The Poison Code	174
13	Invisible Raiders	193
14	Shadow of the Warrior	213
15	It is Rocket Science	232
16	Special Forces	249
17	Viva Glas Vegas	269
18	The Dark Side	288
19	The Uncorruptables	306
20	By Strength and Guile	324

Introduction

Riley had been part of the SBS, the Special Boat Service — the British Royal Navy Special Forces unit. His last link with them was at HMS Excalibur, the submarine base near Helensburgh, Scotland. It was set beside the dark and unfathomable Gare Loch, north of Glasgow in the Firth of Clyde. He was also an experienced historian, raised by his father who was known as the Record Keeper, amid a world of ever changing history. History was to become Riley's future, but first, the past had to be dealt with.

As fate enjoys many cruel twists, his father died around the time Riley decided to leave the Special Forces and assume the supposed anonymity of a civilian. Riley became the new Record Keeper, more through a sense of responsibility rather than choice, but he was fine with that. Being the Record Keeper was his background career, while he concentrated on his own business as a modern private investigator. Riley was a cyber sleuth, an expert in computer related crime, a man at the top of his game, trained by the best — unravelling mysteries and tracing the electronic fingerprints we all leave behind every time we use a computer.

    Riley had been one of the military's most reliable, ruthless and renowned cyber experts. In civvy street, his skills were soon in demand from the police, the government and oh yes, the military. Riley had left their building, but they still wanted him to keep his foot in the door.

Chapter One

The Record Keeper

It had been two years since Riley's past had become history. A former member of the SBS, his last adventure with the military had dealt him his biggest measure of strife. But that was finished with. Now he was a civilian. Twelve years in the British Royal Navy had left their mark. Eight of those years in the Special Forces had scarred him forever. Aside from that, he looked just as fit as he'd always been, over six feet tall and strong, perhaps even stronger than before, and at thirty-four, only slightly older. Older but wiser? Well, probably not wiser. Riley had always been wise beyond his years. The problem was he rarely listened to his own advice . . .

Rain and hail battered against the windows of Riley's study, drumming into him a reminder of how harsh the weather in Scotland could be. October had arrived with a vengeance. Thunderstorms, icy rain that would rip the skin off your face, foggy nights when, if the cold didn't get you, the fog would. Glasgow weather. It was one of the things he'd missed during his missions abroad. Others moaned about the grim, grey, damp days, but when you'd nearly fried in the forests of Columbia, trudged across scorching deserts in rough boots, and floated for a week off the coast of the tropics, a wee bit of drizzle was very welcome.

It was around eight o'clock at night, and he was working from home in a castellated mansion in a secluded area on the outskirts of the city. It was the family house he'd grown up in and which was now empty of life, apart from him and the hundreds of books and data lining the walls of the study like a voluminous library. Charts of star constellations were framed alongside prints of ancient maps of the world. Riley's favourite map was one dating back to the days of the early mariners and explorers, before anyone knew what lay beyond the far side of the great oceans, and which bore the warning message — *Beyond This Place There Be Dragons!* Riley could relate to that sentiment. Life for him had never been easy. Haunted by the mess he'd made of his past, he could appreciate that even in today's world, beyond some limits, physical or personal, there were indeed dragons. Maybe not the sort the map warned of, but treacherous, monstrous characters and places where human nature festered at its worst.

He secured all the windows which were getting a fair rattling from the hailstones. The wind howled like a wounded animal as it whipped through the trees that shrouded his vast garden from prying eyes. The property was protected by the latest high tech security that he'd installed himself, and good luck to anyone who actually managed to break in while Riley was there. And he was there a lot. There was something calming about battening the hatches from the past and keeping off the main radar. The work flowed in via his computer or by phone. The police detectives and government officials rarely chapped his door. It was better for everyone that way. That's how his latest job had arrived, in the form of an e-mail; an e-mail containing a corrupted file that the police hadn't been able to fully open. Riley had been asked by the police in Glasgow to help them investigate the killing of a man whose computer insisted never existed. The man, a forger known as Mackenzie, had been found stabbed while apparently working at his computer. Mackenzie had an unsavoury criminal background, and from the initial data it appeared that he'd compiled a killer's hit list. Unfortunately, Riley discovered his own name was on the hit list, once again providing him with his usual measure of strife.

After almost an hour of reassessing the data, searching remotely through the electronic history of the victim's computer, and seething that his name was on the list, he phoned Detective Chief Inspector Stanley Valentine, the detective responsible for giving him the case. He'd put work Riley's way several times, and although the jobs were always done to everyone's satisfaction, Valentine's glib manner grated on him incessantly.

Main desk at the Glasgow police station picked up the call.

'This is Riley. I'd like to speak to Stanley Valentine.'

'Which one?' the police officer said.

Riley sighed. Only in the Glasgow police force could there be two aggravating bastards called Stanley Valentine. Father and son. 'The lesser of two evils,' he said.

'Hold on, Riley, I'll put you through.'

Stanley Valentine, the son, had risen through the ranks to become a detective on merit, not because his police chief father pulled any strings. Aged thirty, Valentine was ambitious, assertive and annoying. Not necessarily in that order.

Valentine's tone was falsely bright. 'Riley.'

Riley's deep voice poured down the line, a calm warning. 'I'm not happy.'

'You've seen the hit list?'

'My name is on it. You knew I was a target and you didn't flag me.'

Valentine paused, then offered, 'I can off load the case elsewhere and leave you free to watch your back.'

'If anyone should be watching their back right now, it's not me.' Riley's tone contained a threat with a promise.

Valentine backed down. 'I should have mentioned it, but I tell you what, if I were you I'd want the chance to work on a case where I was on someone's hit list rather than leave it to others. You know I'm right.'

'If you're ever right, Stanley, I swear I'll jump in the River Clyde.'

Valentine smiled. 'You're the only man I know who could actually jump in the Clyde, survive the murky depths and climb out still breathing a week later.'

Riley sat back in his chair and studied the list of names that were highlighted on his twin screen computer. His name stared out at him.

'Who do you think wants me dead? No, rephrase that. Why did Mackenzie have the list on his computer data? He was a forger not a killer.'

'You're the computer expert, Riley. You'll figure it out before we do.'

An informal social event that night was in full flow in one of the large offices of the Scottish Parliament building at Holyrood, Edinburgh. A party of around forty government and political figures were enjoying a drink.

Byrn Shaw, fit, tall, good looking, but cold featured, aged around thirty, worked for the government, bordering on politics. He was watching Richard Reece, a self confessed scoundrel and politician, approach a young woman, Catherine Warr. Reece was middle aged, but wearing well, similar in build to Shaw, and had reached a recognisable level of political success. Catherine worked for the government as an in house investigator. She was in her late twenties, very attractive, rich chestnut hair framing a rose and cream complexion.

Reece smiled as he approached her. 'Have I been behaving myself, Catherine?'

'You tell me, Reece.'

'I know you're keeping an eye on me, so I must be up to no good.'

'Everyone has to be accountable, even politicians who think they are a law unto themselves.'

'You should have been a lawyer instead of wasting your talents in the secret halls of government,' Reece said.

'What, and miss out on all the intrigue and throat cutting? Speaking of which, I hear you're challenging Kier Brodie for his seat.'

Reece lifted his glass of wine in a toast. 'May the best man win.'

'He never does, but that's what keeps me in a job.'

'Politics, government, secrets and lies — it's all just a game, Catherine.'

'If only…'

Reece studied her face. 'If only you'd have dinner with me.'

'Tempting but no.'

Reece smiled his acceptance. 'Wish me luck against Brodie.'

'You already have the luck of the devil, Reece. It doesn't get any darker than that.'

He leaned close and whispered, 'You always did intrigue me, Catherine.'

Several others at the party were in a boisterous mood as they approached Reece and swept him into their crowd. Catherine stepped back from them.

'Don't let the bad guys get you,' Catherine said to Reece before walking away.

Reece smiled. 'Don't let them get you first.'

For a second they looked at each other. There was uncertainty in Catherine's eyes. She hurried away.

Byrn Shaw watched her go.

Catherine walked briskly in the cold night to reach her car which was parked in the street. The night was foggy and dimly lit. Few people were about even though it was within Edinburgh's city centre. The fog had kept most of them indoors.

In the icy stillness she pulled her warm coat around her. Only the sound of her high heeled shoes disturbed the lull. She kept glancing around her, more from a sense of being followed than seeing anyone. She saw nothing but the fog, at first. But her instincts were right. A man was shadowing her. Tall and wearing a long, dark coat, his identity was obscured by the gloom.

She hurried on, searching in her handbag for the car keys. Fumbling in her bag, she dropped the keys and as she picked them up, she saw the man stalking her. Sensing danger, she made a run for her car, but didn't make it. Within seconds the man had caught up and made a violent grab for her. Instinct kicked in and she pulled free and started running.

Moments later, she ran straight into Byrn Shaw. He was wearing a long, dark coat, and at first she thought she'd run into her attacker.

'Shaw!'

'Get in the car,' Shaw told her brusquely.

Catherine got into her car quickly and locked the door.

Shaw stood guard, searching the shadows for any sign of the man. He caught a glimpse of him disappearing further along the street, an outline in the mist.

Catherine opened the car window. 'Did you see who he was?'

'Too dark.' Shaw moved closer. 'It's not safe for you to be out at night alone, especially when you have enemies.'

'Enemies?'

'Powerful people resent you prying into their financial affairs and private lives,' he said.

'That's my job.'

'Well try not to be so good at it.'

'Thanks for your help,' she said, and started up the car.

'I'm parked over there. Want me to shadow you home? Make sure you're safe.'

'No thanks, I've had enough shadows for one night,' she said, and drove off.

Shaw stood alone in the street and watched the tail lights of her car disappear into the fog.

Riley was still working at his computer. He glanced out the window into the rainy darkness, seeing only the moving silhouette of the trees outside. Folding a piece of paper listing the names on the killer's agenda, he switched off his computer, shrugged on his black greatcoat, put the paper in his pocket and headed out into the night. There was one man he trusted who would view the list from a scientist's perspective.

Catherine lived in a townhouse in Edinburgh. She drove up, parked her car and hurried inside. Feeling tired, upset and shaken from being menaced, she took her coat off, went through to the lounge and flicked on the soft lighting. Then she heard a noise, like the sound of her front door closing. She crept cautiously through to the hallway. The door was shut. Nothing was out of sorts. She turned the dead bolt on the lock, and put her edginess down to the events of the night.

The Edinburgh street was deserted at 2:30am. Two men, vague figures in the fog, were running along the street, both tall and wearing long dark coats. The chaser caught the first man, grabbed him and forced him against a wall. A fight ensued, very competent fighting, hard and fast punches. One of them had a dagger. The flash of the blade cut through the darkness.

The men ran on again, ending up in an alleyway where a brutal fight took place. The blade glinted as a fierce struggle between the two men ended when one man fell to the ground.

· Riley was having breakfast at his desk and watching the early morning headline news in his study. A reporter was speaking about an incident that had happened the previous night.

'Leading politician, Richard Reece, was stabbed to death late last night in the centre of Edinburgh. There were no eyewitnesses to the brutal murder, and police are asking for anyone with information to come forward. In an unusual twist of events, an ancient parchment scroll was found hanging around Reece's neck, and the dagger which is believed to be the murder weapon, was found lying beside the body.'

Riley's computer alerted him that two men were approaching his house. He turned the television off and checked their identity on his security monitor. Two police detectives were standing on his doorstep. They rang the bell. The senior of the two was Stanley Valentine. The other was Detective Anthony Ferguson, a few years older than Valentine and never likely to catch him up on the career scale.

Riley's heart sank when he saw who it was. He opened the door, left it open, and went back to his study. It was the nearest they were going to get to an invitation to come in. Valentine and Ferguson followed him into the study.

'Are you aware that Richard Reece was murdered last night?' Valentine asked.

'I saw the news,' Riley said, sitting down at his desk.

'I need your help,' said Valentine.

Riley stared at him and did not respond.

Valentine elaborated. 'We're investigating Reece's murder, and I thought you could tell us what's written on this.' He brought out a small, parchment scroll sealed in a clear plastic bag from the pocket of his jacket. He held it up for Riley to see.

'I thought this would be a case for Edinburgh,' said Riley, taking little interest in the evidence.

'We're working in tandem on this one,' said Valentine. 'A long story, but we need this mess cleared up.'

Anthony Ferguson was eyeing Riley's tea and buttered toast. Ferguson wasn't fat, just heavily built, strong arms, big hands, the type who'd be handy in a tug of war. Riley had no gripe with him.

'Help yourself,' Riley said, shoving the plate of toast nearer.

'Cheers,' said Ferguson. He'd only had a pit stop visit to Riley's house over a year ago. He looked around, impressed by the hundreds of books and artefacts in the study. 'You really update all this stuff?'

Riley nodded.

Ferguson munched a piece of toast. 'How far back do the records go? That's what they call you, isn't it — the Record Keeper?'

'Further back than you could imagine. The records are ancient and modern. There's data on most significant events in history,' Riley said, referring to the vast amount of information from past and present sources.'

'Sort of runs in the family, eh? Right back to your grandfather or further than that,' Ferguson said, genuinely interested. 'I studied history in school. Pretty gory stuff. Didn't have forensics then. It was easier to get away with murder.'

Riley disagreed. 'Murder tends to come back and haunt the guilty, whatever the era.'

'You mean like ghosts of the past?' Ferguson said.

'No, it's just that the past often goes full circle. There's truth in the saying that your past comes back to haunt you, not necessarily a ghost, but events in life repeat themselves.' Riley gave Valentine a cold, unwelcoming stare.

Valentine sighed long and hard. 'I know you're pissed with me, Riley, but can we put that aside?' He offered the scroll to Riley. 'The scroll was hanging around Reece's neck. Can you decipher what it says? It's written in Latin or something.'

'While I'm working on why I'm on some freak's computer hit list?' Riley said accusingly.

Valentine didn't wince. 'Here's the hard drive from Mackenzie's computer.' He put it down on the desk.

Riley left the hard drive where it was and reluctantly took the scroll. 'Fingerprints?'

'One set, no match yet,' Valentine said.

Riley studied the scroll under the light of the desk lamp. 'The scroll looks ancient but the paper's not that old. It's stained to give a faded effect, and the writing is a modern version of traditional lettering and symbols.' He took a huge portfolio from a desk drawer and compared the symbols.

'Any idea what the message is?' Valentine asked.

Riley's gut wrenched as he read the message. 'It'll take time to decipher this,' he lied. 'I'll take a copy and get back to you.'

'Not even a rough idea?' Valentine prompted him.

'Nope.' He snapped a couple of photographs of the scroll and then handed it back to Valentine.

Ferguson helped himself to a third slice of toast.

Valentine showed Riley a photograph. 'This is a picture of the dagger he was stabbed with.'

'Have a stab at how old the dagger is,' Ferguson said.

Riley looked at the photograph. 'It dates back to 1410.'

'Are you sure?' Valentine said.

Riley pointed to the ancient markings on the handle. 'These markings show the date. Latin numerals — 1410.'

Valentine checked a message on his mobile phone. 'Right, we need to go. Contact us as soon as possible about the scroll. And bill the department as usual for your time.'

The detectives went to leave. Valentine lifted the last piece of toast.

'Who's the woman?' Riley asked.

The detectives paused. Valentine challenged him. 'What woman?'

'There's usually a woman somewhere,' Riley said.

'Richard Reece was single, but the last woman he spoke to claims she was attacked shortly after speaking to him.'

Riley frowned. 'Attacked?'

'There was a party at the Scottish Parliament building last night. She says a man followed her to her car, made a grab for her but she ran off. Then another man, Byrn Shaw, scared the attacker away.'

Riley hid his reaction toShaw's name. 'Does she work for the government?'

'Yes, she's an in house investigator.'

Riley looked thoughtful. 'Send me some information on her.'

'Just find out what the scroll says,' Valentine told him. 'The woman's involvement is likely to be circumstantial, coincidence.'

'Coincidence is a modern trait, Stanley. There's no coincidence in history, and as that's what we're dealing with, the attack on the woman could be useful.'

Valentine hesitated then agreed. 'I'll e–mail you with an update on her.'

After they left, Riley studied the message on the scroll. If Valentine knew what it said, there would be hell to pay. Not that he cared about rattling Valentine's cage. He just preferred to take a route less obvious. The reason he was on the hit list was clearer now. No coincidences in history. And no rest for the wicked.

Chapter Two

Imagery Intelligence

It was a cold but clear night. Riley was climbing the walls, literally. One of the rooms in his house had a climbing wall right round the inside. His father, Alexander, had built it using stones and pottery jugs set in cement. Artefacts that Alexander had gathered on his adventurous trips abroad were wedged into the walls, giving the entire ensemble a rare but rugged appearance. Alexander had added pieces to it over the years. Riley used it for training. He hated gyms. Running on treadmills wasn't for him. If he wanted to run, he'd go outside, if he wanted to work his muscles, he'd hoist his body weight around the climbing wall — and then there was the diving pool. His grandfather had built it when he retired from the original SBS after the Second World War. Harry knew how to build anything involving water. Set in the centre of the house, it was deep rather than wide and still had the aquamarine blue tiles he'd used to create it. Riley planned to add something useful to the house someday.

He continued to scale the wall, working out, keeping his hand in with his climbing skills. Climbing was good for thinking. And he'd plenty to think about. Byrn Shaw . . . Valentine hadn't clocked his surprise when he'd heard that name, or perhaps he'd hidden his reaction better than he imagined. Shaw now worked for the government, but Riley remembered him when he was in the SAS, an expert in imagery intelligence. How fast the past was unravelling . . .

A green flashing light jolted Riley out of his reminiscing. An intruder alert. No bells, no noise, just a subtle warning that someone uninvited was within the perimeter of his property. Jumping down from the wall, he ran through to the security monitor in his study. Someone was approaching the front door.

Whoever it was rang the doorbell.

Riley scanned the screen. It was a woman. What was she? A journalist? No. Special Branch? Government? A ruse? Options two and three were his best bet.

Wearing his training gear — vest, training trousers, those of a climber rather than someone who trains in a gym, and dark hair swept back from an unsmiling face, he opened the door. She was warmly dressed in a winter coat with the collar hugging her neck, a classically attractive young woman, well groomed and without a hint of hesitation in her wide hazel eyes. Perhaps he did see her glance at him as if acknowledging he was fit, much taller than her and capable of overpowering her, and if she had, she'd immediately dismissed any fear she could have harboured.

'It's freezing out here,' she said in a soft, well spoken voice.

He stepped aside and she walked in, striding elegantly past him into the hall, then seeing a glow from the study, she headed straight there, leaving Riley to close the door and follow her. He found her looking with undisguised fascination at the books and paraphernalia in his study.

'You're wasting your time,' he said, ice grey eyes appraising her. 'I'm in no mood for visitors, strangers or intruders. And I'm particularly unimpressed by pushy women.'

She almost smiled. 'Does that line of derogatory charm usually work?'

'Not so far.'

She stepped closer. 'I know all about you, Riley. I've read your file. I work for the government.'

'Then you'll have seen what they wanted you to read. Nobody gets the full story — not even me.'

'What do I call you — Riley or John?'

'No one calls me John.'

'Not even your family?'

'I've no family left, but you'd know that if you'd read my file.'

She stepped back from him and looked around the study. 'The SBS are said to be very intelligent, highly skilled, and apparently they can do everything other special forces can do on land — but they can also do it on water which is tougher.'

No response.

'You're not going to tell me about your exploits in the SBS, are you, Riley? You're a very secretive lot. To be honest, I'd never heard of the SBS until recently.'

No reply.

Her attention was drawn to several photographs on his desk. The arctic, Amazon jungle and other exotic locations were featured in the frames. 'Where is everyone?'

'I live alone.'

'No, what I mean is, this place is packed with information, books, relics, even photographs of places — but no people. Not a single face to be seen.'

'What is it you want?'

'Nothing. Stanley Valentine was raking through my files — and you wanted to know about the woman. I thought it would save hours of trawling and skulking around in the bushes if I came to your house.'

Riley was impressed, not that he was going to tell her. Not a hint of admiration for her guile and guts. And he wouldn't need to ask about her work. An e-mail would be winging its way soon with every juicy detail. Anything Valentine dug up about her would be far more enlightening and colourful than what she'd tell him, even if she had nothing to hide.

'I'm Catherine. Catherine Warr. And I don't know anything about Reece's murder.'

'What do you know about Byrn Shaw?'

She blinked, surprised at his name being thrown at her. 'He works in the Parliament offices in Edinburgh.'

'A friend of yours?'

'No, but I was glad he was around last night when I got attacked.'

'A handy man to have as a guard.'

'Is he?' She seemed surprised.

'Shaw is ex-forces, but you'd know that if you'd read his file,' Riley said.

'I'd no idea.' He saw no flicker of a lie in the depths of her eyes. 'Was he SBS?' she asked.

'No, SAS.'

Her attractive features lit up with realisation. 'Shaw was a balaclava man?'

'Did you see the man who attacked you? Could you describe him?'

'It was foggy and dark and I . . . I was caught off guard . . .' She seemed angry. 'I dropped my keys, I didn't have them ready. I was fumbling in my bag, doing all the things they warn you not to do.'

'Who are *they*?'

'You know — safety advisors. Women in my line of work, we get advice, but it applies to most women. The usual stuff, don't go to dark creepy places on your own —'

'Why did you?' Riley's voice was tinged with accusation.

She seemed flustered and ran her hands through her silky, shoulder length hair. 'It had been one of those nights. Reece had been . . . he had a way of unnerving me. He'd been up to no good, as always, nothing vile, just diddling extra funds for personal use, abusing the system. But it's what he said before I left the party. No, not what he said, more the way he said it, as if he knew something.'

'Knew what?'

'I'd said jokingly, don't let the bad guys get you, and he'd said in that roguish tone of his, don't let them get you first. And they nearly did, didn't they?'

'So you were edgy when you left the parliament building?' Riley said.

'Yes.'

'Had you anything to fear from Reece, anything apart from the flack for rapping him over the knuckles for skimming the cream?'

'No, I thought I had Reece's measure. We were almost friends. I didn't feel threatened, not until last night. Before that it was just a case of better the devil you know.'

'Better the devil who doesn't know you. Someone who knows your strengths and weaknesses can exploit them. It's a harder fight to get clear of.'

She steered the conversation back to Riley. 'You're known as the Record Keeper.'

Riley nodded.

She looked at a few of the artefacts in the study including a large, weather beaten book. She flicked through the pages. 'You can't rewrite history even though you'd like to.'

Riley closed the book carefully. 'No, but you can update and correct it when new information comes to light. Few things are ever what they appear to be.'

'I'd better go,' she said suddenly aware of his closeness, and walked out of the study to the front door.

He opened the door for her.

She breathed in the cold night air. 'Maybe I'm getting paranoid, but I thought I heard someone in my house last night. Was it you?'

'No. If it had been, you wouldn't have heard me.'

Catherine smiled and stepped outside. 'I suppose you've got me on three different security cameras,' she remarked flippantly, looking around her for any sign of a lens.

He let her walk away towards her car before replying. 'Four.'

'Hmm. Life for you must be a bundle of laughs,' she said.

Riley didn't say anything. He watched her get into her car and drive off, leaving behind her an impression in his thoughts that was hard not to like.

Valentine phoned him later. 'The cases are linked.'

'Where's the e-mail information on Catherine Warr?'

Valentine hesitated. 'Who told you her name?'

'She did. She turned up at my house to save you and me raking through her files.'

'What did she tell you?'

'She doesn't know who killed Reece. If she was lying, we should bottle her technique.'

Valentine sounded frustrated. 'Have you managed to decipher the message on the scroll?'

Riley considered his options, and then thought — what the hell. 'It says — *this one is for the Record Keeper.*' It was almost worth it to rattle Valentine.

'Someone's playing games with you. We found a copy of the list in Richard Reece's office. This links the cases.'

'I never met Reece.'

'As I say, someone's playing games with you.' Valentine accessed the data on Catherine Warr. 'I'm forwarding the e-mail.' It arrived moments later in Riley's inbox. Subject heading: The woman. The mail had an attachment. Riley opened it and skimmed the information. Photographs were included.

'She's got an interesting history,' Riley summarised.

'So have you.'

'Is that an accusation?'

'Can you explain why you're mentioned on the scroll and why you're on the hit list?' Valentine said.

'Maybe someone wants to settle an old score.'

'What score would that be?'

'Take your pick. As you say, I've got an interesting history.'

'You've got kudos in all the right places, Riley, so no one is going to be breathing down your neck accusing you of being involved in Reece's murder.'

'I can sleep easy then.'

'But you know as well as I do that this is going to get messy. I'd prefer we worked on the same side, so I'll make a deal with you. I'll try not to be an aggravating bastard on this one, if you'll be less secretive and share information.'

'Deal.'

Valentine seemed happy with this. 'Let me know if you think of anything else.'

'Run a check on Byrn Shaw. He's ex–SAS, specialised in imagery intelligence — images gathered and interpreted from satellite and aerial photography and radar sensors. He'll be clean, but we'll need to make sure he doesn't get used as a pawn.'

'Consider it done.'

After the phone call, Riley studied the information about Catherine. She'd spent several years as an in house investigator with Scottish Government. Hobbies — astronomy and space. Riley frowned, and then phoned her home in Edinburgh.

'It's Riley. Question for you.'

'How did you get my private number?' she said.

'You saw the maps on the wall of my study?' he continued.

'Yes.'

'What else did you see?'

'Ah, you've read my file,' she said.

'Hobbies — astronomy and space'.

'Your constellation charts. You're wondering why I didn't gasp in awe or at the very least show my knowledge of them.'

'Why didn't you?'

'Is that the question?'

'Yes,' he said.

'Because your charts are incomplete and outdated.'

'Fair enough. Could you recommend improving them?' he said.

'I'd recommend you update them. Other planets have been discovered recently, planets have been relegated, and some of the constellation information is out of date. If you're the Record Keeper, you need to keep up with what's happening in space, the future, not just the past.'

He took the criticism on the chin. 'Will do. Point taken.' He hesitated and then said, 'Would you like to have dinner with me tomorrow night?'

'Are you asking me for a date?' There was a hint of a smile in her tone.

'No, I'm offering you a meal and maybe we can talk about the charts. Have you ever seen the night sky through one of the best private telescopes in the country?'

'Can't say I have.'

'Then you're in for a treat. Meet me tomorrow night at my house. Seven o'clock. We'll walk from there.'

'Walk to where?' she asked.

'The best view in the city.'

Riley was hoovering the diving pool. He'd flicked a switch on the automatic pool cleaner that looked like a mechanical beetle and worked its way around the blue tiles ridding them of mildew and keeping them glistening.

Lit by spotlights, the water reminded him of the sea in the tropics — this was his little bit of paradise in Glasgow. More importantly, it kept his underwater swimming techniques strong and sharp. He never wanted to loose those abilities. Harry had proved you didn't have to. Age had failed to wither his late grandfather. Harry had been one of those men who'd kept whipcord lean well into his twilight years, never giving age a chance to diminish his physique. Riley aimed to be like that. In contrast, Harry used to joke that Riley's father, Alexander, was the suave and sophisticated palaeographer, travelling to far off lands like a classic adventurer. Even in the remotest of areas, Alexander managed to have a cup of tea with two sugars — and a digestive biscuit. Harry was more inclined to eat what he could kill, cook or get his hands on. Riley was nearer the latter, though living in civvy street he'd not had to nut roast a squirrel in a long time. He got his groceries delivered via the Internet, and like many ex-forces men, he kept his house clean and tidy.

Looking at the water in the pool helped him think. Why was his name on the list he found on Mackenzie's computer data? And what about Mackenzie? Stabbed to death beside his computer. A computer that wasn't registered to anyone, and that insisted no one of that name existed. Mackenzie had a dubious background as a forger but it didn't mean that even his computer could disown him. Then there was Richard Reece. The media were still reeling from his demise. Who would use an antique dagger as a murder weapon these days? And who would be stupid enough to leave it at the scene of the crime?

Riley's mobile phone rang. It was Mul McAra.

'Are you busy?'

'Just hoovering,' Riley said.

'Right, I'll be over in a jiffy.'

Mul McAra lived a ten minute drive away from Riley. McAra could run it in seven, six if it was snowing. Friends since they were wee boys, McAra was the grandson of Harry's best friend who had served with Harry during the SBS training on the Scottish Isle of Arran in the 1940s. Mul McAra hadn't ventured into the forces. Science was his game, rocket science to be precise. As a rocket scientist in Scotland, McAra did very well for himself and was known as one of the leading space scientists in his line of expertise — astrobiology and space robotics. When he wasn't peering bleary eyed through a telescope at the solar system, McAra liked to run. At thirty-five, he had a lot of running years left in him. Riley imagined he'd still be pounding the highlands when he was in his seventies. Riley had given him a copy of the names on the computer list to see what McAra made of them. One of the names was familiar to Riley, something to do with science, and he hoped McAra would know.

By the time the kettle had boiled and Riley had made a mug of tea for both of them, McAra was at the door.

'The list's a corker!' he said, hardly out of breath from the sprint. His gingery hair stuck up in wild peaks, not from the speed of running, just a natural quirk of fate. He slugged a mouthful of sweet tea. 'The names belong to scientists. Two of them are already toes up in the bone yard. Copped it years ago. I haven't checked the other four. Maybe you or Valentine can do that, but I've a sneaky feeling it's a dead man's list.'

McAra was grinning as if this was good news. Riley wasn't convinced. 'If I'm the last man breathing on the list, you know what that means.'

'Not an inkling.'

'It means it's a hunter's game the bastard's playing,' said Riley, 'and I'm going to have to go after him before he comes after me.'

'Ah, not so good, eh? Still, I wouldn't like to be them.'

Riley sat down at his computer and checked the remaining four names on the list. The computer began the search. McAra read the outcome. 'All dead.' He sucked the air through the gap in his front teeth. 'What's your plan?'

'What are you doing tomorrow night?'

'Apparently I'm up for a science award in Glasgow,' said McAra, sounding vaguely disinterested.

Riley took a swig of his tea. 'Is it a trophy, a medal?'

'Ach, I wasn't listening properly,' McAra said. 'I'm not into all that. I wish they'd just let me get on with my work. I'll phone them up and ask them to post the award to me.'

'No, you go to your party. I need to borrow your house for the evening. I've invited a woman, Catherine Warr, to have dinner with me.' Riley rarely referred to McAra having a house. It was more like an observatory with a bed and kitchen, telescopes and a glass domed roof. McAra had converted the substantial size house over the years into a high tech observatory that he just happened to live in.

'There's nothing to eat in the house. I haven't done my grocery shopping,' McAra said.

'No problem. I'll sort out the food.'

'She must be gorgeous,' McAra remarked.

'That's got nothing to do with it. She's part of the investigation.'

'Well, for the sake of the investigation, I wouldn't cook if I were you. When it comes to rustling up a survival dinner in the wilds of nowhere you're an absolute gourmet, but take my advice and order something in.'

Chapter Three

A Hunter's Game

A lethal looking hunting knife lay on a shelf in Riley's study. Despite its worn appearance, it was as handy as ever. He'd taken it with him to various parts of the world, used it when diving, to cut through a parachute cord when entangled in trees during a mission in one of the darkest jungles on Earth, and when ice climbing in the arctic circle. The knife bore the scars of its travels, and so did he. He picked up the knife and turned it skilfully in his hand. It was a fixed blade, strong and reliable, with the metal running through the centre of the handle. It was very different from the dagger used to murder Reece.

The day had been a blur of gathering information. He'd already recovered ninety-nine percent of the information from Mackenzie's computer hard drive that refused to reveal all its secrets. It had been made to look like the computer had crashed, but Riley discovered this wasn't true. The data he'd found, and passed on to

Valentine, didn't reveal why he was on the hit list, but it had to be his past. Someone involved in the underside of all this had an axe to grind, someone he'd crossed swords with. He could sense it in his bones. There was something about the way the information on the hard drive had been tampered with, something in the electronic fingerprints they'd left behind that seemed strangely and chillingly familiar.

And whatever Mackenzie was into, he didn't like a noisy computer. From Riley's experience, men who liked silent computers tended to be thinkers, loners, experts who specialised in meticulous work. Mackenzie the forger certainly fitted that profile, despite his computer's denial of ever knowing him. Maybe that was it? Riley had come across forgers who'd erased their identities so perfectly and so often they'd lost themselves in a labyrinth of fake IDs and pseudonyms. Even he knew how that felt.

He put the knife back, and shelved his thoughts about the silent computer. Gut instinct warned him he was being blindsided by the dead man's list. The next few answers he needed were in Edinburgh, and the one woman who held a key to the solution was on her way to his house.

He'd taken McAra's advice about not cooking a meal for Catherine and ordered a buffet for two from a catering firm. McAra confirmed it had arrived before dashing off to the awards ceremony in the city centre. Riley checked his watch — five to seven. His surveillance camera showed Catherine's car in the driveway. He put his greatcoat on over his dark grey and black clothes and went out to meet her.

The air was crisp and clear with a hint of frost glistening on the ground. 'You'll need your coat,' Riley said as she got out of her car.

While she reached into the passenger seat for her cream wool coat, he noticed she was wearing a dress and fashionable boots with impractical high heels.

'Where are we going?'

He motioned up the street towards several large houses set on a hill. 'The house with the big glass dome on the roof. It belongs to a friend of mine, Mul McAra, he's into rocket science.'

'Mul McAra's a friend of yours?' She sounded surprised.

'You know him?'

'No, but I've heard of him. He's supposed to be brilliant.'

Riley smiled to himself as they reached the long stretch of pavement McAra liked to slide down when it was covered in snow or frost. It cut a minute off his time getting to Riley's house. 'He's getting an award tonight — for being brilliant. Not that he's too fussed about it, but he's happy for us to use his telescope and have something to eat at his house.'

They continued walking.

'I'm still not entirely sure what I'm doing here,' she said, her breath filtering through the icy air.

Riley looked down at her. Even with her boots on, she was only up to his shoulders. Before he could explain that he wanted to talk to her about the political games being played in the Scottish Parliament in Edinburgh, and about the constellation charts, he saw a figure, a man, step into the shadows of the trees at the bottom of the hill below the houses. Riley scanned the vicinity, gauging the danger.

Catherine rambled on light heartedly. 'If you think I'm going to tell you any more about Reece's —'

Riley grabbed hold of her arm and pulled her near him, his eyes willing her to be quiet. He smiled and then whispered, 'We're being watched. Stay close.'

Catherine swallowed her fear, hoping Riley was as good as his reputation said he was. She tried to look like she hadn't been told of the threat and continued to walk beside him, shielded by his arm around her waist.

'I need to see who it is,' Riley whispered, 'but I'll make sure you're safe first.'

She smiled nervously and kept her voice low. 'Don't go leaving me on my own while you play the hero.'

Taking her by surprise, he lifted her up, put her over his shoulder and made a run for McAra's house. He was strong, fast and reached the front door in less than two minutes — a record, even by McAra's standards. He unlocked the door, put Catherine inside, locked it securely and then went after the shadow in the trees.

Whoever it was had got as big a shock as Catherine and had decided to make a run for it. The man got into a car, whose vehicle number plates had been blocked out, and was speeding away as Riley got close, leaving him to watch the car disappear into the traffic. But they'd be back. He was sure of it — and even surer that this had become a hunter's game with a vengeance.

Riley walked briskly back to McAra's house, thinking about the man. He couldn't be Special Forces, unless he'd deliberately wanted Riley to see him, otherwise he'd have blended into the shadows like a dark ghost. Riley pulled up the collar of his coat and walked on. Sometimes the past came back to haunt him — pieces of his former life. Tonight was one of those times. The sparkling frost, the icy chill, and the possible threat to Catherine caused the memories to come flickering back. He remembered a mission in North America when he'd had to rescue a woman from the clutches of drug dealing killers and run the gauntlet with her over the snow covered landscape to safety . . .

. . . ice — the worst thing in the world to run on. It was winter, and their SBS mission, a narcotics import operation, was proving difficult. Riley and three other SBS were there, including Nick Deacon, a man who would eventually cause Riley more strife than anyone else. A solitary ship was anchored in a remote landscape at the edge of a freezing cold bay. Nearby was a warehouse complex. The four–man SBS team, wearing white Arctic clothing and comms gear for stealth communication, were preparing to raid the drug import base. They were armed with guns and knives. The objective was to secure the warehouse, capture the dealers, dead or alive, and rescue their hostage, a young woman, like Catherine, who'd got caught up in their filthy game.

The four split into two pairs. Riley and Deacon made their way cautiously around the edge of the bay, over rocks and ice, having stashed their boat further along the coast. The other pair took the opposite route. Riley and Deacon ice climbed to the top of a ridge where they watched the drugs being unloaded from the ship and transferred to the warehouse complex. Twelve men were involved in the unloading. Others were inside the warehouse, packaging the drugs ready for distribution. Several armed guards were on patrol. The SBS lay hidden on the snow covered ground, watching and evaluating the situation.

Riley used his comms to communicate with his men. 'Ready to move in?'

Deacon nodded and prepared his gun. The two others confirmed they were poised to attack.

'Deacon and I will take the north entrance,' Riley said. 'Fireworks in ten minutes.'

Riley checked the time on his watch, gave Deacon the thumbs up, then all four of them moved in stealth down towards the warehouses, merging into the snow like white ghosts.

Although armed with guns, Riley and his men used silent combat techniques to disarm several guards and knock them unconscious, permanently or otherwise. They continued, fast, competent and silent until the warehouse and almost all dealers had been taken. During the fighting, Riley climbed through a window and found the woman who had been badly beaten and tied up. With no time to loose, he set a charge in the building that would ignite within minutes, illuminating the warehouse and torching the stockpile of illegal drugs. Then he put the woman over his shoulder and ran with her, through the fighting, towards the safety of the boat. Deacon and the others watched his back, but there were a few times when he'd had to shoot while running, and then, in the freezing conditions his gun wouldn't fire.

Forced to take swift evasive action, Riley physically fought one of the guards, defending the woman, and finally threw his hunting knife across the remaining distance to overpower the last man standing in his way. He pulled his knife out of the man's chest, and then hurried on, carrying the woman to safety. It was another successful mission . . .

Riley hated running on ice, and yet here he was, in civilian life, still treading a wary path.

Catherine was slightly shaken but glad to see Riley when he opened the door to McAra's home. She'd had the sense to arm herself with a . . . he wasn't sure what it was . . . a long metal pole, one of McAra's weird gadgets, but it made a useful weapon. He took it off her and put it aside.

'Did you get him?' she said hopefully.

'He drove off before I got there.'

Riley led her up the stairs to the glass observatory where the buffet had been left for them. Soft lights lit up the dome to give maximum viewing of the night sky. She sat down on a sofa and he poured her a glass of water before phoning Valentine.

'Catherine was a possible target again tonight,' he said, explaining the details of what happened.

'Is she there with you right now?' Valentine said quietly.

'Yes.'

'Can she hear me?'

Riley walked over to the window to ensure she was well out of earshot. 'No.'

'We brought Byrn Shaw in for questioning. Apparently he was shadowing Catherine the night Reece was murdered because he has a crush on her and was worried about her safety. He'd heard rumours about Kier Brodie, the man Reece was hoping to oust.'

Riley kept his voice low. 'What rumours?'

'Nothing tangible. Kier Brodie was gaining a reputation as an up and coming political candidate that you wouldn't like to cross. Catherine had some damning information on Brodie. The rumour was they'd made a deal. She'd keep her mouth shut and he wouldn't have her beaten and nailed to the floorboards of her house.'

'Something stinks. It doesn't run true,' said Riley, noticing that Catherine was busy making them a drink.

'Shaw says he used some of his former contacts in the SAS and a private investigator in Glasgow to dig deeper into Brodie's business. What he found wasn't pretty. Plenty of dirt and daggers as they say.'

'Daggers?'

'Not literally, just a turn of phrase. Anyway, one of the other rumours flying around was that someone was going to get poisoned. Shaw wanted to warn Catherine, and he planned to tell her during the party, but Reece monopolised her time and then she left early.'

Catherine came over, handed Riley a drink, and then went to gaze through the large telescope at the view of the night sky.

'Was Brodie going to have Catherine poisoned? Or Reece?' Riley whispered.

'We don't know,' said Valentine. 'Call me old fashioned, but I always think of poison as a woman's weapon.'

Riley eyed the glass in his hand, looking at the liquid with chilling suspicion.

Valentine continued, 'I'm not saying Catherine's a suspect. No one's been poisoned yet, but the last time I didn't flag you about information you weren't too happy. And I'm trying not to be the aggravating bastard you think I am.'

Catherine walked over to Riley. He cut the call short. 'Thanks, I'll be in touch.'

Catherine held up her glass and said, 'Cheers, Riley. I shudder to think what would've happened tonight if you hadn't been there. No one's ever run off with me over his shoulder before.' She touched her glass against his.

'Cheers,' he said, pretending to sip his drink.

'Was that Detective Valentine you were speaking to?' she said, going back over to the telescope.

'Yes,' he said, and then carefully stashed the glass with the intention of having it analysed later. He replaced his glass with another, making it look like he'd finished his drink.

Catherine looked through the telescope at the night sky. 'What did Valentine have to say?'

'He said you have a secret admirer.'

She turned her attention back to him. 'Did he mention who it was?'

'Byrn Shaw.'

'Really?' She appeared to be flattered.

'You didn't know?'

'Absolutely not, I thought I annoyed him.'

'What gave you that idea?'

'Kier Brodie told me to watch my back. He said Shaw wasn't pleased with my investigations because they undermined his authority,' she said.

'Shaw's job doesn't clash with yours surely?'

'I wouldn't have thought so. Shaw's a shadow, one of those men in the background of government whose work is a vague outline. Kier Brodie hinted that Shaw had aspirations to venture into the political arena, but no one thought he had the charisma or the guts for it. Of course, I didn't know he was ex–SAS, so perhaps he's very capable of making his mark.'

'Shaw's certainly not the type of man others could threaten.'

Riley studied her face for any hint of reaction or deception. Catherine didn't flinch. Not a flicker in those gorgeous hazel eyes. Neither did she study him to see if the drink had affected him. If she'd spiked it, she wasn't concerned it hadn't worked. Bloody Valentine and his stupid suspicions! And then he heard a noise from downstairs.

'What?' she said.

'Stay here,' he whispered and crept down the stairs to the front door. A letter was lying on the floor. No envelope, just a piece of paper. Being careful not to destroy any fingerprints, Riley read it. It said: *Fortune Favours the Brave.*

'Lock the door behind me,' Riley said to Catherine, and then hurried out into the night.

He'd been right. It was a hunter's game.

Chapter Four

Fortune Favours the Brave

Riley's dark clothing made him the shadow he needed to be as he hunted down the man. McAra's house was hidden from the street by a bank of trees that led to a driveway. The scientist liked to illuminate anything that wasn't moving and had installed blue lights near the bottom of the trees. Riley ran full speed, a deep blue figure in the cyan glow.

The man was already in his car but the engine had stalled. Perhaps the icy weather was to blame or the man had panicked at the speed with which Riley, who suddenly appeared out of the darkness, had closed the gap between them. On the third attempt the car roared into life and sped off, narrowly escaping Riley's wrath.

Riley didn't give up the chase. He ran on, taking the racing line down the hill towards his house, got into his car and drove after him. Whoever it was didn't know the lie of the land and had taken the high road leading to the main city route. If Riley was quick he'd catch him up within minutes at the next exit. And he was quick enough. He was now only a few metres behind the man's car and wasn't letting him out of his sight. It was the same vehicle he'd seen earlier with the number plates blocked out. Had he calculated that Riley would come after him? If so, the man was obviously willing to take that risk.

And who would dare mention *Fortune Favours the Brave* — the motto Riley associated with HMS Excalibur, the last military base he'd been attached to before leaving the SBS?

While his mind eliminated various possibilities, he tried to phone Valentine but the clicking noises and scattered signal sounded familiar. 'Bastard!' The car in front was using a high powered mobile phone jammer. The signal improved when the distance between the cars increased. Riley pulled back from the car in front, buying himself time before his phone cut off. 'This is Riley. Put me through to Stanley Valentine — it's urgent.'

'Putting you through, Riley,' the police officer said.

Riley estimated he'd have a minute, maybe less, before the line went dead.

'Riley?' a man's voice said, unsure what was happening, hearing the unusual breaks in the connection.

'Shit!' Riley cursed to himself. It was the wrong bloody Stanley. Stanley senior was the last man he needed to talk to. He relayed his predicament anyway in the extreme hope that the old bastard would actually give a toss about what he said. 'I'm near the Clyde Arc bridge. Need assistance . . . possible suspect . . .' Then the mobile phone connection went dead.

Riley looked ahead. In the distance he saw the lights of the bridge arc across the River Clyde — a blaze of glory, lit by purple and blue spotlights reflecting off the water. It crossed his mind that the man could swerve at the last moment and take another route, so he pulled back to see which way he went.

The distance re-established his phone connection. A call came through from McAra. He was phoning from the awards party. Riley took the call while keeping an eye on the bridge.

'I've been trying to phone you. Something's just dawned on me,' McAra said. 'The scientists on the dead man's list — they were all involved in *dark projects* for the military. I've been doing a bit of sniffing around —'

'Tell me later. Contact Valentine —' Riley said, and then suddenly cut short his conversation when he saw the man's car skid to a halt on the bridge beside a group of young women wearing glittering fairy wings and sparkling fluffy ears having a girls' night out.

Riley raced in his car to catch up as the driver got out of the vehicle.

The girls were a lively group, a bit drunk, and were startled by the sudden brutality of the man as he grabbed one of them, a pretty blonde with fairy wings, lifted her up and without any hesitation threw her over the metal barrier of the bridge into the freezing cold river. The other girls were too drunk or too shocked and frightened to stop him.

'There's an incident on the Clyde Arc. Get the emergency services and tell Valentine someone's thrown a girl over the bridge into the river,' Riley told McAra then hung up.

Something about the man and his cold brutality was familiar. He wore black clothing and a woollen hat to disguise his hair. A sense of the past shot through Riley, and a feeling of foreboding jarred his thoughts. But this wasn't the time to search his memories. He had to focus on the current threat.

The car sped off seconds before Riley reached the girls. They were screaming and panicking. One of them had phoned the police on her mobile, but the others were too distraught to do anything.

'Stay here! Help's on the way,' Riley shouted to them. Then he jumped over the barrier and dived into the icy river to save the girl.

McAra was running. It was quicker than driving round the one–way system to get to the bridge which was literally a stone's throw from the party. He left his jacket at the party and ran in the black trousers and white shirt he'd made an effort to wear for the awards dinner. He still had his trophy in his hand, but it didn't slow him down. He held it like a gold–plated baton as he raced through the streets, taking a short cut to the bridge. Driving would have taken him at least twelve minutes, taking into account the heavy traffic in the city. Instead he ran it in under three minutes, a record even by his standards.

A crowd had gathered on the bridge with most people looking down at the river. He didn't have to ask where Riley was because he could see him, lit up in the water by the long bands of colourful lights illuminating the bridge like a work of art.

Riley powered against the strong undercurrents of the dark water that threatened to pull swimmers down into its depths. The surface, smooth as black ice, shone with the lights, reflecting the colours like a mirror.

'Riley!' McAra shouted, his voice sounding like a desperate echo in the night.

A quick flick of the head as Riley heard his friend indicated he knew that help was on its way. Nonetheless, he increased his pace, swimming with long, powerful movements, gaining on the young woman floating unconscious in the water. Even in the darkness her glittering fairy wings sparkled and seemed to be the only life coming from her fragile body. The fall alone could have killed her, but maybe she'd be lucky. He knew from the state of her friends they'd all been drinking. If her body was relaxed when she hit the water she stood a better chance of surviving the impact. If the fall hadn't killed her the freezing temperature of the water would. He had to get her out as fast as possible.

Police and ambulance sirens blared in the distance. Flashing emergency lights shone from the bridge and crowds gathered to watch the spectacle. A television news crew turned up at the scene, but what Riley needed right now was practical help. It arrived in the most unexpected way.

Riley reached out and grabbed hold of the woman. Her body was completely limp like a discarded rag doll but the undercurrents were dangerously strong. He could survive the extended length of time in the water but she couldn't. He continued powering against the currents, and every minute he was swimming nearer to the water's edge.

A rescue crew divided into two teams to cover both banks, ready to pull them out of the water when Riley got close enough. Then he saw a figure in the water just ahead. The man's face bore an expression of sheer determination. It was Byrn Shaw.

'She's not breathing,' Riley said to Shaw, who started swimming on the opposite side of the girl. They swam together against the undercurrents, doubling their power and speed. Soon they were at the edge of the river being pulled out by the emergency team. Riley could only watch as the medics fought to save her.

Shaw stood next to him, looking up at the bridge which was alive with activity. Police were waving on crowds of onlookers who'd stopped their cars to look at the incident and were now causing a traffic jam across the bridge. The television cameras captured every dramatic moment.

'We've got a pulse,' a medic announced. The woman coughed up water and was then taken away in an ambulance.

Riley and Shaw made their way back up to the bridge. McAra was standing beside Riley's car. He gave a nod of acknowledgement to Byrn Shaw, who glanced at the gold trophy in McAra's grip. They'd met a few times, though they were no more than passing acquaintances.

'I heard the girls tell the police what happened,' McAra said. 'Apparently he threw her into the water. What the hell was he thinking?'

Riley's shook his head in disgust. 'He used her as a weakener. What was I supposed to do? I couldn't let her drown.' He stripped his soaking wet top off, threw it into the boot of his car and put on a warm climber's fleece, offering a spare one to Shaw who took him up on his offer. Although a seasoned outdoor runner, even McAra shivered looking at Riley and Shaw standing there in the freezing night air. Neither one of them flinched, complained or made an issue out of it. No macho bravado or seeking glory either.

'And when he threw her over the edge apparently he said something like, *let's see if you can fly pretty thing*,' McAra added.

Riley felt his blood rise. He'd get the bastard for that.

Valentine and Ferguson approached them. Valentine was talking on his mobile phone. 'Yes, Riley's here with me right now. We're on our way.'

'On our way where?' Riley said.

'McAra's house. My dad's waiting for us. And he's fuckin' pissed off.'

This was the least of Riley's worries. He got into his car along with McAra and Shaw and followed Valentine and Ferguson back to McAra's house. Shaw left his car parked nearby with the intention of picking it up later. For the moment, he wanted to talk to Riley.

'Did you get a good look at the bastard?' Shaw asked Riley as they drove away from the bridge. McAra sat in the front passenger seat and Shaw was in the back. McAra could hear Riley's shoes squelch every time he used the accelerator but made no comment knowing his friend would dismiss it as just a wee bit of water.

'He was wearing black — civilian not military,' Riley said. 'I didn't see his face, but there was something about him . . . I get the feeling we've crossed swords in the past.'

Shaw nodded his understanding, and then Riley asked, 'What are you doing here tonight? I thought you lived in Edinburgh. Just passing by were you?' It wasn't an accusation, more a subtle inquisition.

A heavy sigh escaped Shaw's firm mouth. 'I was keeping an eye on Catherine Warr. She told me she was having dinner at McAra's house, and with the attack on her the other night, I . . .'

'Save it,' Riley said, smirking. 'You were checking up to see if she was on a date with me.'

No more was said for several seconds. Shaw knew Riley well enough to know there was no point in denying he liked Catherine. 'Did Valentine tell you?' he said finally, 'or was it someone else?'

'Valentine mentioned it. Catherine certainly didn't. She seemed genuinely surprised and flattered that she had a secret admirer.' He paused. 'A balaclava man I think she called you.'

Shaw smiled for the first time that night. 'Catherine hardly knows I exist and it's probably best for everyone that way. I'd only cause her grief.'

'I thought women loved action men,' McAra said. 'Scientists like me well . . . we don't get a second glance from the female of the species.'

Shaw's smile faded to a cynical, lopsided smirk. 'Women love the idea of us, but the reality's too raw to live with. Too many secrets. It's like living with a shadow. At least with a scientist they know he'll come home at night more or less in one piece.'

'Oh don't bet on it,' McAra said. 'I've botched a few dodgy experiments in my time.' He said to Riley, 'Remember the time I blew one of my eyebrows off and it was Rachel's birthday and I'd promised I'd take her out to dinner?'

'You should've gone with my idea,' Riley said.

McAra explained to Shaw. 'His idea was to shave the other eyebrow off rather than just have one. But I thought I'd be inventive and glued a snippet of my hair to my bare brow.'

Shaw cracked a smile again. 'What happened?'

'Well,' said McAra, 'we were having our soup, and it must have been the heat of the steam rising up, but all of a sudden my eyebrow took a nosedive right into her dinner. I never saw her again after that.'

As the laughter subsided, Riley said to Shaw, 'What else do you know about Catherine? Valentine mentioned a rumour that someone involved in this whole fiasco was going to get poisoned. He said that poison was a woman's weapon.'

Shaw shook his head adamantly. 'I heard that rumour, but I don't think Catherine is involved. More likely it's whoever killed Richard Reece.'

'Poison?' McAra said.

'Trust me,' Shaw emphasised. 'Catherine is not a poisoner.'

Riley looked at him. 'Better be absolutely sure of that.'

'I'll check out the source of the rumour,' Shaw assured him.

The three of them were still discussing this as they drove up to McAra's house. Numerous police and the formidable, silver-haired and fiercely distinguished figure of police chief, Stanley Valentine senior, were waiting for them in the driveway. A forensic team was scouring the grounds searching for evidence of the girl's attacker. Catherine, who stood near the front door of the house drinking a cup of hot coffee, had been told to wait for further questioning. She wasn't a top suspect in the incident, but Stanley senior had a reputation for being a stickler for procedures. Catherine's name and the word poison having been mentioned in the same sentence was reason enough for Stanley senior to grill her.

As Riley's car drove up, she was surprised to see Shaw was with them and went over to talk to him.

Valentine and Ferguson got out of their car. Stanley senior's greeting to his son was a cold, hard grimace. His expression was even less friendly when he saw Riley.

'You're turning this into a fuckin' circus,' he said to Riley. 'And I'm in danger of being made to look like a bastard clown.' Stanley senior's rich, Scottish brogue and colourful vocabulary got his point across loud and clear.

Valentine stepped into the fray. 'We'll catch him soon. We've several leads we're working on,' he said to his father.

'Tell that to the next woman he tries to kill,' Stanley senior roared. 'He threw a drunken fairy into the Clyde! Can you imagine the fuckin' headlines in the news tomorrow?'

Everyone present could, and it didn't seem pretty.

Stanley senior railed on Riley. 'Just do what's asked of you. Don't go muck raking where you don't belong.'

Riley didn't flinch.

Stanley senior gave him his best stare, the one that made lesser mortals shrivel.

Riley still didn't flinch.

'Give us a moment,' Stanley senior said to everyone around them. He didn't have to ask twice. They cleared the area, leaving him and Riley to thrash out their differences. McAra and Shaw's money was on Riley. Valentine thought it could go either way.

'I know your name's on that bloody hit list, Riley, and the message on the scroll is a nod to you,' Stanley senior said. 'I'm in no mood to be fucked over on this case. I've got snide arse politicians who can make everyone's life hell biting at my throat. So if you've any ideas how to clear this mess up, spit them out.'

'You're in danger of denting your reputation,' Riley said. 'I never thought you'd let the criminals call the shots.'

'What do you mean?'

'The political arena always closes ranks when they're guilty. You're being pressured to clear this up quickly. To find out who murdered Reece, all nice and tidy.'

The muscles in Stanley senior's jaw jerked in silent aggravation.

'From the evidence I've seen,' Riley said, 'Reece wasn't stabbed by anyone in the Special Forces. It was too messy and they wouldn't have left the dagger lying on the ground. And it wasn't a petty criminal either because they wouldn't hang a scroll around his neck.'

'So who do you think killed him?'

'A rival, a grudge bearer, someone who knew him well.'

The aggravation in Stanley senior's face eased to a firm determination. 'Another politician did it?'

'Very likely, or whoever the political rival was involved with. Mackenzie the forger was a middle man for quite a few people. I'm planning to ask a contact of mine tomorrow if he's got any information on Mackenzie.'

'Let me know what you find out,' Stanley senior said firmly. Then he leaned close and whispered, 'And try to keep off the fuckin' radar.'

Riley and Stanley senior went back over to the others. Catherine was drinking her coffee at the front door. 'Can I make everyone a coffee?' she offered.

There was a unanimous and emphatic, 'No thanks,' from Riley, both the Stanley Valentines, Ferguson and even Shaw who despite what he'd said earlier didn't seem willing to risk it. Only McAra, momentarily forgetting about Catherine and the poison issue, said, 'Yes,' and then almost immediately retracted it. 'Eh, no, I'll not bother.'

If Catherine knew why her offer had received such a vehement reaction, she didn't show it. 'Well it's been an eventful night, but I'd like to go home now,' she said.

It was agreed she could leave and that Valentine and Ferguson would talk to her tomorrow at the Scottish Parliament in Edinburgh. Police gave her a lift back to Riley's house where her car was parked, and then took Shaw to pick up his car at the bridge.

In the background, Valentine indicated to Riley that the glass Catherine gave to him would be tested for traces of poison.

'Let me know what you find out,' Stanley senior emphasised again to Riley, bringing the evening to a close. 'If forensics turn up anything, I'll phone you.'

Riley nodded.

Stanley senior left them to it. Most of the police cars went with him, leaving only the forensic team scouring the area for evidence.

McAra and Riley went into the house and McAra made them both a strong, sweet tea and they talked for a while in the kitchen.

'What was that you mentioned earlier?' Riley said. 'Something about the scientists involved in dark projects.'

'Yes, I asked some friends at the award's party about the scientists who were on the list. Of course I didn't mention the list or stuff like that. It turns out that they were the sort of scientists who invented new devices to give the military the edge. Sneaky stuff. Dark science.'

'Do you think there's a link to the projects? Was it first strike weaponry or surveillance equipment?'

'There was no link that I could see. The projects were really diverse,' said McAra, gulping down a mouthful of hot tea. 'I still can't fathom why your name was on the list. Unless there's a link to you and one of the scientists.'

'I didn't know any of them,' Riley said.

McAra shrugged and smiled. 'Never mind. It was just a wild theory. I'm sure it'll all come out in the wash.'

'It always does.'

'Do you think your escapade on the bridge tonight will be in the newspapers tomorrow?'

'I hope not,' Riley said. 'I'd rather keep well below the radar. The last thing we need is for the press to take an interest in this.'

Chapter Five

Luck of the Devil

The Scottish Parliament building in Edinburgh was crawling with newspaper journalists the next morning. Catherine made her way through the chaos to get to her office. A television news team were filming her and she was jostled by the media who pressurised her with questions. Word had got out that Catherine had been attacked in the street the night Richard Reece was murdered.

She pushed her way past the throng as journalists bombarded her with questions.

'Can you identify the man who attacked you?' a journalist asked.

'No. It was dark,' Catherine said.

'What was your involvement in the incident?' another journalist said.

'I have no further comments,' Catherine said.

Journalists continued to question her, and the situation escalated into a mild frenzy of flashing cameras and microphones being thrust in her face.

From out of the melee a strong arm grabbed hold of her and shielded her from the onslaught. It was Byrn Shaw. He hustled her through the crowds and into the building. Then he took her into her office and closed the door.

Catherine shrugged off her coat to reveal a smart black business suit and blouse. 'You're always coming to my rescue, Shaw,' she said, looking at him in a different light. Shaw was her secret admirer. That was either creepy or comforting. Right now she preferred the latter.

The office was small but sufficient, with a window that allowed plenty of daylight to shine in. Not that there was much light this morning. A murky dawn had merely brightened to a pale mist that hung over the city like a clouded veil. Shaw stood near the window watching the crowd outside. Richard Reece's murder had stirred up quite a hornet's nest.

Shaw and Catherine were alone in the office, but he had no intention of telling her how he felt about her, and besides, Valentine and Riley had already let that particular cat out of the bag. Part of him was pleased she knew that he cared about her, but equally he'd felt more at ease in her company when she was none the wiser.

'I can't believe how anxious I felt. I didn't know what to say to the press,' Catherine admitted.

Shaw continued to watch out the window. 'The pressure gets to everyone.'

She studied his chiselled profile stern against the world. 'It doesn't seem to get to you.'

Cold blue eyes looked round at her. He said nothing.

'I suppose your Special Forces training gives you a different perspective on things.'

He listened without making any comment.

'Of course you're not part of that anymore,' she rambled, clearly still on edge.

He fixed her with a direct gaze. 'It's never really over,' he said quietly, and then turned to look out the window again.

'I'm sorry. I'm saying all the wrong things this morning. This isn't like me. I'm just . . . a bit paranoid,' she confessed. 'It was horrible that Reece was murdered, but someone tried to attack me that night. I can't help but wonder what would've happened if you hadn't been there. And then last night, with Riley, another man, or the same man, following us to McAra's house. Am I the target? Was I the original target?' She paused. 'I even thought I heard someone in my house the other night.'

Shaw took a deep breath. 'That was me,' he said. There was no point adding to her paranoia.

'You were in my house?'

'I was worried for your safety. I checked the house was secure, and then I left. I won't invade your privacy again. You have my word.'

Catherine looked suddenly drained. 'Do you believe I was the target?'

'No. Reece had some bad enemies.'

'You said I had enemies.'

'Yes, but not anyone who'd murder you and hang a scroll around your neck.'

'Have you any idea who could've killed Reece?' She was looking for reassurance more than straight answers.

'Kier Brodie's mixed up in this. I think we both know that,' he said, hinting that he knew of her arrangement with the politician. 'I was going to talk to you at the party, but Reece monopolised your time.'

'Talk to me about what?'

'About the rumour that Brodie had pressurised you into keeping your mouth shut about things he'd been up to. Things you weren't supposed to find out, but as always, you're too good at your job, Catherine.'

She didn't deny his accusation.

Shaw continued, 'We all knew that Reece fleeced the system, but he wasn't into anything violent. Brodie on the other hand . . .'

'I've been gathering information on Brodie,' she said, defending her actions. 'Veiled threats were made that I should keep my investigations out of Brodie's business. I was hoping Brodie would eventually meet his match. Unfortunately it wasn't me. If I'd known you were ex–SAS perhaps I'd have acted differently but I thought I'd have to deal with the flack on my own.'

'You won't have to deal with Brodie on your own. You have my word on that as well.' Then he saw Valentine and Ferguson making their way through the journalists outside. 'The police detectives are here.'

'They want to question me. What should I tell them?' she said.

'The truth.'

Moments later Valentine and Ferguson knocked on the office door. Shaw let them in and then went to leave.

'Can Shaw stay?' Catherine asked Valentine.

Valentine nodded. She looked like she needed back up. He wasn't a complete bastard. Besides, it would save time. He wanted to talk to Shaw too.

For the next half hour Valentine and Ferguson asked Catherine about the sequence of events on the night Reece was murdered. Nothing new came to light.

She'd been followed, attacked, broken free, then Shaw had come to her rescue and the man had run off. She didn't know who he was and couldn't give a description. Neither could Shaw but he did have security video footage taken in the men's cloakroom of the parliament building. Footage of Reece and Kier Brodie. It didn't show either of them in a good light.

Shaw set up the video in the office. All four of them watched what had happened.

'There's Reece,' Shaw said, giving a running commentary of the footage that had been overlooked when the police had collected the main security video tapes. This particular camera had caught a small but very valuable few minutes in the gents' cloakroom.

'What's he doing?' Valentine said.

Numerous coats were hanging up in the cloakroom. The angle of the camera gave a close up of the scene and they could identify Reece quite clearly.

'He's going through Brodie's coat pockets,' Shaw said.

They watched as Reece found a dagger hidden in the inside breast pocket of the coat. It was encased in a leather cover. Reece pulled the knife free and studied the blade.

Catherine's blood ran cold when she saw the weapon. 'Is it the dagger he was attacked with?'

Valentine studied the dagger. 'It looks very like it. I'll get forensics to run a check but I'd say it's the same weapon.'

Reece rummaged through the rest of Brodie's pockets and found a second item — a scroll. It was carefully wrapped in a piece of dark material. He unravelled it, read it quickly and rolled it up tight again. Then he put his coat on and hid the dagger and the scroll in his pocket seconds before Brodie walked into the cloakroom. There was no sound on the recording, but from their manner, they weren't friendly. A few harsh words were exchanged and then Reece left the cloakroom. Brodie waited for a few moments, deep in thought, shrugged his coat on and hurried out.

Shaw clicked the video off, ejected the tape and gave it to Valentine. 'Maybe a lip reader could tell you what was said,' Shaw suggested.

'Any idea what may have been mentioned?' Ferguson said.

'Brodie's a collector. He likes antique weapons, especially short swords and daggers,' Shaw said. 'Apparently he's got quite a private collection.'

'Why did Brodie have a dagger in his coat pocket?' Valentine said. 'After all, he was at a party, a social evening in parliament.'

'And why did he have the scroll?' Ferguson said.

Shaw didn't know. 'Riley's your man to ask about the scroll.'

Valentine had every intention of asking Riley. The video tape put a whole new slant on things. He also needed to question Kier Brodie again.

'Do you know what the message was on the scroll?' Catherine said.

'No,' Valentine lied. 'We're working on it.'

Catherine took Valentine at his word. Shaw sensed he was lying.

'Is Brodie in the building today?' Valentine said to Shaw.

'Yes. I'll show you where he is.'

Valentine and Ferguson turned up unannounced to talk to Brodie. Ever the politician, Brodie, a fiercely ambitious man in his early forties who mixed in all the right social circles for all the wrong reasons, swallowed the unwelcome surprise and invited them in.

The rain was bearing down on Glasgow, adding weight to the day. Riley darted through the busy traffic, his greatcoat a shield against the weather. In the high fashion centre of the city he was heading for a niche that time forgot. At least that's how it appeared to Riley. He was going into the underworld of Glasgow to find out what he could about Mackenzie. Glasgow was a modern metropolis these days, but there was one particular labyrinth of back alleyways that had managed to avoid the twenty-first century, maybe even the twentieth century by the looks of it.

He turned into a narrow cobbled alley and dipped his head under a heavy tarpaulin that was stretched above the walls and tied with ropes to keep the rain off Lucky's empire. Lucky, who didn't have an ounce of flesh to spare on his scrawny frame, sat on his comfy chair watching open air television. In fact it was two silver, flat screen TVs showing two different shopping channels. Barking Bob the scabby dog, another quirk of nature, of indefinable age and breed, was snuggled at his feet on a remnant of thick pile cream carpet that was a good match for his fur.

Living up to his name, the dog barked as Riley approached, and then fell quiet when he recognised Riley.

Riley noted the resemblance between mutt and master; both lean, grizzled and borderline mangy with light-haired colouring and a kicked-in persona.

'Looks like you've been through the wars,' Riley said.

'You talking to me or the dog?' Lucky said, smiling with one less tooth than the last time they'd met a year ago.

Riley smiled. 'What happened to your ear?' he said. Lucky's right ear was less than it used to be. A large piece of the top half was missing but the lobe with its gold earring was still intact.

'I lost it,' Lucky said.

'What, did it fall off or blow away in the wind?'

'Ach, I was in a fight. Couldn't be arsed getting it sewn back on. Don't fuckin' need it anyway. I've still got the bit with my lucky earring in it.'

'Who came off the worst?'

'You know what women are like,' Lucky said. 'Unpre–fuckin'dictable. She just went for me. I didn't like to smack her around the chops. Don't want the name of being a chick–beater.'

Riley stifled a laugh. 'You've got your reputation to think of.'

'Exactly,' Lucky said seriously. 'Not that you'll associate with chicks of her calibre though, eh? Your women will be all hoity–toity.'

Maybe Lucky was right, but Riley wasn't about to discuss his love life, or distinct lack of it. Few women had been a close part of his life, mainly through circumstance. Shaw had been right when he'd said that living with a Special Forces man was fine in theory but the reality was too harsh for some women to deal with.

And for those women he'd cared deeply enough about, it was better to step aside and give them a better chance at happiness. He'd always attracted trouble like a magnet and he wouldn't wish that on any woman.

Perhaps things would change in the future. His new life as a civilian was supposed to have given him hope of eventually settling down. So far it had been like ether in the air.

'So what can I do for you, Riley? What is it you need?'

'Information. Does the name Mackenzie mean anything to you? A forger. Very skilled. Managed to wipe himself off the map.'

'From what I hear, someone did a better job of it — he's dead.'

'I know, but what's his history? Who was he involved with?'

'Mackenzie was in tow with dirty politicians and a weirdo scientist. A right creep, but a smart one. Don't know the scientist's name. He's a gadget freak.'

'Where can I find him?' Riley said.

'He eats in Jamesie's restaurant. Jamesie's the chef. You'll remember him.'

'The question is, does Jamesie remember anything these days?'

'Oh yes, he's a lot sharper. The dent in his head's barely noticeable. And the chefing work has really calmed him down. Better than the nightclub bouncing. Ironic, isn't it, he was an expert in martial arts and filthy fighting techniques. In all the years he worked the doors he never came a cropper on the job. Then one of his ex–

girlfriends clobbers him with her shoe, sticking the stiletto in the back of his head.'

'Is his memory reliable?' Riley said.

'It's like tuning in a dodgy radio to some obscure station. It takes a few goes before you're on the right wavelength with Jamesie.'

'Sounds like the ideal informant.' Riley didn't even try to hide the sarcasm in his voice.

'I'll contact Jamesie,' Lucky said. 'I'll find out when the scientist's going to eat at the restaurant and give you a bell.'

'How much will this cost me?'

'No charge. I just want to see the fury. I'd like a front row seat to see that scientist get what's coming to him.'

'You've met him?'

'I've passed him a couple of time. He glares at me like I'm a piece of scum.'

'Describe him,' Riley said.

'At a distance he could look like you on a bad day, only he's blonde. Got a wee bit of a power trip going on. Thinks he's got the world by the balls.'

'In what way?'

Lucky shrugged his bony shoulders. 'Don't know, just the impression, the look in his eyes like he's something special. A man with secrets.'

'We've all got secrets.'

'Especially you, eh Riley? But your secrets and mine have a habit of haunting ourselves. This weirdo's secrets . . . I've a feeling they're going to haunt other people.'

There were times when Riley thought Lucky's talents for selling stolen goods, clothes for the discerning male that had fallen off the back of a lorry, were wasted. An astute observer of human nature, he'd have made a first rate profiler.

'What about the politicians Mackenzie was hanging around with. Any names?' Riley said.

'Kier Brodie was one of them. He collects *daggers*,' Lucky said with a wink.

'Like the dagger that killed Richard Reece the politician?'

Lucky gave him a knowing look. 'The dagger and the scroll were all over the news. If you were into political intrigue and stuff you could put two and two together. Reece was after Kier Brodie's seat in parliament. No one will kill you surer than a dirty rival.'

Riley seemed surprised at the extent of Lucky's knowledge.

'Don't look so surprised. I watch the telly. I keep up with what's going on, especially politics. I love the hatred in it.'

Riley understood the politics of love and war only too well. 'Right, let me know when you've contacted Jamesie. And try to keep a low profile on this.'

Lucky laughed. 'Low profile! I'm not the one who jumped in the Clyde to rescue a drunken fairy!'

'Word travels fast.'

Lucky smirked. 'You've no idea.'

Riley put an envelope of money down. 'For the dog,' he said, and then walked away.

'If I hear anything else about Mackenzie, I'll let you know,' Lucky called after him, opening the envelope, having a quick tote up of the folded notes and then stuffing the money in his trouser pocket. 'I'll keep my ear to the ground — the good one.'

By the afternoon Lucky phoned Riley with the information he needed.

'Got a snippet for you about Mackenzie,' Lucky said. 'He was a loner, lived in his own wee world where everything was forged and no one was ever who they were supposed to be. He knew about you though. He knew you were the Record Keeper. Word was that he'd been paid to make a really good forgery of a document, make it look ancient.'

'The scroll?'

'I would think so. I don't know anything else,' Lucky said. And I spoke to Jamesie. The scientist will be in the restaurant for dinner tomorrow night, 8:30. He'll be alone. That's your chance.'

'Tell Jamesie I'll be there,' Riley confirmed.

'Oh and . . . I know you're well capable, but I hear the scientist's handy in a fight — and they say he's got the luck of the devil on his side. So watch your back.'

Lucky was still as superstitious as ever, but Riley made a mental note to keep the warning in mind.

Chapter Six

No Rest for the Wicked

The early evening offered a brief pocket of calm at the end of a busy day. The information from Lucky had given Riley plenty to think about. He stood at the edge of his diving pool at home gazing down into the blue depths. This was the ideal place to think. What would the scientist do when he confronted him tomorrow night at the restaurant? A public place, it wouldn't be easy, especially if a fight kicked off. Then there was Catherine. Valentine had contacted him about the forensic tests. No fingerprints had been found on the piece of paper that bore the message — *Fortune Favours the Brave*. And there were no traces of poison in the glass Catherine had given him. He was disappointed about the first and relieved about the latter. He liked Catherine. He hardly knew her but he liked her. It was enough for now.

He took a deep breath and dived into the water. His senses were filled with the dazzling blue liquid lit by spotlights all the way down. The pressure of the water at the bottom of the pool felt like the weight of the day, and lifted as he turned his hands and body upward to rise to the surface again. The temperature was colder than normal. He'd not bothered heating it fully. The coolness gave a jolt to his system, reminding him how alive the water could make him feel. Reminding him too of one of the last times he'd dived into a bright turquoise sea that promised more warmth than it really offered . . .

Every one of the eight SBS men were kitted out in blue wetsuits, the colour of the sky, to blend in with the tropical sea. Black wetsuits would have made them too visible, an easy target. Winter in the tropics was rarely less than warm, so they'd been surprised by the lack of heat in the water. Riley put it down to the depth of the sea. A British Royal Navy frigate, using a waterborne insertion technique, had dropped them off miles from the shore at the start of their mission. Their objective was to board a ship suspected of holding hostage four British undercover agents who'd been ratted on during an espionage assignment.

Riley could see the ship, a private vessel belonging to a business magnet who was being blackmailed to go along with the kidnappers plans. This had to be a clean sweep. Board the ship. Take control, regain the agents and deal with the perpetrators.

The water was calm, affording them little margin for error. If ever the SBS needed to live up to their reputation as the *Invisible Raiders* this was a prime time. In bright daylight in a flat calm sea, the eight men had to utilize ever part of their swimming techniques to approach the vessel without being compromised. The non–reflective blue material of their gear was the camouflage of choice, but it was vital to literally go with the flow of the water, each individual swimming like a thin arrow through the surface, submerging when necessary on Riley's low key signal whenever they were at risk of being seen by the two armed patrol guards who were stalking back and forth across the main deck. And they had to be quick. Intelligence had advised Riley that the ship followed a pattern whereby it would anchor for one hour, then proceed to its next coordinates. Riley checked the time on his diver's watch. They had fifteen minutes max to get there.

They made it in twelve.

Silently, the SBS split into two, four–man teams. Nick Deacon headed the second team. Riley took his men around the hull and then climbed up on the blind side of the guards, capturing both of them without incident. Each guard was armed with two heavy duty automatic weapons. Riley and his three men now had one weapon each. This was in addition to the small, light, but effective weapons they had stashed in their fully watertight bags.

Riley signalled to Deacon and his team who were now within listening distance of the ship's bridge. Five men were milling around inside the bridge, unaware of their visitors. Riley and Deacon exchanged a nod. Complete dependability. No hesitation. They'd go in on three. Two different angles. A fast take down, minimum fuss, few casualties and even fewer fatalities as had been requested by the military hierarchy.

One . . . two . . . and in! Only one of the kidnappers had time to fire a shot, but it was more a misfire from his gun due to being overpowered by one of Deacon's men. It hit nothing but glass, shattering the panoramic bevelled window of the bridge, sending the fragments scattering out on to the deck.

Footsteps, running from below the deck gathered pace. Another nod exchanged between Riley and Deacon. Let them come up, straight into the fly trap.

Deacon made the first strike. One enemy down, then another four, minor injuries, fully disarmed.

Riley led the way below deck, sliding down the outward metal of the stairs without touching a single step. Deacon's men held the upper level while Riley's team and Deacon located the agents. Muffled sounds mixed with aggressive arguing could be heard as the kidnappers who were left guarding their captives failed to agree on how to handle the situation. Riley could smell their panic. Violence had its merits because it tended to follow a distinct pattern. You could see it coming, guns blazing, hard and uncompromising. Panic was erratic. Wild shots, maybe even killing the hostages for the hell of it if they thought there was no way out. This could get messy.

Riley pulled out his knife, the hunting knife that had seen every piece of action since he'd become a member of the SBS. The blade could pierce metal if thrown with sheer voracity and force.

Deacon and the others separated, each man hunting the lower decks like a blue ghost that haunts the enemy and defends the weak.

Riley stood where he was. Beside him a red flashing light signalled an emergency on board. Indeed there was. Blood had already been spilt, in moderation, with the potential for more if the mission turned grim. Then he saw a figure, a shadow at the far end of the corridor, dart across from one room to another, a gun forced into the back of one of the agents. He recognised the agent from the photographs they'd seen before the outset of the mission. He'd familiarised himself with each of the faces, but this agent was distinctive — slight with white–blonde hair.

Riley held his knife, angling the blade into a long throw strike. He was anticipating a situation. Here it came.

'Let me go or I'll kill him!' the kidnapper shouted at Riley, forcing a gun into the agent's torso while grabbing his neck from behind in a choke hold. 'Drop the fuckin' gun!'

Riley put his gun down on the floor and kicked it forward until it was out of reach, lying between him and the kidnapper. He was anticipating the next move. The kidnapper must have been reading the standard book of what not to do when faced with an unknown enemy.

Under the blood red glow of the flashing light, Riley kept his eyes focussed on the kidnapper's gun. He would surely turn the weapon on Riley, feeling he was now in a position of power to kill the military adversary while still keeping a grip on the hostage.

Within seconds this was played out for real. A split second before the kidnapper had a chance to fire, Riley's hunting knife cut through the air and embedded itself into the centre of his skull. No shot was fired. The kidnapper slid to the floor, his limp hand trailing down the shocked body of the agent.

Deacon swept up from behind the agent, and with the other SBS having gathered all the kidnappers and other hostages, they were hustled back up on deck. Mission accomplished. Job done . . .

. . . the sound of the phone ringing incessantly brought Riley back to the present. He climbed out of the diving pool and grabbed the phone. It was McAra.

'Turn the television news on,' McAra said, sounding desperate yet elated.

Riley ran through to his study, activated the television remote and flicked through the channels to the early evening news. He was on it, seen swimming in the Clyde and saving the girl. Valentine was being asked questions by the television crew who were on the bridge capturing every moment of the incident that night.

A reporter who'd been at the scene was speaking. '*An un-named hero dived into the freezing cold River Clyde last night to rescue a young woman, a so-called drunken fairy. Another man also helped in the rescue. The girl is now recovering in hospital. Thanks to the swift action of these two local heroes, she survived being thrown into the icy water during an unprovoked attack. Her injuries are said to be minor. What was supposed to be a girls' night out to celebrate her birthday turned into a nightmare. For once, the fact that she'd been drinking and was relaxed when she hit the water, may have helped to save her life.*'

The news cut to a view of Valentine. '*Do you know the man who rescued her?*' the reporter asked, thrusting a microphone at Valentine.

'*Just a man who was driving past and dived in to save her,*' Valentine said. He pushed past the television crew who were then cordoned off by Ferguson and other officers, creating a barrier to keep them away from Riley.

Riley's muscles tensed in anger as he watched the footage of him and Shaw rescuing the girl from the river. The cameras focussed on Riley and Shaw's bare torsos as they stripped off their soaking wet tops, revealing their scarred back, chests and shoulders.

'The clarity is amazing,' McAra said. He couldn't help but enthuse. The scientist in him loved technology. 'Some of it is amateur footage from mobile phones.'

'No detail spared,' Riley said standing in his study, dripping wet from diving in the pool.

'You can even see the bullet hole scars and the marks of the ice axe wound on your back. Some cameras nowadays are powerful enough to see a gumdrop on Mars.'

Riley didn't know about Mars but it was blatantly obvious that Shaw and Riley weren't your average Joe. Shaw had marks on his torso, old wounds from his SAS past. Part of his shoulder, Riley remembered, because he'd been there when it happened, had been set alight with a cocktail of alcohol and a dirty rag stuffed into a glass bottle, lit and thrown at Shaw. The bottle had hit off the wall and shattered, sending flames on to his clothes. Before Riley had time to pull Shaw's burning jacket off him, the fire had seared his skin and some of the fabric had melted into his raw flesh. Riley's hands had taken a fair scalding but Shaw had come off the worst. He still bore the scars, visible now to everyone who was watching the news. And they would see the scars across Riley's back. The bullet holes were left by the slugs pumped into his back from a long distance. The bullets hadn't penetrated too deep. The gun was a short range weapon that had struck lucky with its target. Deacon had prised the bullets out of Riley's back with a scalding hot knife, poured disinfectant over the wounds, slapped on a dressing and they'd continued with their mission. As for the ice axe wound, it happened during a climbing recce when an enemy tried to stop Riley scaling the sheer face of a frozen cliff by embedding an ice axe in his shoulder. Riley had kicked the man unconscious and continued to climb with the axe sticking out of his body. The axe had two components on either end of the head. One end was flat, used to gouge steps into the ice, and the other end, the pick, was a long, pointed hook serrated with teeth for a vice-like grip. It was the pick that had pierced his shoulder and the resulting wound still bore the marks of the serrations.

Despite the scars of past conflict, neither of them had a tattoo on their bodies. Riley wasn't sure what

Shaw's reasons were but they were probably the same as his. A tattoo was a tag, a label. He'd have been as well having his name inked on to his skin. The lack of any tattoo helped protect his life of anonymity — a grey ghost.

'Oh, and I had a thought,' McAra said. 'If this is the type of footage gleaned from mobiles at night, what about cameras picking up Richard Reece getting stabbed.'

'I'd have thought the police would've checked their own sources for that,' Riley said.

McAra wasn't convinced. 'I've been raking around the weather charts. It was a foggy night in Edinburgh. We know that Scotland is the best place in the world to hide from satellite imagery. Nothing except the top equipment can penetrate the ruddy grey clouds, but it was cold that night. There's a chance that any high powered satellite image system could've captured the fight, maybe even seen Catherine being attacked.'

'I'll talk to Shaw,' Riley said. 'He's the expert on imagery intelligence. If it's available to be picked right out of the air, he's the man to do it.'

The television news reporter concluded, '*Police are appealing for information from anyone who recognises the man who cruelly threw the drunken fairy into the Clyde. And here is a message for the two mystery men from the girl's father.*'

A man was shown, his face worn and distressed. He looked straight at the camera. '*Whoever you are, thank you, thank you for saving my wee girl.*'

Riley was glad that the girl was okay, but angry at what had happened to her.

He thanked McAra, and then checked a list of telephone contacts, found Shaw's number and gave him a call. 'Have you seen the news?'

'Yes, just what we don't need. Things are getting messy,' Shaw said.

'Want to help me clean up?'

'Your house or mine?'

'Still got your imagery intelligence contacts?'

'I can do better than that,' Shaw said. 'Right now I'm pouring over a particular area of Edinburgh. The images were taken that night. So if you're not busy . . .'

'Are you living at the same place?' Riley said. There was a tendency for people to imagine that forces men never settled in the one place for long or constantly changed their contact numbers. Riley thought it the opposite. Forces men, including him, could often be located by their friends, even years later at the same address. If someone happened to get hold of the information and was brave enough to chap their door or phone a number they'd no right knowing, the welcome could be less than friendly.

Shaw confirmed he was at the same house in the centre of Edinburgh.

'I'm on my way,' Riley said. Another long night — and still no rest for the wicked.

Chapter Seven

Beyond This There Be Dragons

Riley made sure he wasn't followed to Edinburgh. No forces man, ex–forces or otherwise, would ever compromise a colleague. Riley had been watched as he'd gone to McAra's house with Catherine, and there was a chance he'd be followed again. Despite Shaw being capable of looking after himself it just wasn't done. He was extra vigilant as he drove to Shaw's house in Edinburgh. He didn't want to be the one who highlighted it like a marker.

It was dark by the time Riley arrived outside the narrow, three–storey, grey stone building that merged into an ancient part of the historic city. A light shone from one of the windows on the top floor, indicating that someone did actually live there. It was difficult to distinguish the outline of the house because the structure blended into the medieval stonework, creating a home that was camouflaged as part of the landscape.

Shaw opened the ground floor level door. There was one way in and three optional exists as far as Riley remembered, including one via the roof but you'd need nerves of steel to venture across the sheer drop to reach it, or be a very capable climber. Riley thought the house was the perfect place for a man with Byrn Shaw's background. A shadow living in the heart of everything that was going on. Even his current role, working for the government in some indistinct capacity, was ideal for a man, similar to himself, who lived a life in shades of grey. As if to emphasise this, Shaw's house, although stylishly furnished, was a monochrome home. White, cream, greys and blacks were the predominant colours of the decor. If Riley had taken a photograph of any of the rooms, the image could have been mistaken for a black and white snap. Riley liked it.

They went up to the top floor. It had a view of Prince's Street, alight with traffic, shops and famous monuments silhouetted against the night sky in the Scottish capital. A large screen computer sat on the spacious desk and showed satellite images that changed every five seconds.

'I contacted a friend to get access to these,' Shaw said.

Riley had brought his laptop with him. Between them they began to piece together the events leading up to the murder of Richard Reece.

Shaw pointed at the screen. 'It's dark, overcast and the fog is obscuring parts of the view, but the freezing cold gives us gaps to see through. If you look closely you can see a figure, which we know to be Catherine, coming out of the parliament building and walking towards the street where she'd parked her car.'

'I see her.' Riley said, and then leaned closer. 'Is that someone over there? Looks like a man further along the street.'

'Yes, he's watching her. There he goes, he's following her now. And then you'll catch a glimpse of me leaving the building.'

The five second intervals moved the sequence of events on quite quickly. It was hard to see where the man disappeared to after he lost his hold on Catherine and Shaw scared him off. Although the images were reasonably high–resolution and Shaw was adept at imagery analysis and had already sharpened the pictures, some details remained shrouded in the fog.

Now that Riley had a better idea of how the imagery could be interpreted, he was ready to study further satellite footage of Reece's murder. While Shaw set up the computer with the next range of images, he told Riley about showing Valentine and Ferguson the security video of Reece taking the dagger and scroll from Kier Brodie's coat.

'So Brodie's the prime suspect?' Riley said.

'Yes, but Valentine seemed frustrated after talking to him. Even without his lawyer Brodie managed to create an alibi. The two things that were left at the crime scene were stolen from him by Reece and it's all on camera.'

'Do you think Brodie did it?'

Shaw hesitated. It was answer enough.

'This was taken from a different satellite,' Shaw said. Two vague figures were seen running along the street. 'The images aren't quite as sharp but we can focus in on the location because we know where Reece was murdered.'

'Can we assume the two figures are Reece and Brodie?'

'Yes, I've analysed the images and cross referenced them with the time Reece and Brodie left the party. You'll see them fight here and then run on.'

'Presuming it was Reece running away, he seemed able to fight Brodie. Was he known to be a good fighter?'

'Reece used to belong to a posh boxing club in his youth and was said to be competent in a scrap. He could really pack a punch. Some politicians could give you a run for your money.'

'What about Brodie?' Riley said.

'Let's just say you wouldn't want to meet him in a dark alley. Rough background. Would annihilate anyone who got in his way — and Reece was planning to challenge him for his seat in parliament.'

'Was it Brodie who attacked Catherine?'

'No, he was still at the party. He didn't leave until later in the night. Neither did Reece, so it wasn't either of them.'

Riley leaned back in his chair. 'So we've got a third man mixed in with this somewhere.'

'Catherine's worried she was the original target. I doubt it. But maybe she was just another problem digging up dirt on Brodie and he'd paid someone else to deal with her.'

'The same man who was in Glasgow last night?'

Shaw nodded. 'Here's where the fight ends,' he said, focussing again on the images.

They watched the final moments of Reece's life. It was too dark to see the dagger being drawn but the struggle was obviously vicious. Then the image changed to reveal the distinct outline of a body lying lifeless on the ground. The killer stood over the body for at least three of the five second frames.

'Why is he waiting?' Shaw said.

'He's thinking,' Riley said. 'He probably didn't intend to kill Reece. Perhaps he just wanted to threaten him, get Reece to back off, rough him up a bit, but things got out of hand.'

Shaw nodded. 'By the way, Valentine was lying today.'

'About what?'

'Catherine asked him what the message was on the scroll and he said he didn't know, but I knew he was lying.'

'The message on the scroll was for me.'

Shaw couldn't hide his surprise. 'You? How are you involved?'

Riley shrugged his shoulders. 'It says — *this one is for the Record Keeper.* That's all I know.'

Shaw rewound the satellite images of Reece's murder. They watched as the figure that was standing over the body finally ran away.

'The images stop there,' Shaw said.

'Can we see where he runs to?'

'No. The fog was too thick over that area, so I lost track of him after that. I'd hoped I could follow him to a residence but no such luck.'

'Well this gives us a lot more to go on. Are you going to pass it on to Valentine?' Riley said.

'Yes.' Shaw got up from his chair and looked out the window at the city. 'I spoke to a private investigator in Glasgow. It's clear that Brodie's a devious bastard but there's no hint he could've made the scroll.'

'Whoever made it knew a bit about what they were doing. Not brilliant but not a bad forgery. And the only forger in the mix is Mackenzie.'

There was a strange feeling to the day. Riley worked in his study, ripping Mackenzie's computer files apart, checking for anything he'd missed, taking into account the new information that had come to light, searching for the electronic fingerprints Mackenzie had left behind. But in the back of his mind something didn't seem right. There was an edginess in the air, a sense of something coming up, and his instincts had rarely let him down. Instincts played a bigger part in military life than people realised. It wasn't as if he felt someone had him in their sights, more like a sense that the past was coming back to cause him yet another measure of strife.

He looked around the study and one of the maps caught his attention. He read the warning message on the ancient map of the great oceans — *Beyond This Place There Be Dragons!* His senses jarred. Something was definitely ahead of him, a conflict from years ago coming back to have another run at him.

The most likely event was the meeting with the scientist tonight. He remembered what Lucky had said. According to him the scientist had the luck of the devil on his side. Riley wasn't superstitious — but he'd be ready to deal with the human equivalent of any dragon that reared its head tonight.

Riley was stripped to the waist and training on his climbing wall when Valentine and Ferguson turned up at his house in the early evening. Riley let them in and went back through to the climbing room to grab a vest. The detectives followed him.

'Unusual decor,' Valentine said looking around the cement walls that were embedded with pieces of ancient pottery jugs, stones and rugged artefacts.

Ferguson was fascinated. 'What do you use this for?'

'It's a climbing wall. I use it for training.'

He could see the enthusiasm rise in Ferguson. 'What do you do?' He pulled at a couple of the jugs to test how firmly they were stuck into the wall.

Valentine and Riley exchanged a glance. Riley sighed and took a moment to show Ferguson the technique. He climbed along the wall and then jumped down on to the polished wooden floor.

'Can I try?' Ferguson said. He was already slipping his shoes off and didn't seem likely to take no for an answer.

'Knock yourself out,' Riley said.

Valentine had no objections. He spoke to Riley while Ferguson challenged himself on the wall. The detective had a grip like a bear and was determined not to fall off as he made his way along the wall rather than climbing too high. His determination lost out several times but he'd no more than a few feet to drop and kept climbing back on again.

'Shaw gave us the satellite images,' Valentine began. 'Very useful. Off the record, we're keeping an eye on Brodie. A slippery customer, but that'll be his downfall. He'll slip up and make a mistake. When he does we'll nail him.'

Ferguson took a hard tumble off the climbing wall.

Valentine continued, 'Any idea why Brodie had the scroll with a message on it for you? He denies even having it. Claims it was stashed in his pocket by someone else and then Reece stole it. But he does own up to the dagger. He's even listed as a collector.'

Riley shook his head. 'I've no links with Brodie. Never met him.'

'We're presuming he hung the scroll around Reece's neck to take the heat of himself, maybe even to implicate you in the murder. So we also have to assume he has a link with you, whether you know it or not.'

'Someone who knows both of us?' Riley said.

'Yes, a go–between. Brodie has all sorts of people in his back pocket.'

'From everything I've seen, there's only two other rats in the sewer — Mackenzie, who could've forged the scroll, or the scientist.'

'All the scientists on the list are dead,' Valentine reminded him.

'Ah but there's another one. He was, and probably still is, tagged to Brodie.'

'Who told you that?'

'Lucky.'

Valentine blew out a mouthful of hot air. Lucky was always a pile of trouble but his information had an uncanny habit of being within range of the truth.

'Lucky has set up a situation for me with the scientist,' Riley said.

Valentine raised a cautious eyebrow.

'Borderline legal,' Riley assured him. 'I just want to talk to him. However he's known to be a difficult bastard.'

'Got a name for the scientist that we can go on?'

'No, Lucky's contact has a memory problem for details so I'm going in with only the basics.'

Valentine kept his voice down. 'Talk to him, find out who he is and what he knows. Don't go kicking up a storm though.'

Ferguson came a cropper off the wall again. Sweat was pouring from his brow and the tips of his fingers were starting to feel like sandpaper. 'I could get used to this,' he said, slightly out of breath.

Riley and Valentine continued their conversation while Ferguson put his shoes back on.

'Lucky told me that Mackenzie knew I was the Record Keeper,' Riley said.

'Could he be the link between you and Brodie?' Valentine suggested.

'Very possibly because it's likely that Mackenzie was paid to make the scroll with the message on it for me.'

'Did you find anything about that on his computer?'

'No, only that I was on the list. But something bothers me. Mackenzie kept his computer clean. It didn't even register that he existed. So why would he be stupid enough to have a copy of a hit list on his files? Very sloppy and that just doesn't fit his profile. I think it was put there by someone else.'

'The scientist?'

'Well it was a list of scientists who'd died in mysterious circumstances. According to Lucky this guy's a gadget freak so he's bound to be good at computing.'

'When do you meet the scientist?' Valentine said.

Riley checked his watch. 'In a couple of hours.'

'Want back up?' Ferguson offered.

'No. He's a sharp one and he eats regularly at the restaurant. Any change in the water mark and he might run.'

The restaurant was in the one of the busiest areas of the city centre a couple of minutes from Sauchiehall Street. Glasgow was winding down for the day and gearing up for the nightlife. It was 8:15pm. A river of brightly lit traffic poured through the streets and although most of the shops and stylish malls had closed for the evening, numerous window displays were filled with vibrant orange, black and gold Hallowe'en decorations that kept the place alive during the twilight hours. Spooks, skeletons, luminous pumpkins and witches on brooms had arrived early in October, ready for the end of the month fancy dress parties.

Riley sat in his car watching the street, looking for the scientist, waiting for him to arrive. He had a view of the restaurant, an elegant upmarket eatery. How Jamesie ended up being the chef there was a minor miracle. A few couples entered while he was watching. Two large front windows with tinted glass gave an element of privacy but allowed him to glimpse what was going on inside. A beautifully carved pumpkin lit with candles flickered in one of the windows, a subtle nod to the Hallowe'en scene. Candles lit each table and most tables were busy.

Jamesie's face peered out the window several times. His chef's hat did him no favours but it helped to hide the stiletto chunk missing from his skull. His bobbing and weaving near the window was at least a sign that Jamesie had actually remembered Riley was due to arrive. There was hope the evening wouldn't turn into a complete fiasco.

As if on cue the second element of trouble sauntered past Riley's car. Lucky had arrived early, no doubt to claim his front row seat to see the fury. Lucky was shrewd enough not to acknowledge Riley's presence and walked past like a stranger in the night. He went across the street and stood near a lamp post. Riley guessed he was anticipating the fury wouldn't take place while everyone was enjoying their meal and was more likely to kick off outside in the street after he'd confronted the scientist. Yes, Lucky would've made an excellent profiler.

The street was getting busier with people on their way to a night out. So who was he looking for? At a distance, the scientist was supposed to be a blonde mirror image of him on a bad day. No one fitted that description. Riley checked his watch. Almost time and the scientist was never late. Among the many faces going by, who was the man with secrets? The man who thought he was something special.

The thought had barely manifested when Riley saw the one face that stood out from the crowd. A cold shiver like a jagged blade of ice cut through Riley. This man indeed had secrets. He walked towards the restaurant, his tall, stylishly suited stature and long unbuttoned, beige coat clearly visible within the crowd. He had an attitude that dared anyone to stand in his way. No one did. No one really noticed the man who was expensively dressed in dark brown and beige. They were too busy in their own happy revelry.

Riley sat back into the seat of the car, pressing himself into the shadows. The man was about two hundred yards straight ahead and would be turning left to go into the restaurant, leaving Riley to study him without being seen.

As he turned the corner the Hallowe'en lights from a window display of spooks and ghouls highlighted his tall, blonde stature. It had been four years since Riley had encountered this particular ghost. Ruary Strang, a man in his early thirties, had been a scientist, a civilian working on the naval base at HMS Excalibur. He'd messed up his chances of going the distance by developing projects that the navy hadn't authorised. Projects that were classified as dangerous.

Without the slightest inclination that he was being watched by Riley, Lucky and a jittery looking Jamesie,

Strang went into the restaurant and was seated at his favourite table in the corner beside one of the windows.

Lucky gave Riley a bone–jarring stare though nothing in his body moved to give the game away. Riley got out of the car, acknowledgment that he'd seen the target. He flicked a glance at Lucky, a silent nod that it was game on but with an extra look that said things weren't going to end well tonight.

The muscles on either side of Lucky's prominent cheekbones tightened. It was a cold, bleak night to be standing against a lamp post in Glasgow but Riley's silent message assured him the fury was on its way.

Jamesie had taken care of the reservation for Riley. A waiter showed Riley to his table and gave him a menu. He was seated directly behind Strang who was unaware of what was to come. Riley evaluated the situation. Of all the scientists it had to be this bastard — the worst of all dragons tonight. His instincts had been right, and this was one man who really did have the luck of the devil on his side. There were too many people in the restaurant to risk a set–to here. Strang hadn't yet taken his coat off but it was obvious he'd kept himself fit and strong. Riley had no problem taking him on and if it had been Strang who'd thrown the girl in the Clyde he welcomed the chance to get his hands around the weasel's throat. No wonder there had been a sense of familiarity about the man on the bridge. He just never thought he'd see this ghost again. The navy had seen to that, disposing of Strang's services, burning his bridges for him and locking the door forever. But here he was, turning up again, niggling like an old war wound that refused to fade into the past. So be it.

Riley got up and approached Strang's table. The scientist was reading the menu, head down, engrossed in the selection, taking a sip from a large glass of whisky.

Strang didn't flinch as he suddenly realised someone was standing right next to him, barring his exit from the table. He looked up. Cool blue eyes full of recognition, arrogance and deep-seated hostility stared out from a face that many would consider handsome. He ran a hand through his thick blonde hair, the only giveaway to his edginess. 'I'd recommend the steak,' he said calmly.

Riley leaned down. 'I'd recommend we take this outside,' he said, his voice a bitter whisper.

Strang sat back in defiance. 'I don't think so.'

Riley watched his every move, his hands, whether he was carrying a weapon, any tricks he was likely to use. Out the corner of his eye he could see Jamesie bobbing his head over the swing door of the kitchen like a demented chicken. He wished he would bloody calm down.

'Did you throw the girl off the bridge?' Riley said quietly.

Strang's sly smile was his answer.

Riley swallowed his rage.

'Why don't you sit down and we can talk about this calmly over dinner,' Strang said, believing Riley couldn't cause a scene in public without just cause. If he remained undisturbed he took the fight away from Riley.

If anyone came close to being wrong about that it was Strang. Riley preferred to play an intelligent game but he had no qualms about grabbing Strang in a neck lock and dragging him out of the restaurant. Fate had other plans.

Jamesie came hurrying out of the kitchen towards Strang in an attempt to cause a distraction. It worked, but not to Riley's advantage.

'We've got a special menu this evening,' Jamesie said nervously to Strang.

Strang looked him up and down. 'You look guilty. Been telling tales?'

'No, no . . . nothing like that Mr Strang.'

The scientist cut him dead. 'I'd say he's lying. What do you think, Riley?'

Riley glanced out the window. Across the street Lucky was watching them like a hawk. 'Get back into the kitchen,' Riley said to Jamesie.

In the split second it took Jamesie to register what Riley was saying, Strang threw his glass of whisky on to the tablecloth and set it alight with the burning candle. The cloth burst into flames — and so did the edge of Jamesie's chef whites.

Immediate chaos ignited in the restaurant and some of the diners scurried out into the street. Others stayed where they were, transfixed by the madness nearby.

While Riley tried to contain the fire, and Jamesie battered out the flames on his apron, Strang took advantage of the distraction. He punched Jamesie in the back of the head to get him out of the way so he could make a run for it. If he'd hit the chef on any other part of the body the retaliation would have been milder, but the stiletto injury had left its mark in more ways than one. Jamesie couldn't stand being hit on the back of the head. Not ever. It sent him crazy. Years ago, when he'd worked on the doors of the nightclubs, he'd used his martial arts expertise to deal with awkward customers. As if the past were yesterday, Jamesie launched into martial mode, the look in his wild eyes sheer frenzy. The highly strung and forgetful chef was back in his box and standing in the restaurant was Mad Jamesie.

Riley was stamping the flames out on the carpet, but even he did a double take at Jamesie. Tackling a skilled martial arts expert was difficult. Taking on a hardened street fighter was just as tough. A combination of the two was highly dangerous, but there was nothing more deadly and unpredictable than being attacked by a madman. It was, in Riley's experience, a hard fight to get clear of. Strang was about to live the experience.

Strang had almost made it through the chaos to the door. Almost but not quite. Jamesie launched himself at him, kicking him full force in the back, sending the scientist tumbling out into the street. Riley hoped Lucky was getting his money's worth of the fury.

A red flashing light in a corner of the restaurant signalled the fire brigade had been alerted without deafening the customers. Riley had the fire under basic control but no one else seemed capable of handling it so he was stuck with the task. The fumes were beginning to stink and he told everyone else to get out the back exit. No one argued.

On the street Strang was fighting Jamesie. It was getting messy. Lucky had been right again. The scientist's reputation for being handy in a fight was obvious, his style of choice a combination of combat techniques and boxing. Despite Strang's size and skill, Riley knew who his money was on.

Jamesie let rip a debilitating kick but Strang blocked it with his arms and countered with a punch to the jaw. The force would've sent lesser men reeling but the madness in Jamesie absorbed the blow and he retaliated with a punch of equal force. Strang saw it coming and jerked his head aside. The strike grazed his face and in the flurry of punches that Jamesie continued to rain on to him, Strang managed to duck and dive the worst of them. Moments later the fight went to the ground and some grappling action was seen by crowds of onlookers who were wary of trying to separate the ferocious pair. No one was prepared to step in and tame the beasts. The fight went on with them grappling and rolling around in the street. Strang struggled to his feet but Jamesie got up and was ready to fight on. He scored a perfect roundhouse kick to Strang's upper body. The scientist reeled back from that one, then reached into his coat pocket and pulled a knife on Jamesie. The crowd moved back.

Lucky was tearing across the street to help Jamesie but stopped when he heard the sound of police car sirens blaring towards the restaurant. His scrawny silhouette disappeared into the shadows. He wasn't the only one. Strang made a similar exit, leaving Jamesie to face the police alone.

Three police cars screeched to a halt from different angles, blocking off the street in front of the restaurant. Jamesie stood in the middle, caught in the headlights, his mouth and nose dripping blood from the punches inflicted by Strang. He didn't feel the pain. He didn't feel anything. He was too pumped with adrenalin and the remnants of blind fury. Blow for blow, Jamesie had been the victor. Strang had taken a vicious hammering.

The restaurant manager, who had made himself scarce when the trouble kicked off, came running forward, praising Jamesie to the police, putting his arm around his shoulder and thanking him for tackling an armed attacker single handed. A pay rise was in order and the insurance would cover the fire damage. The restaurant needed a new ambiance anyway.

The fire brigade were on the scene minutes later but someone told them that one of the diners had contained the blaze so there was little for them to do except extinguish the smouldering carpet. Where Riley had disappeared to, no one knew. A leading officer from the brigade searched for the booking register so that everyone could be accounted for safely, and the police needed it anyway for eye witness reports. Jamesie made sure it had gone missing, presumably destroyed in the fire. Before the ambulance took him to the hospital to clean up his wounds, and before he forgot, Jamesie slid the register down a drain at the back of the kitchen. It was no one's business who'd been at the restaurant that night or what any of them had been up to.

Riley sat in his car watching from a distance. A figure made his way up the street ahead, keeping close to the buildings, merging with the night. There was blood on the long beige coat and a touch of scarlet in the blonde hair. The man was walking away from him, moving with less confidence and arrogance. Riley's eyes bored holes into his shoulder blades. He'd let him go, for now, until he'd told Valentine what had happened.

Strang must have sensed Riley watching him, sensed the hatred searing into his back. He paused and glanced over his shoulder at Riley's car. It was a look with a promise of vengeance.

Three phone calls from Riley put the night to a close. He told Valentine what had happened at the restaurant with Strang. Then he got information from Lucky about where the scientist lived. Glasgow and Helensburgh were two locations but exact details weren't available. Hearing the name Helensburgh had been the trigger for the third call to his military contact at HMS Excalibur – Captain Henry Davenport. Riley arranged to go to HMS Excalibur the next morning. If Strang was back on the scene Henry needed to know about it especially as all hell was likely to break loose. Part of it already had.

Standing in his study Riley looked at the map on the wall, lit by the glow of his desk lamp. The warning of dragons had been right and whatever lay beyond them was still unknown.

Chapter Eight

HMS Excalibur

HMS Excalibur was an impressive sight. The naval base was set beside one of the deepest sea lochs in Scotland about twenty five miles north of Glasgow — a striking shadow in the heavy rain with the unmistakable black outline of submarines waiting silently in the dark water. Riley drove towards the main gates. To his left he could see the loch with a solitary sub heading away from the coast. The crew probably wouldn't see daylight for weeks, something he'd experienced a few times. The last surveillance and intelligence gathering mission on a sub had taken him up to the Arctic Circle. After several days underwater there was nothing quite like a breath of freezing sea air and the spectacular view of icebergs that seemed close enough to touch.

Two security guards checked his car at the gates. One of them phoned Captain Henry Davenport to confirm Riley's identity before issuing him with a pass and opening the gates to let him drive in. Riley hadn't been back to Excalibur for two years although he had done work for them remotely — everything from advising on security issues to cyber sleuth work. Nothing much had changed. Excalibur still gave him the same sense of raw excitement and intrigue it always had, only now there was the added element of the past, his past, a part of his life that could never be rewound. He remembered a lifetime of faces, characters and conversations. How many of those faces were still within the base? Not many — a handful at the most. Henry was one of them and today that's all that mattered.

He pulled up in the car park and walked past the main buildings to Henry's office which was set on the hillside with a view over the loch. The rain was spitting bullets at the tarmac and the scent of the wet grass on the hill was starkly potent. The air at Excalibur always smelled of the cold loch and the unmistakable mix of salt, metal and sadness.

Riley put the memories aside and hurried towards Henry's office. The door was already open in welcome. Four officers in full naval uniform were leaving. Not one face was familiar but each of them nodded in acknowledgement as they passed Riley on their way out. Henry stood in the office smiling at him, dressed immaculately from head to toe, a shining example of how sharp a top ranking officer could look in the crisp white shirt, dark suit with its gold buttons, gold braided cuffs and polished peak cap with naval insignia. If ever anyone suited full naval uniform it was Henry.

'We've just had a meeting with the top brass,' Henry said, his vivid blue eyes looking out from under his cap. 'The usual hullabaloo. There's always something happening somewhere.' The eyes hadn't faded. Henry had probably seen every variation in human military trauma and there was probably nothing left that would make a substantial dent. If it had, he was hiding it well, and again if ever anyone could do that it was Henry.

Riley didn't ask about the hullabaloo. It was true. There was always something going on. Right now Strang was his priority.

Henry took his cap off, shook hands with Riley, phoned for tea to be brought in, and they settled down on either side of a large, sturdy desk to talk.

'I saw you on the news,' Henry said. 'I take it there was more to the story and you weren't just in the wrong place at the right time to jump in the Clyde.'

'I'm on a dead man's hit list and I'm working with the police on a murder case that's linked with the killing of Richard Reece.'

'The politician who was stabbed in Edinburgh?'

'Yes. The police wanted me to decipher the scroll that was round his neck. Unfortunately it was a message for me. And I'm on a dead forger's hit list, and involved in a hunter's game with Strang.'

'So you've been keeping busy then eh?' Henry said.

'You know me, Henry.'

Henry did know Riley. They'd been on SBS missions together many times. He relaxed back in his chair. 'I've heard rumours that Strang has popped his head back up on the radar. I thought we'd seen the last of him.'

'I had a run in with him in Glasgow last night. A contact says he's based there and in Helensburgh.'

'He's got a nerve showing his face around here again but there was always an element of a moth to the flame about him. I don't know exactly what he's up to, but I hear it's something to do with his science experiments — and you know what that means.'

A strong and heavy sigh came from Riley. 'This is going to be a bastard to sort out.'

Strang had been one of several scientists working at Excalibur. Around twenty-five percent of the military base was made up of civilian personnel — office workers, research and development technicians. Strang worked as a scientist but he secretly wanted to be a cyber expert like Riley — a computer code breaker. Computer security coding and decoding was headed by military officers but there were civilian techies and science buffs working alongside them. Strang was a scientific researcher developing communications hardware and was a specialist in silent projects — anything that could be adapted for silence and stealth whether it was a computer or a defence weapon. Strang was one of the best, but he had a problem — he wanted to join the navy, become a marine and then be a member of the SBS. The navy had turned him down several times in the past. His psychological profile was officially incompatible with the forces. Unofficially he was an egomaniac, a dangerous man to have around when you had to take orders and save on the glory. Strang was smart there was no doubt about that. On the intelligence scale he was off the marker and that's why the naval military hired him as a scientist. However he lacked the buffer of self discipline. Strang was a wild card in the darkest sense and there was no place for a man like that in the forces.

Initially Strang had seemed to accept his limitations but gradually the cracks began to show, especially when he encountered Riley. Both fascinated and deeply envious of Riley's capability and credit, the worst aspects of Strang's nature seeped to the surface, at first masquerading as scientific innovation and eventually manifesting as someone who was a potential risk to security. His involvement in *dark projects*, dangerous experiments that could cause chaos in society and put civilians in jeopardy had prompted the navy to ask him to leave. Strang had refused to go quietly. One of the less tolerant Excalibur officers had him thrown unceremoniously off the base, wrapped his bank account in enough red tape to bankrupt him, withdrew all accommodation and virtually dumped him out on to the streets of Glasgow at 2am on a Saturday night. It had been a harsh goodbye.

'I've heard he's got political backing for his science work,' Henry said.

Riley suspected as much. 'We've got a hornet's nest unravelling.'

The tea and biscuits arrived.

Henry poured the tea when they were alone again. 'The name Kier Brodie has been brought up in connection with Strang but you didn't hear it from me. He's got a lot of power and political clout behind him.'

'The police are keeping an eye on Brodie.'

'Will he manage to buy them off?'

'No, not these police. It's the Stanley Valentines.'

Even Henry knew them. 'Thank goodness it's the Uncorruptables.' The Valentines reputation for being awkward bastards had its merits. 'Brodie's stuffed if he's got those two buggers after him. So that just leaves Strang — and whoever's got your name on the list.'

'I'm wondering if Strang's got something to do with it,' Riley said.

'I'd have thought he would want to prove he's better than you rather than let someone else do the dirty work. He always wanted to outshine you and I doubt that'll have changed.'

'He had a go last night.' Riley said. He relayed the details.

'Maybe Strang's playing a stronger game than we give him credit for,' Henry said.

In the distance an alarm went off. Riley went to the window. Armed security was running across the base, blurred by the heavy downpour.

Henry activated the intercom on his desk. 'What's going on?'

'Intruder alert,' a voice said over the com. 'Someone cut through the security fence on the east hill.'

Henry clicked the com off, grabbed his greatcoat and cap and hurried out of the office followed by Riley.

'I'm not saying you're a jinx, Riley, but does anyone know you're at Excalibur?'

'No one who would pose a threat. Only McAra.'

Henry knew McAra was the last man to do anything to jeopardise Riley's safety. 'Could you have been followed to the base?'

Riley thought about it. Had he been extra vigilant on the drive up here? Yes. It was second nature to look for any cars who could've been tailing him. 'I didn't see anyone.'

Outside in the rain security was running past them up the hill. Henry shrugged his coat on and pulled the peak of his cap down as a shield against the weather.

'Anyone sighted?' Henry asked one of the men.

'No one yet, Sir.' He ran on.

Riley's eyes searched through the sheeting rain that was so heavy it created a mist of water over the landscape. Everyone was scanning the east hill area. That was logical. But what would an illogical or devious intruder do? He'd run further along. He'd head north taking the long route down to the base. A man like Strang could figure that move out. That's if it was Strang. He couldn't be sure.

'What about your car?' Henry said. 'Could there be a tracer on it?'

It was possible.

Riley ran to his car, kneeling down, checking under the wheel arches, the bumpers and . . . there it was, attached to his offside mirror. He wrenched it free and took it over to Henry.

Henry turned it over in the palm of his hand. 'Very sophisticated. Probably got quite a range on it. Leave it with me. I'll have our security check it. He put it into the pocket of his coat.

The weather buffeted against their greatcoats but neither of them flinched, intent only in finding whoever had broken into the base.

'It's Strang, isn't it?' Henry said, his warm breath visible in the cold air.

Riley nodded. No emotion. He'd a feeling in his bones that Strang was toying with them.

Henry stared out from under the brim of his cap as the rain pelted down around them. 'Shall we . . .?'

Riley knew exactly what he meant. Coats off — and run! Riley led the way, taking the north route across the rugged ground running parallel with the loch. Riley felt the icy rain soak his black jumper in seconds making it sleek against his muscled physique. His boots were waterproof with toughened soles. Even in the city he wore them and they'd always served him well. He could run fast and strong in them. Henry kept pace with him, his white shirt almost transparent now, soaked to the skin but with the same level of grit he'd always had when they'd been on missions together. Riley stopped when he reached the trees, pressing his body against one of them, making himself part of the landscape. Henry faded in behind him.

'He could be armed,' Riley said, listening for any sound from the depths of the trees. Nothing.

'He's a sly bastard. He's probably left a present for us — a trap, a device, something to cause damage or a distraction.'

Crack! A sound resonated through the trees. Riley stepped further back.

Henry signalled he'd take one route while Riley took another and they'd meet on the other side of the trees.

No hesitation. They were off, sprinting, keeping close to the shadows, their boots forcing a pace through the squelching ground.

Riley saw a flash, a light then another, like an intermittent beacon in the shaded hollow. Whatever it was, it moved in small circles, making a mechanical noise.

Henry saw it too.

Riley approached with caution, telling Henry to stay put. He wiped the rain from his brow. It was dripping into his eyes, blurring the accuracy of his determination. What the hell was it? He moved closer again.

The frantic noise of a car revving up and driving off at speed, tyres screeching in the wet, sounded nearby, further up the hill beyond the end of the wooded area.

Henry ran after it, leaving Riley to deal with the device. Riley took another few steps nearer. And then he saw it — a silver mechanical object about the size of a toaster, a robotic gadget like a small remote control vehicle.

Riley backed away. Tempting as it was to have a good look, taking chances was for idiots. The bomb disposal unit could deal with it, though instinct was telling him it was merely a sharp poke in the ribs from Strang, a virtually harmless device to prove that he could penetrate Excalibur's security and escape cleanly. Any footmarks or other evidence was being washed away by the torrent of water. Only the robot, its mechanisms whirring wildly and lights flashing was left in Strang's wake.

Riley went to find Henry who was trudging back down the slope.

'He's gone,' Henry said. 'We won't catch him. Not this time. There are too many cars on the main road. He could be anywhere by now.'

Riley felt the blood rage through his veins. 'But he'll have another run at us.'

'Next time we'll be ready for him. His ego thrives on stuff like this but you know what they say about high flying ego junkies.'

'Yes,' Riley said with quiet determination. 'It's a long way down.'

The disposal unit dealt with the robot. It was deactivated and found to contain nothing of merit or menace. Strang had used a very sophisticated and high powered device to cause disruption to the security camera system around the east side of the fence surrounding Excalibur. When security footage was played to confirm the identity of the intruder, it was faulty, as if a rogue signal had blocked it. Riley and Henry knew Strang had messed with it. The naval hierarchy who were informed of the break in took them at their word. That's where the military had the edge over the police.

Riley drove away from Excalibur later in the day. The black water of the loch was disturbed only by the sight of a submarine submerging into its depths, the long dark shadow vanishing before his eyes. Within moments the wake had smoothed like liquid glass under a stormy sky. It was still raining, shrouding the day in a perpetual grey watery mist. There was nothing quite like the weather in Scotland. The rain battered against anything in its path yet it caused everything around it to be muffled. The silence was haunting. Just like the ghosts of Riley's past who refused to lie down and die.

Chapter Nine

Dark Matter

Old habits die hard. Even after the day he'd had at Excalibur, Riley headed up the driveway to McAra's house having received a phone call from his friend at 2am.

A security keypad was beside the front door. McAra always changed the numbers on it and Riley always decoded it and got in. It hadn't beaten Riley yet and became a habit that neither wanted to lessen.

Riley went upstairs to the glass dome observatory that overlooked the glowing lights of the city beneath the dark blue sky. McAra had phoned with information about the projects Strang was rumoured to be involved in. The two night owls had a lot to talk about.

'I spoke to some of the scientists I know who are less than thrilled that Strang's on the scene again. He could be more dangerous than ever because he's dabbling in dark matter experiments.'

'Sounds like science fiction,' Riley said.

'Science fact I'm afraid. You can say what you like about Strang but he's a bloody genius — the type of scientist who can come up with the most brilliant scientific achievements. If only he'd been less of a savage bastard the world could've benefited from his work, but I doubt that's what he's got in mind.'

'What's the worst damage he can do?'

McAra sucked the air through the gap in his teeth and grimaced. 'Create a vortex, a black hole that could potentially become uncontrollable and destroy a large chuck of the Earth.'

Riley was silent.

'But that would require a considerable amount of money and backing and it would take years before he reached that level,' McAra said, diffusing the tension.

'The potential is there though?'

'Yes, definitely, so he's got to be monitored, controlled and certainly not given money to develop any form of dark matter experiments.'

'What is dark matter?' Riley said.

McAra went over to the telescope. 'Have a look through that.'

Riley peered out into the night. The sky was clear with a scattering of stars and edged with the warm glow of the city's nightlife. 'What am I supposed to see?'

'Ah, that's the problem. You can't actually see dark matter. It doesn't emit any radiation, it's not luminous so it's not visible to us, but we know it's there. We can detect it by the gravitational effect it has on galaxies and star clusters, like an invisible source of gravity. An enormous amount of the mass of our universe is made up of dark matter.'

Riley stepped away from the telescope. 'So if Strang is able to manipulate or create it even on the smallest scale, it would be a threat.'

'Absolutely. If he's dabbling in fundamental particle developments or dark energy projects it's potentially very dangerous. Proving he's a threat is the hard part. Strang's work is likely to seem fine on the surface with nothing much to see.'

Riley had learned never to underestimate what was possible in any given time. Dark matter and black holes may have seemed like science fiction but if McAra was right, Riley was prepared to accept that the danger was real.

'Strang would need a substantial amount of monetary backing and political support,' McAra said.

Riley gazed thoughtfully through the glass dome at the city. 'I got an e-mail from Valentine today. He'd already told me that a copy of Mackenzie's list was found in Reece's office. This linked the two murder cases. But police forensics has been pouring over Reece's diary. They've found several references to Mackenzie and Kier Brodie — and Strang. The four of them are linked. Two are dead and Strang's back in play. If anyone's giving him financial and political backing it's got to be Brodie.'

'Do you think Strang murdered Reece?' McAra said.

'No, even Valentine's sure it was Brodie. Finding hard evidence and making it stick is the problem.'

'Brodie would need to be extremely wealthy to give Strang the kind of money he'd need. I understand that Brodie's got his fingers in a lot of dirty pies and isn't short of a bob or two, but even he would need another source of cash. Money that could legally disappear.'

'Where would you go for that type of money in Glasgow?' Riley said, theorising out loud.

'Not an inkling.'

'Gambling. There's a lot of cash in the gambling industry. When I was having another look at Mackenzie's computer data I found a fragment of a file with a note about money and the name of a new casino. A casino in Glasgow. I also found out that Mackenzie was a member of a private intranet.'

'Internet?'

'No, an intranet, a private Internet. It contained around ten pages that were only accessible if you were on that intranet.'

'What is it exactly?'

'It's a small version of the Internet, like being a member of an exclusive club except you couldn't access this from the Internet even if you tried. It's not in a public place. It's on a separate sub–network.'

'Why didn't Mackenzie just put it on a normal website and password protect it?' McAra said.

'Because anyone in the world could have a go at cracking the password and hack in, but an intranet only exists on the few computers that are actually using it.'

'So Mackenzie and others were on a separate network from the Internet?'

'Yes,' Riley said. 'When the users aren't connected and communicating, the intranet doesn't exist. It's a secure way of exchanging valuable information. The Internet itself is like ether. If everybody stopped connecting to it, it wouldn't be there either. It's intangible. And Mackenzie's intranet was an extreme version of this. It didn't exist.'

'Mackenzie managed to forge himself out of that as well,' McAra said.

'Yes, and I think Kier Brodie was part of it. Politicians need secure exchanges of information but few are computer savvy enough to set up an intranet for themselves, so the likes of Mackenzie became the middle man — the geek. And maybe he knew too much and someone had him murdered.'

'Brodie?'

'Or Strang.'

Riley's mobile phone rang with an alert, a picture message linked to the security system of his house. The picture showed an intruder on his property.

'Someone's paying me a visit.'

'At this time of night?' McAra said, craning to see who was captured on the image. He blinked. 'Isn't that Catherine Warr?'

Riley nodded and grabbed his coat.

'What do you think she's up to?' McAra said.

'I'll find out.'

Riley ran down the hill, reaching his house in minutes. Catherine was about to drive off when she caught sight of his tall figure in the headlamps, blocking the driveway.

'Not that anything would surprise me when it comes to women,' Riley said through the window of her car, 'but isn't this an unusual hour for a social visit?'

'I was dropping something off for you,' she said calmly. 'I was at a political dinner in Glasgow, one of those boring events that really dragged on.' She reached into the back seat of the car and brought out three long cardboard packages. 'I didn't think you'd be a clock watcher so I decided to hand these in to you before I headed back up to Edinburgh.'

'What are they?'

'Star charts — with all the latest updates. I imagined you'd be too busy saving damsels in distress and fighting shadows to have time to get any new charts.'

Riley was secretly surprised. 'Do you want to come in for a coffee,' he said, taking in everything about her. She was wearing a long cream coat, diamond earrings, and her chestnut hair was pinned up in a classy chignon.

She hesitated and he sensed she was going to say no. Instead she said, 'Can I show you something? It wouldn't take long.' She made no move to get out of the car.

'What is it?' Riley asked.

'There's something I think you should see. It's not far from here.'

He got into her car. 'Where are we going?'

'Are you a gambling man, Riley?'

'No.'

'Good. I want you to see the new casino that's opened up in the city. I found out that Kier Brodie's got shares in it.'

'A gambling politician, now there's a rare beast.'

'The casino's above board. It's Brodie who's the dark element,' Catherine said.

He told her about Strang and the incident at Excalibur.

'Can't the police pick Strang up?' Catherine said, as they drove over one of the colourfully lit bridges spanning the Clyde.

'There's not enough evidence to arrest him. Valentine's hands are tied.'

Catherine couldn't help but smile. 'Which Valentine?'

'Take your choice. If neither of them can nail Strang it'll give you a rough idea how badly we're losing this particular game.'

'It's not a game though, is it,' she said. 'Not when people are getting murdered.'

'It's a hunter's game, Catherine. Strang's out to settle an old score. He won't give up until he's beaten me.'

'It's not going to end well, is it?'

Riley didn't need to answer. His silence gave her his reply.

The bright lights of the casino shone like a beacon in the night. Catherine parked the car nearby and they sat for a moment looking out at the stylishly dressed people going in and out of the front entrance.

'It's busy like this most nights,' Catherine said. 'Brodie's in there tonight.'

'Are we going in?'

Catherine looked surprised. 'No, we'd be recognised. At least I would be.'

'What did you want me to see?'

Catherine sighed deeply. 'I just . . . I'm not sure. I thought you should see where Brodie's getting some of his money. As I said, the casino is clean, they're above board, but Brodie's manipulated his way into getting a cut of the profits.'

'Have you any idea who his contacts are?'

She shook her head.

'I could go in and ask him.'

Her hazel eyes widened at the thought of it. 'No way!'

'Well we're going to have to find out somehow.'

'Yes but I'm trying to go around Brodie, get information from people who know him —'

'That'll take time, and we don't have time to waste.'

'I'm certainly not asking you to go in and confront him.'

Riley opened the car door. 'I've no intention of doing that.' He got out of the car.

'Wait! What are you doing?'

Riley leaned down and spoke quietly. 'I'm going to have a look at the casino's computer system. It should have all the answers we need.'

'Someone will see you. You'll be on more cameras than even you've got if you walk through that front door.'

Riley nodded and smiled. 'That's why I'm going in the other route.'

Catherine frowned. 'There's no back entrance to the building.'

'That makes it easier then, doesn't it?'

Before she could object further he'd taken his coat off, thrown it on the seat and closed the door.

She opened the driver's window.

'Keep the doors and windows locked,' Riley said. 'If I'm not back in half an hour phone Valentine.'

'Which one?' she said, without a hint of humour in her voice.

'The lesser of two evils,' he said, and then hurried across the street and disappeared into a dark alley.

The side of the casino was cast in shadows. Riley scaled it easily. The structure had a patterned brick facia making it a straightforward climb for a man of his expertise. Fast and agile, he reached the third floor in minutes. On his second attempt he found an unlocked window and climbed through into a carpeted hallway. Luck was on his side. Appropriate he thought for this particular venue. Maybe he was a gambling man after all because although he'd never admit it to Catherine he'd taken a risk entering the property, especially if he was compromised.

He wore smart casual clothes — dark shirt and trousers. With the right attitude he could pass for a guest who'd simply taken his jacket and tie off and lost his way in the casino.

Several doors lined the hallway. One was marked — *office*. He listened. No sounds, no voices. He tried the door handle. The door was locked. He had two choices. Pick the lock using one of the accessories attached to the keys in his pocket or kick the door in. He went for the silent option. He picked the lock, clicked the door open and went inside. The room was in semi–darkness, lit only by the neon light from the casino signage pouring in through the window. Nothing too bright, just enough to prevent him having to flick a lamp on to see what he was doing. And what was he doing? He was looking for the nearest computer with a mind to hacking into the system, getting the information on Brodie, or at least accessing a link to how to hack into it at a later time, and then getting the hell out of there.

He was in luck again. Two computers in the office were on stand–by mode. All he had to do was flick the monitors on and key in the details. He took a guess at how the system was set up, a calculated guess. Few civilian systems contained many surprises. The majority of computer programmes were variations on a main theme. This one was designed for day workers but presented the ideal route into the cache of information he needed.

Footsteps sounded nearby. He held his fingers a fraction off the keys waiting for them to go by, and then typed again at speed, accessing the information. He accessed their private files in less than five minutes.

The monitor lit up with a goldmine of data. He found Brodie's name in several links so rather than waste time reading over it he logged in remotely to his home computer and sent the information to himself as an e–mail attachment. Then he deleted all traces of this, leaving no electronic fingerprints behind. On the other computer he saw a link to the security cameras. He clicked on it and scanned the numerous small screen images to see if he had a clear exit from the building. No one was in the hallway. Then he saw the foyer of the casino on one of the security cameras — and Catherine. She was trying to look like she belonged to the crowd, and was certainly dressed for the part but he could tell she was edgy even if others hadn't noticed.

Trouble was heading in her direction. Kier Brodie was on a collision course with Catherine, both heading towards the same gambling area from different directions and unaware of the other's approach. It had to stay like that.

Riley identified Brodie from photographs he'd seen, although they'd never met. The politician was a strong, robust man, his height reduced by the illusion of his muscular stature. His hair was brown, sleek, and the clean shaven face had a distant history of fist fight hardness. Brodie was too wily to buy any excuse Catherine could give him for being in the casino. Brodie could accept that Catherine was an in-house investigator at the Scottish Parliament but he'd know she wasn't at the casino to play blackjack. She was outside her territory — and that would make her a target.

Riley reacted immediately. He wiped his fingerprints off the keyboards, switched the computers back to standby and left the office, locking the door behind him. He hurried to the elevator and took it to the ground floor. He had to reach Catherine before Brodie did. No easy task. If he ran or caused a scene he'd risk drawing attention to himself, so he walked as if his purpose was to join one of the gaming tables. No one gave him a second glance. He picked up an empty cocktail glass from a silver tray and held it in clear view like a badge of belonging to the casino crowd.

Brodie was in sight, positioned at Riley's nine o'clock with Catherine at ten o'clock. The clash was fast approaching. Riley walked quicker, making his way through the guests without causing any ripples of suspicion. He saw Catherine. She hadn't seen him yet. Brodie hadn't seen him either but they were about to walk right past each other face to face. For a split second Riley's eyes met the politician's gaze. Brodie had a casual social smile, the smile of a man who thought he was safe in the centre of his turf. How wrong he was.

Riley walked on and intercepted Catherine before Brodie saw her. She gasped when she saw Riley and he greeted her with a kiss on her glossy lips to silence her. His eyes warned her something was wrong. The surprise of seeing him blatantly walk past Brodie or the stolen passion of his kiss disarmed any remarks from her.

'We have to get out of here now,' Riley said, smiling as if nothing was troubling him.

Catherine smiled and linked her arm through his as he escorted her from the casino.

Two doormen bid them good night and they left unchallenged.

Outside, the cold air felt like ice against the fabric of Riley's shirt. Catherine instinctively pulled her coat around her for warmth and they walked across the street to her car.

'I got the information,' Riley said, deciding he should drive. She looked pale and anxious.

'What you did was illegal!' she snapped.

'Would you rather I deleted it?'

She sighed angrily. 'No . . . but I don't want to get entangled in . . .'

'In my strife,' Riley said, driving off.

Catherine didn't answer and they didn't speak during the few minutes it took to drive back to his house. He parked in the driveway, left the engine running and got out of the car. She reached over and turned the engine off. 'Is that coffee still on offer?'

It was. They went into Riley's house taking the star charts with them.

Riley lit the fire in his study, made them tea and coffee served with biscuits, and then accessed the data he'd sent in the e–mail, while Catherine cupped the hot coffee in her hands and stood in front of the log fire for warmth.

The computer screens and the lamp on his desk cast a glow over the study. Riley concentrated on searching for anything relevant about Brodie in the files. 'It seems he owns shares in the casino and there's an agreement to pay him a regular amount direct into one of his bank accounts.

'*One* of his accounts?' Catherine said. 'How many does he have?'

'Four different account numbers are listed. It's like a spider's web of money being routed to various banks making it hard to trace any one cache.'

'We couldn't use that as evidence. We'd have to say where the information came from and I couldn't exactly lie and say, well actually a former Special Forces cyber sleuth broke into a casino, hacked into their computer records and found that Brodie was siphoning off money into hidden accounts.'

Riley studied her. 'I think you're missing the point. Take a look at this.' He pointed to the computer monitor.

Catherine slipped her coat off to reveal a black cocktail dress which she wore with black high heeled shoes. The fabric of the dress was shot through with fine glittering threads giving it an understated hint of gold. Riley could see why Byrn Shaw was crazy about her but he'd no intention of overstepping the mark tonight. Neither did he think she was attempting to entice him. Her manner was straightforward, a gorgeous woman concentrating on how to beat a political adversary.

'What am I looking for?' she said, standing beside him gazing at the screen.

'If you think of Brodie's account system as a web, we can bait him and set a trap to rattle him, cause him to make mistakes.'

'What kind of trap?'

'I could make two of his accounts inaccessible and change some basic information that would alert him or his accountant that something wasn't right.'

'A fly in the ointment?' Catherine said.

'It would be a temporary blip but it could cause him to pop his head above the parapet long enough for Valentine to find evidence to nail him.'

'Or for me to nail him. I obviously don't have powers of arrest but the government pay me to be part of their internal affairs system.'

'Shall I press the buttons?' Riley said.

'I couldn't be part of it,' Catherine said.

Riley smiled. 'Part of what?'

Catherine smiled back at him. 'It's really late, thanks for the coffee. I'd better head back up to Edinburgh. I've got a meeting at 10am.'

Riley helped her on with her coat. 'Remember this is borderline legal because technically Brodie's accounts aren't bonafide.'

She nodded and glanced around the room taking it all in before leaving. 'I hope the star charts help you update your record keeping.'

'I appreciate them.'

'You're welcome.' She hesitated. 'I keep telling myself I should spend more time on my astronomy interests.'

'Have you ever thought of it as a career?'

'Yes. I've made a number of wrong choices on that scale. My parents had a fashion design business and they assumed I'd become part of it but fashion's never been where my interests lie.'

'And government is?'

'No not exactly but we all make mistakes in the past and you can't rewrite history.'

'That's the second time you've said that.' He remembered she'd said it the first time she'd been in his study and it had stuck in his memory.

'You can't though, can you?'

'No, but you can rewrite it when it's based on mistakes.'

'Sounds like my career. Maybe one day I'll just walk away from it all.'

The look in her eyes told him she'd seriously thought about it.

She pulled her coat around her. 'Sometimes I get tired of living in a web of lies. Politics is such a deceitful business.'

He knew exactly what she meant. 'If you ever want to walk away don't let anyone stop you.'

'Is that what happened when you left the SBS?'

'Sort of. There was nothing left for me in that world.'

'Did you make the right decision to leave the forces?'

'Under the circumstances, yes, but things feel like they'll always be less than they might have been.'

She lifted one of the framed photographs from a dresser. It showed a scene of the desert, miles of sand and scorching sunlight. 'Still no people in any of your pictures, Riley. Aren't there any faces belonging to your past?'

'Too many to forget.'

She studied the picture. 'Were you ever in this desert?'

'I was there several times with my father, Alexander. He took the photograph.'

'Was he a forces man?'

'Not quite,' he said, giving her an unfinished answer. 'He was more of a palaeographer and the Record Keeper of his day. He travelled to many countries throughout the world and I often went with him.'

'That explains your accent,' she said. 'It isn't that of anywhere. You're like a shadow in the background that never quite belongs.'

'It's better that way.'

'Is it really?'

'For now.'

Chapter Ten

The Edge of Nowhere

Henry was in a hurry. He phoned Riley from HMS Excalibur. Riley was finishing his breakfast in his study, checking his e-mails and planning the day. All plans were set aside.

'We're flying down from Excalibur to Glasgow airport,' Henry said. There was a calm urgency in his voice. 'Strang's been sighted up north. He's been testing things he shouldn't in one of our training zones. No major damage so far but he needs to be shut down. I'm deploying a team. The appropriate people have been informed and confirm the deployment.'

Riley was poised for the invitation.

'Get over to Glasgow airport – and bring your wet gear,' Henry said. 'We're flying down by Sea King. We'll refuel at Glasgow, pick you up and head to the edge of nowhere.'

'Cape Wrath! What the hell's Strang doing up there? Riley said.

'Messing with the wrong people.'

Riley grabbed his gear. A backpack was always on standby filled with the essentials. It was a habit he'd yet to break.

Before he left, he e–mailed Shaw asking for satellite images of Cape Wrath during the past twenty–four hours and gave a brief explanation why he needed them. He took his laptop with him and drove to the airport.

He saw the Sea King in the distance when he arrived. The low roar of its power rippled through the air. It was a Henry special — a Sea King with the guts ripped out, precisely kitted for immediate action and stripped of any superlatives so it could go quicker, but still with full attack capacity. A fast deployment helicopter, tough and dependable, it was perfect for a trip to the edge of nowhere.

An apt description Riley thought. It was situated at the North West tip of Scotland overlooking the sea. In Cape Wrath you were nearer to the Arctic Circle than you were to the bottom of England. It had some of the highest sheer cliffs in Britain and the terrain was wild in the extreme. It was also alleged to be haunted with strange phenomena of past ghosts. One of the last untamed landscapes, it was sometimes used for military training courses because it was the ideal locale for the forces to pit their skills against the most remote, rugged and wild landscapes of sea, cliffs, unforgiving terrain and storms that were the stuff of nightmares. The courses incorporated the navy's brown water training. Brown water assignments were close to the coast, rarely more than a hundred miles off land and generally used for defence. Green water missions extended further out, around a thousand miles from land and were used for offence and defence objectives. Blue water missions were on the global scale so all three had their place and purpose. Cape Wrath was an outstanding area to train for survival in a fierce brown water location. And that's where they were heading.

The Sea King landed in a section of Glasgow airport and was immediately refuelled. Henry slid open the side door of the helicopter and waved Riley through security.

Riley ran across the runway. The weather was blustery and it was starting to rain. The air was heavy with the smell of fuel and adventure.

Henry stood in the doorway kitted out in full SBS wet gear. Henry did four years with the SBS with a two year break as a captain in the regular navy in between. He looked fit and strong — and was clearly pleased to see Riley. He grabbed Riley's hand with a firm grip, partly in handshake and party to pull him on board as he leaped from the tarmac into the Sea King. They stood in the doorway for a minute being buffeted by the wind and the sound of the rotary blades whirring into action.

'Glad you could make it,' Henry said. He turned to introduce the others. Pilots one and two were in their seats ready for take off. Four SBS, also in wet gear, were sitting in the hub. The men knew who Riley was and Henry introduced them to him briefly.

Pilot one gave Henry the thumbs up as he was given clearance for immediate take off. Henry slid the door shut and the noise inside the Sea King burned up a couple of levels. The only way to hear what anyone said was to put the headgear on and speak via the comms on the helmet. Riley adjusted the volume on his comms and clipped the extension wire into the system, making himself part of the communication loop. He flipped down one of the basic seats, belted himself in securely and as always he never felt the initial lift off as the helicopter rose upwards with tremendous force from the runway. That was the thing with this type of aircraft. The main surge happened moments after the helicopter was in the air. Then the force of it hit the body like a stream of fast–pressured energy.

Riley looked around the interior. Apart from the seats and the SBS team's equipment, it was stripped to the bone. Metal with no embellishments. Yellow tape was stuck to emergency exit panels and doors. This was usual. If you needed to get out in a hurry all you had to do was whack a yellow strip and the panel would open and out you would go. This was fine as long as you remembered never to lean on any of the yellow bits when you were mid–flight.

Henry stood holding on to the back of the pilots' seats and looked through the front windows. 'There's more yellow than ever, Riley, so don't go leaving us early.'

Riley smiled. 'Any further news on Strang?'

'Intelligence tells us he's working alone. He'll be a bastard to find but at least he doesn't know were on our way.'

Pilot one was receiving instructions from the airport flight path control tower. 'Okay, will do,' he said to the controller. He turned to Henry. 'We're going to take the racing line under the Erskine Bridge. The flight paths are crowded and the weather's getting worse. We can't risk flying over the bridge. Another emergency is in progress with a flight nearby heading for the hospital heli–pad.'

'Under the bridge it is,' Henry said. 'We'll stick to the river line as much as possible.'

Riley got ready. Erskine Bridge was minutes from Glasgow Airport. The bridge, which had a high structure and wide span, ran across the River Clyde and was often heavy with traffic.

The Sea King banked to the right and lined up over the river. Riley could see the water beneath them and the impressive structure of the bridge straight ahead. Henry kept a tight hold of the back of the seats as he stood behind the pilots.

'We're going under the bridge, lads,' Henry said to the others. 'Hold steady.'

Pilot one flicked on the windscreen wipers to clear the front windows. The rain was becoming heavier. Everything looked like it was coloured in shades of varying grey — the river, the rain and mist, and the dark outline of the bridge as they approached.

Henry didn't flinch. He had complete confidence in the pilot. An experienced forces pilot could take a helicopter to within inches off a cliff face during rescue missions. Flying under the Erskine Bridge was something they'd done more than once.

Car drivers and pedestrians stopped to watch the Sea King soar under the deck of the bridge. A clean fly through.

The Sea King gathered pace and height as it headed north.

A message came through on pilot one's comms. He listened and then asked Riley, 'Does the name Byrn Shaw mean anything?'

'Yes, I asked him for satellite images of Cape Wrath.'

'He's got the data for you,' Pilot one said. 'I'll arrange to have it relayed to the drop point.'

'Can you ask him a question?' Riley said.

'Go ahead.'

'Is Strang using any type of weaponry?'

Minutes later the reply came through. 'No weaponry. He's alone. It looks like he's testing equipment with high powered lighting and possible laser gear.'

Henry shot Riley a look of despair. 'He's up to his old tricks again.'

'It could be a trap,' Riley said.

The other members of the SBS team listened intently.

'Be aware,' Henry told them. 'Riley and I have encountered Strang before. He doesn't play by the standard rules. He'll use every trick in the book and believe me he's got the technology to do it.'

'What level of force is acceptable to bring him in?' one of the team said.

'Reasonable force,' Henry said. 'You've all trained at Cape Wrath so you know what we're dealing with. The weather's not going to be on our side.'

The Sea King picked up pace, heading north towards the edge of nowhere. Riley sat back in his seat and mentally went over the possibilities. The weather definitely wasn't going to be on their side. Judging by the darkening day the further north they flew, they'd receive a stormy welcome when they arrived. They'd be lucky if the Sea King could make it near the drop point. Strang was the one with the luck of the devil on his side, and he hoped Cape Wrath wasn't going to play the devil's advocate.

A car drove up to McAra's house. A man got out, went up to the door and rang the bell. McAra opened the door to the stranger.

'Is Riley here?'

'No, he doesn't actually live here. Is there something wrong?' McAra said.

'I'm an acquaintance of his . . . probably more like an annoyance of his.'

'Do you want me to give him a message?'

'Lucky's gone missing. I don't know what to do.'

'Lucky?'

'Yes, Lucky's —'

'I know who he is,' McAra said.

'I'm Jamesie.'

'Oh you're the chef.'

'That's right. I thought Riley lived at this address, but I get things mixed up in my head sometimes. You must be the rocket scientist.'

'Yes. Mul McAra. What do you think's happened to your friend?'

'I'd arranged to give him a steak pie through the back window of the kitchen. I work in the restaurant and some nights I give him his dinner out the back. A wee perk of the job.'

McAra nodded.

'But he didn't turn up, and it's not like him to miss the chance of a free steak pie and roast potatoes. So I went round to his place late last night when I'd finished in the restaurant and he wasn't in.'

'Doesn't he have various . . . business dealings?'

'The dodgy deliveries were dumped in the alley in front of his door. He hadn't sorted them.' Jamesie leaned closer. 'And he hadn't fed the dog.'

'Right. Maybe you should call the police.'

Jamesie nearly choked. 'I don't think so. No offence Mr Mul but they wouldn't give a toss about finding Lucky. They'd likely have a party to celebrate that he'd finally got shafted.'

'Not too popular with the local police then eh?' He sucked the air through his teeth.

'You can get that fixed,' Jamesie said.

McAra's brows furrowed.

'That big glaring gap in your teeth. I used to have a gap you could drive a truck through and I got mine fixed.' He lifted his top lip to show a fine set of molars.

'No, no, I'm used to it. I'd feel strange without it, but thanks all the same.'

Jamesie nodded. 'Yeah, I know what you mean. I only got mine fixed because the women don't like gaps. They like a nice cheery smile.'

For a second, McAra caught himself considering the wisdom of this. Had the gap played a part in his trail of failures with the fairer sex?

'So Riley's not here then,' Jamesie said, more to make it clear in his own thoughts.

'No, he's eh, he's busy today.' Riley had e-mailed McAra with brief details of his trip to Cape Wrath.

'Before I did the cheffing, I worked on the nightclub doors,' Jamesie said, giving a knowing wink. 'I got to understand human nature at its worst and I've got a feeling that weirdo scientist has played the payback card.'

McAra took a moment to decode the jargon. 'Strang's done something to Lucky because he set him up?'

Jamesie nodded.

'Not wanting to fan the flames of suspicion but wouldn't Strang have come after you first. After all you're the one who makes his dinner and knew when he'd be in the restaurant.'

'Correct, but he's not daft.' Jamesie pointed to his head. 'He knows I go a bit crazy in a fight whereas Lucky's not so handy on the knuckle front.'

'Okay,' McAra said thoughtfully. 'So you'd be a harder target and he's gone for Lucky instead.'

'Jamesie clenched his gap-free teeth. 'I'll kill that fucker if he's done anything to my pal.'

'Come on in. Perhaps if I spoke to the police they'd help.'

Jamesie stepped inside, willing to take any help he could get but reluctant to get his hopes up.

McAra phoned Stanley Valentine and was met with the response Jamesie had predicted. Lucky had long been a thorn in the side of the police. An all out search for him wasn't going to be a priority for them.

McAra put the phone down and slumped into an armchair.

'You phoned the wrong Stanley, didn't you?' Jamesie said.

McAra rubbed his hands across his face in frustration that he'd mucked up.

'Try again. Phone the other one and don't mention the steak pie this time.'

'I've never heard anyone laugh like that,' McAra said, redialling the police and asking to speak to the lesser of two evils.

Ferguson took the call and was prepared to accept McAra's explanation of Lucky being missing.

'It ties in with a report we had yesterday,' Ferguson said. 'We got a call about two men with blonde hair having a knife fight in the street in Lucky's area. One was well built, well dressed and the other was rough and scrawny. Officers were sent to investigate the incident but by the time they arrived whoever it was had gone. We assumed it was a local squabble but obviously it could be a grudge attack from Strang. We'll certainly take your report seriously.'

'I'd appreciate it,' McAra said.

'Is Riley there?' Ferguson said.

'No, he eh . . .' He turned to Jamesie. 'Any chance of making us a cuppa?'

'Coming right up,' Jamesie said, understanding that he wanted to talk to the detective in private, and figuring he could find his way around the kitchen.

McAra explained that Riley was on his way to Cape Wrath in pursuit of Strang.

'What kind of experiments is Strang testing up there?'

'Nothing that will do any of us any good.'

Jamesie came through with the tea as McAra finished the call.

'I took the liberty of making us sandwiches.' The plate was piled with beautifully cut sandwiches that looked good enough to be an advertisement.

'Great.'

'Thanks for you help,' Jamesie said. 'I'll have this and then go and feed Lucky's dog. I thought I'd have a shifty round his house and see if I can find anything that'll give us a hint of what's happened to him. He had information about that man, the politician, what's his name . . . Brodie, Kier Brodie. He was going to tell Riley. Something about a computer and a hit list.'

McAra went with Jamesie to Lucky's house. Barking Bob was snarling behind the front door.

'I've got sweeties for him,' Jamesie said, bringing out a packet of chocolate toffees. 'These stick to his teeth so he doesn't have time to bite. He's fine once he's calmed down. Just don't touch him because his bite's worse than his bark.'

Jamesie fished out a key from a drainpipe and opened the door while simultaneous throwing a handful of sweets at the dog. It worked a treat. Barking Bob chewed on a mouthful of toffees and was happy to let Jamesie put a collar and lead on him.

'Are you taking him for a walk?' McAra said.

'Bob would've made a great sniffer dog. I thought if Lucky was anywhere near here he'd sniff him out.'

'Good thinking.'

Jamesie smiled. 'It's not rocket science, eh?'

Barking Bob was hot on the trail of something as soon as Jamesie took him outside. McAra went with them. The dog was straining on the lead and the pace quickened through the labyrinth of alleyways and nooks and crannies until he stopped dead outside a half hidden door that was barred with a metal lock plate. It was an old, red brick shelter left over from the Second World War, another niche that time had forgotten.

Jamesie and McAra exchanged a wary look. The dog began barking.

McAra took a gadget from his pocket that had several attachments on a key ring including a mini screwdriver and wire cutter. He sifted through the items and used a combination of two to pry the lock plate open.

'Quiet!' Jamesie said to the dog.

McAra took a deep breath and pulled the door open. A stench of blood mixed with rotting damp wafted out of the darkness.

The dog became quiet.

Jamesie rummaged in his pockets, found a lighter and handed it to McAra who sparked it on and turned up the flame to full strength. He put his hand into the shelter carefully, not knowing what it would brush against. The flame lit up the inside enough for them to see that the walls were splattered with blood and a knife was lying on the ground.

Jamesie bent down to lift it up.

'Don't touch it. We'll let the police do that,' McAra said.

Jamesie left it where it was. 'It's Lucky's knife.'

Neither said what they thought. The chances of Lucky being alive were narrow.

McAra phoned Ferguson.

'I'm on my way,' Ferguson said.

McAra closed the door to the shelter. A savage fight or torturing had taken place there. If Lucky had survived he certainly warranted his name.

The police were crawling all over Lucky's house within half an hour. Valentine and Ferguson were there talking to McAra outside in the alleyway. A forensic team were tackling the bloodied shelter.

'Any word about Riley from Cape Wrath?' Valentine said.

McAra checked his watch. 'He should be arriving there soon.'

Jamesie was inside the house getting in the police's way.

'You'll have to go outside, Sir,' an officer said. 'You're interfering with the evidence.'

Jamesie continued to make a nuisance of himself for a few moments longer. 'Lucky's my friend. I'm just trying to help.'

One word shouted by Valentine made Jamesie vacate the premises. 'Out!'

Jamesie grumbled to himself and scurried away.

'We'll need to talk to you later,' Ferguson said.

'Fine. You know where to find me. I'm away to start my shift at the restaurant.' He looked at McAra. 'Don't worry about Barking Bob. I've left him with a neighbour. She's good with dogs. He'll think he's on holiday. And I've got that table booked for you at six o'clock tonight.'

McAra didn't know what Jamesie was talking about but went along with it nonetheless. 'Great. I'll be there.'

The secret arrangement went unnoticed by Ferguson.

Valentine smiled shrewdly and leaned closer to McAra. 'Whatever the chef has in mind let me know will you?'

'Will do,' McAra said.

Valentine and Ferguson went into Lucky's house leaving McAra standing alone.

At the top of the alley Jamesie caught McAra's attention without anyone else seeing him. He held up a notebook, nodded to McAra, hid the book inside his jacket again and hurried away.

Chapter Eleven

Cape Wrath

The water at Cape Wrath was seething. Waves that could swallow the bow of a ship swept towards the coast and were broken by the towering cliffs. A storm raged around the cape with death defying winds roaring across the bleak landscape. The Sea King fought through the onslaught to deposit Riley, Henry and the SBS team as close as possible to the drop point. A pre-arranged pick up time had been organised. The Sea King took off again escaping the brunt of the weather.

Henry shouted at Riley as they stood on top of the cliffs. The wind buffeted his voice, making hand signals necessary to indicate where they were heading. Riley nodded, pulled the straps of his backpack tight and together they forced their way through the elements to where Strang had been sighted.

The weather attacked them with biting winds and rain. The force of it was enough to leave a welt across their faces but they were wearing balaclavas and high necked, hooded jackets to protect them from the onslaught. Riley had also worn his waterproof boots, specially designed to grip slippery terrain with a curved flexibility that could double for climbing. Not that he intended climbing in this weather but if the situation got worse he may have no other option.

Below him he saw the wild sea. No man would survive in the treacherous water today — not even him, and his ability as a swimmer–canoeist was strong. Only the foolish would venture near it under these conditions, or those with a dangerous element in their nature. It crossed his mind that Strang was the type to attempt it if cornered and this was his only route out. If so, perhaps they wouldn't need to bring him in. The tide would do it for them days later when his body was washed up on the coast. No sooner had he thought this than he dismissed the possiblity. Strang was many things, on the borderline of grand obsession, but he was a wily bastard and more likely to ensnare one of them into the teeth of the waves than himself. Riley would be wary and watchful that the others didn't suffer this fate.

Henry signalled to him and pointed towards a path no wider than the breadth of a man's shoulders. It wound down towards an overhang above an inlet of caves. The slope fell away at a terrifying angle. Riley took the ice axe from his belt. Henry and the others stopped and chose similar pieces of kit from their backpacks. It was standard practise when tackling Cape Wrath. Although there was no ice, the efficiency of this type of axe in gripping tight to the hardened ground was excellent.

With axes at the ready Henry led the way. Riley took the strong point at the rear. He knew his abilities and those of Henry. The other four men were an unknown, but the fact that they were members of the SBS and chosen by Henry to go on this mission was testament to each and every one of them being at the top of their game.

The first few metres of the descent were precarious but it was the quickest and only way to reach the caves where, according to intelligence sources, Strang was last seen.

The further down they went, the fiercer the wind attacked them, rising up at double the force from the mouth of the largest cave. The roar of the water resonating from its core was deafening and one of the eeriest sounds imaginable.

Henry glanced over his shoulder at Riley as if to say — here we go. Riley's eyes, peering out from his black balaclava acknowledged him.

They scaled down to the first overhang. Henry wedged his ice axe into the ground and leaned over the edge to look into the front of the cave. A light, the size of a domestic satellite dish, was sending a beam outwards towards the sea. Riley went down for a closer look.

'A signal,' Henry shouted.

Riley nodded.

Intelligence had reported this. It was one factor on their agenda they'd been tasked to eliminate.

'One of us will have to take the shot,' Henry said, willing to do it, but knowing Riley's marksmanship was better. It was a skill he'd always had. Riley had been trained along with others in the forces, but he was one of the few whose ability was something that could never be learned. He rarely missed. They needed that type of shot.

As a civilian, Riley wasn't armed but the others were. 'I'll do it,' Riley said, shouting so he could be heard above the raging torrents. Henry's rifle was ideal for a long range sniper shot. He handed the weapon to Riley who lined up the sights to suit his purposes, focussing on the near horizon until he had the adjustments correct. The gun was another Henry special, customised to become his favourite long range weapon. Riley didn't have favourites. Favourites always let him down and everything else was invariably less in comparison. No favourites meant no mistakes. He could use whatever was available, altering his technique and adapting to the elements.

Henry linked the end of a climbing rope securely around Riley's waist, attached it to his belt and effectively tied them together leaving enough rope to allow Riley to reach over the precipice and take the shot. Two of the SBS secured Henry and made a human chain so that no man would fall.

Riley gave Henry the thumbs up and then leaned out over the edge. The noise of the sea pounded against the sides of the caves in a resonating roar but he kept his concentration and his balance steady. Far below him he saw the water, a torrent of dark grey liquid that matched the stormy sky.

'Hang tight, Riley,' Henry shouted. His words hardly penetrated the rain that was now shot through with hailstones as the temperature continued to drop.

The skin on Riley's hands tightened with the cold and his knuckles felt the bite of the hail striking off them. Fingerless gloves weren't for him, never had been, not when it came to shooting. Riley held steady as the noise and rain intensified around him. He was calm. Some would call it a quirk of his nature — the ability to centre himself in the eye of any storm and do what needed to be done. His eyes, dripping with rain, connected with the target. He closed one eye and lined up the sight. Not an easy shot especially in high winds. The target was a long way off. Despite digging the heels of his boots into the edge of the cliff, the gale buffeted against him. If he missed he could afford one, perhaps two other shots, but each time he fired he risked alerting Strang, who was nowhere to be seen, that they were here to get him. He needed to do it in one.

Compensating for the wind and the updraft from the cave he aimed slightly to the left of target and more importantly, above it. The air pressure in the cave was formidable. No wonder Strang had chosen it as a hidden location. He wouldn't be pleased that he'd been compromised and that his precious equipment had been taken out of action.

Riley's breathing was slow and controlled, almost in sync with the flow of the water. It seemed like forever yet was less than a few seconds. He took the shot, hearing it cut through the atmosphere. Bang! The light shattered and the metal structure holding the light tumbled into the sea.

Henry hauled him back up. 'That was a million to one shot. You haven't lost your touch, Riley.' He untied the ropes and slapped him on the back.

'Movement at five o'clock,' one of the SBS said. He didn't point in the direction or give any indication that he'd seen a figure scrambling across the rocks on the shoreline.

Riley and Henry kept their backs to the view. 'Is it Strang?' Henry said.

'Yes.' Images of Strang had been studied by all members of the team. Strang wore standard black wet gear but nothing covered his distinctive blonde hair that even when wet was his trademark. He wasn't expecting company and hadn't attempted to disguise his appearance. A backpack was slung across his shoulders. It looked heavy.

The SBS backed away from the edge of the cliff to a vantage point further along where they could watch him without being seen.

'He's alone,' Henry said, scanning the coastline with his binoculars.

'He always works alone,' Riley said. Another reason why Strang wouldn't have cut it in the forces. He couldn't be relied on and he wouldn't rely on others to be part of a team. Strang was an extreme loner and there was no place in the forces for those. Even lone wolves could become part of a pack when needed and then break away again when the time was right. Riley was a borderline loner who could go off on missions where he'd had little contact with the outside world for weeks on end, but equally he could slot back into the mainstream when it was over. He could be content when he got home from wherever he'd been, a trait he considered one of his most valuable. Without it, he could easily have become one of the lost souls who were never at ease and a nightmare to themselves. Strang had become lost a long time ago, resulting in a loner, one of life's malcontents. It had driven him to the extremes of his scientific experiments but he'd clearly lost the ability to know where to draw the line. Strang spent his time in his own thoughts. And it was never good for any man to spend too much time steeped in his own perspectives.

'Will he run or fight?' Henry asked Riley.

'Run. He's a strategist. He'll know he's outnumbered. His only hope is to disappear.'

Henry shielded his eyes from the elements and searched for Strang. There were so many places to disappear to in Cape Wrath.

Riley looked down at the rocks below and then at Henry. 'Shall we . . .?'

It was Henry's turn to know exactly what Riley meant. They'd scale down the cliffs and give Strang a run for his money.

Henry tightened his belt and got his climbing rope ready, as did Riley. The SBS split into three groups of two men. Two groups covered different areas of the upper part of the Cape. Riley and Henry took the harsh way down, using their ropes to scale to a ledge that led on to a narrow path where their ice axes came in handy. They got bombarded by hail as they faced the full onslaught of the weather on the sheer cliff where there was no shelter whatsoever.

'Just like old times, Riley,' Henry shouted across to him.

Riley smiled. 'It never ends, does it?'

'No, not for men like us.'

Would he have had it any other way? Riley wasn't sure. Too many things had happened in his own history, diverting him to other paths in his career that he may or may not have chosen.

They got nearer the bottom of the cliffs and abseiled the last stretch to the jagged rocks below. From there they headed to where they'd seen Strang moving at a fast pace across the black rocks whose edges cut like razors. The flow of the sea failed to smooth their ragged structure and the landscape was as untamed as it had been thousands of years ago.

'What do you think the light in the cave was for?' Henry said. 'I remember he had something like it at Excalibur.'

'It's probably a form of hi-tech weaponry. That was his speciality.'

'I must be getting old. Some of the stuff these days sounds more like science fiction.'

'That's what I said to McAra recently but he says it's science fact.'

One of the SBS radioed Henry. 'Strang's heading north. We can see him from here. He's about five minutes away from you.'

Riley and Henry had closed the gap. 'Radio the Sea King to pick us up at the drop point.'

Riley pointed ahead towards an inlet where the sea had cut them off from going any further. He craned his neck searching for another route. 'We'll need to climb up then cut across the cliff edge.'

Henry cursed to himself. 'Beaten by the bloody tide!'

They scaled the cliff face and over the arc of a cave. Henry looked at his watch. It had added several minutes to their route. He signalled to Riley that they needed to move fast to make up for lost time.

Riley nodded, and then he heard the noise of an electric motor whirring below them. He stopped and scanned for any sign of a boat. Nothing, then a black inflatable dingy came skimming across the water from one of the caves. Strang was in it, getting soaked by the sea. He glanced up at Riley and Henry. There was no hint of triumph in Strang's face, just sheer determination, almost shock that he'd been compromised and how close he'd come to being caught. He hadn't escaped yet but Riley and Henry knew he would. By the time they reached the sand he'd be long gone. Their only advantage was the treacherous sea conditions. The dingy was similar to those used by the Special Forces. Strang had chosen well. It could take a fair pounding, and being light, sturdy and agile, it could handle severe seas.

The look exchanged between Riley and Henry said one thing. They'd need to climb up to the top of the cape if they'd any chance of seeing where Strang was going. Riley led the way, climbing strong and sure.

The top was flat, covered in grass and rocks. Both men now secured their backpacks ready for the run, for that was the only option available. Riley and Henry were nearest north, making them the two man team most likely to see where Strang was heading.

Henry radioed the other SBS teams. 'Everyone rendezvous at the drop point. Wait for our arrival.'

'Affirmative.'

Riley was ready to run. 'Let's go!'

Henry and Riley raced against the wind along the top edge of the cape, single file, giving double the chance for each man to sight their target in the water below. The tide had beaten them the last time, but now it thwarted Strang. Even if he'd wanted to, the dingy couldn't have turned and forced its way south. The tide and the elements were too strong. So the race was on. Two men on foot running against the boat in the churning sea.

'Sighted at nine o'clock,' Riley shouted, putting on a burst of speed.

Henry kept pace but danger was in front of them.

'Ahead!' Henry said.

Riley had seen it. Mist — the likes of which he'd rarely seen was rolling in over the sea and shrouding the cape. It was moving in fast. Too fast. Within minutes they'd be running the gauntlet in it, barely able to see the edge of cliffs. He hadn't encountered Scottish mist like this since climbing on Ben Nevis, the highest mountain in Britain. The Ben's cliffs had been challenging enough to climb but the most dangerous aspect happened when he reached the summit and couldn't see more than a metre in front of him because of the mist. One false step and he could've been over the edge. The same could so easily happen now at the cape.

The Sea King soared above them heading to the drop point. A fog light signalled a warning to them. Henry raised his arm in acknowledgement as the helicopter flew on.

Riley stopped running and took in their bearings. The drop point was sharp east. He glanced down at the sea. The weather had beaten Strang. He was going nowhere fast.

'He'll head into the caves,' Riley said.

'There are numerous routes from there,' Henry said. 'We'll be lucky to find him today. At least we've scuppered his experiments.'

Riley agreed. 'Drop point?'

'Yes, before this place disappears.'

The mist had blurred everything in shadowy grey by the time they reached the Sea King. Riley and Henry ran towards the helicopter. The whirring blades wafted a vague clearing in the mist as they climbed on board. It took off and banked across the sea, taking a last sweep over the violent water in search of Strang.

'Strang's a ghost,' Riley said over the comms.

'One that'll be back to haunt us,' Henry said.

'Images from Byrn Shaw have come through for you,' Pilot one said, passing the printouts over his shoulder to Riley.

Riley studied them. Shaw was good. He'd located the figure of a man taking equipment into one of the caves. The man could be identified as Strang. The images confirmed that Strang had been alone, and it looked like the only experiment was the one taken out with the long range shot. The laser gear had been part of the dingy equipment.

Pilot two indicated something in the sea just outside the area of the caves. The searchlights penetrated the mist which was less dense at lower altitudes. 'There's the dingy.' The black inflatable was being thrown around in the water and hit off the rocks.

Riley and Henry got up from their seats to look out the pilot's window. 'It's getting ripped to shreds,' Henry said.

'No sign of Strang,' Pilot two said.

'We'll take another run over the area,' Pilot one said. The Sea King did a search of the coast using the full beam of the searchlights. Nothing.

'If Strang's in the water he'll have been torn to pieces,' Pilot two said. 'No chance of locating him in this sea.'

'I don't buy it,' Riley said to Henry.

Neither did Henry. 'Anyone I've ever known who had the luck of the devil on his side never went out in anything less than a blaze of glory.'

As the Sea King turned around to head south to Glasgow and HMS Excalibur, Riley had a feeling in his bones that Strang was watching them. He looked over at Henry and pointed two fingers towards his eyes, indicating that they were undoubtedly being watched by Strang as they flew off.

Henry nodded.

The Sea King faded into the mist, leaving Cape Wrath behind. From the shadow of a cave Strang's eyes followed the lights of the helicopter. He wiped the sea spray from his face and spat out a mouthful of blood. Had he fooled them into believing he was dead? Perhaps the others thought so, but not Riley. There had always been a strange sense of understanding the other's objectives. Riley knew he was still breathing and that there would be payback for what they'd done. Hunting him to the edge of nowhere showed how far they'd go to destroy him. It was time to bring the hunter's game back closer to Riley's home.

Chapter Twelve

The Poison Code

The night had a brittle quality to it. The streets in the centre of Glasgow sparkled with a thin layer of frost that seemed to drain the last of the vibrant colour out of the city. Everything was cast in a cold blue glow.

McAra parked his car near Sauchiehall Street and walked briskly to the restaurant, rubbing his hands together for warmth as the air chilled him to the bone. Jamesie peered nervously out the window of the restaurant. It was almost six o'clock. McAra had cut it neat.

Jamesie took McAra's coat as soon as he walked in, folded it over his arm and showed McAra to his table. Waiters were busy arranging cutlery and settings for a pre–booked party, and two guests who'd arrived early for the party enjoyed a drink in the corner.

'Do you think I would suit a coat like this?' Jamesie said, admiring McAra's long, dark overcoat.

'I'm sure you would,' McAra said, wondering if the chef was fishing to try it on.

'I'm not going to put it on. I wouldn't want to muck it up. It's just that every winter I think to myself I should get a snazzy coat, like one of those businessmen's coats, a money coat.'

'Try it on if you want to,' McAra said.

Jamesie took his chef's hat off, put the coat on and looked at his reflection in the window. 'Very posh. Posh but practical.'

'They're quite expensive but last for years,' McAra said.

Jamesie had another look at his reflection and then took the coat off, carefully folding it over his arm again. 'I'll maybe treat myself. Great for cold nights like this. The dark ones like yours are nice but I fancy a lighter colour, like Strang's coat — a caramel colour but that wouldn't suit a gingernut like you.'

McAra smiled to himself. He knew no offence was intended.

'I've got a good eye for colour,' Jamesie said. 'See that painting over there — that's one of mine.'

McAra looked at the painting hanging on the main wall of the restaurant, a stylishly colourful depiction of Glasgow nightlife. 'You're an artist?'

'I dabble. I'm self taught.'

'It's excellent.'

'I started painting when I worked at the nightclubs. I used to draw the different faces I saw and the colours of the fashions and the drinks.'

'You could make a living out of it.'

'Quite a few of the pubs and nightclubs have got one of my paintings. I still get the odd commission, especially when somewhere new opens up. I'm working on a painting for the new casino.' He indicated towards the restaurant painting. 'That one there was supposed to be for the casino but I brought it in to cover up the scorch marks from the fire.'

McAra looked around. 'I thought the restaurant would be closed for a while due to the damage.'

'Nah, it'll take more than a fire and a fight to close us down. There was a wee bit of smoke damage but that got repapered, and a new carpet's been laid. And we've got new curtains. So we're sorted again.'

'Indeed,' McAra said.

'Right, I'll get the notebook and we'll have a chat.' He hurried off, hung the coat up and then hurried back. 'Fancy something to eat?'

McAra hesitated.

'How about a nice piece of salmon?' Jamesie offered.

This sounded good to McAra. 'Lovely.'

'Back in a minute.'

While Jamesie went away for the notebook, and to serve up the salmon, a waiter brought McAra a bowl of hot soup and fresh baked crusty bread. It was very welcome because he'd hardly had anything proper to eat all day.

Several minutes later Jamesie arrived with the salmon and served it up with all the trimmings. Then he sat down at the table and opened Lucky's notebook.

'I'm worried about Lucky,' Jamesie said, emphasising the point. 'I may seem chirpy and okay, but I'm far from it. We've been friends for years. But I'm no good to him if I get rattled.'

McAra nodded and continued eating his dinner. He didn't even want to hint that Lucky may not be alive.

Jamesie turned over the pages. 'I've been reading the notes he's written about that politician, Kier Brodie. He'd told Riley he'd find out what he could and this is what he came up with. Some of it I don't understand.' He pushed the notebook over to McAra. 'It says that Brodie and Mackenzie were involved in an intranet. He probably meant the Internet.'

'No he got it right. An intranet's different. It's like a small version of the net — a secure way to pass on information.' McAra traced his finger down the list of names, numbers and scribbled notes.

Jamesie sounded anxious. 'Riley's name is listed. Lucky says the others are dead. I don't like to say, but that's a hit list.'

'Riley knows about it. The other men are scientists.'

'Dead scientists.' Jamesie paused and stared at McAra.

'Yes, I'm a scientist and my name wasn't on the list,' McAra said, anticipating the chef's thoughts.

'Do you know why?' Jamesie said.

'I've never been involved in dark projects.'

'I'm guessing that's dodgy stuff.'

'Dangerous stuff if it got into the wrong hands.'

'Like Strang?'

'Yes.'

'Lucky reckons Strang killed them and stole their work,' Jamesie said.

'There's no proof of that.'

'But he did, didn't he?'

'It seems likely,' McAra said.

'Why don't the police bring Strang in for questioning?'

'He's gone underground. Riley and others are trying to find him,' McAra said, keeping the details of the Cape Wrath incident quiet.

'So they don't know where Strang is?'

'Not exactly.'

'Why don't they phone him and trace where he is?' Jamesie said.

'No one has his number.'

Jamesie searched in the back pocket of his trousers and brought out his mobile phone. 'I've got his number.' There was a tinge of guilt in his voice.

'Did you copy it off the diners booking register?'

'No, Strang never left his address or phone number. He was a sly fucker. There was something creepy about him. I've always said you can tell a lot from the things you find on someone's mobile phone. I used to nick customers phones at the nightclubs, read their messages, take a note of their numbers, then put it back in their pockets without them even knowing.'

'Is that what you did with Strang?'

'Old habits and all that . . .' Jamesie flipped to the back page of the notebook and wrote the number down. 'Riley will know what to do with it. Give him the notebook.'

'Where did Lucky find this information about Brodie and Mackenzie?' McAra said, putting his knife and fork down and flicking through the notes.

'From Mackenzie's cronies. With him being dead they don't need to keep their mouths shut any more. Everyone tells their stories to Lucky.'

'Is there any mention of a scroll, a parchment scroll? Or anything about poison?'

'Poison's a code word.' He took the book from McAra. 'Here it is. It was Brodie's computer password. Mackenzie had a note of it. Not sure what it was about.'

'I'll ask Riley.' McAra checked his watch. 'He should be here in about half an hour.'

'Riley's coming here?'

'Is that a problem?'

'No, no, that's superb. If anybody can help us find Lucky, it's him.' He paused, and the colour drained from his face. 'Do you think Lucky's still alive?'

'There's always hope,' McAra said, wishing it wasn't a white lie.

Riley had driven home from Glasgow airport after a briefing at HMS Excalibur with Henry. One of the naval personnel gave him a lift back to the airport. It had been a long day. He stored his wet gear near the diving pool ready for action again and was due to meet up with McAra. He lit the fire in the study to warm the house which felt especially cold and dark. The trip to Cape Wrath had made its mark, leaving a haunting feeling, a silent unsettledness that was hard to shake off. Strang hadn't died in the sea today though he wished he had. It was good to work with Henry again although it was a stark reminder of how different his life had become since leaving the SBS. Part of him would always be with the forces.

A call from Byrn Shaw interrupted his thoughts. He was phoning him urgently from the Scottish Parliament office in Edinburgh.

'Brodie's been watching Catherine like a vulture. I've got a bad feeling about it.'

'Have you spoken to her?' Riley said.

'No she seemed distracted and I never got a chance.'

'Is she still in Edinburgh?'

'Yes but she's gone home.'

'Keep an eye on her.'

'I will. Brodie's up to something. I can sense it,' Shaw said.

'Be careful. Don't take any chances.'

'Any news on Strang?' Shaw said.

'Nothing yet. Henry's lot are working on it, and I'm meeting McAra tonight. A contact has information that could be useful.'

'I'll keep the satellite checks open. If he pops up on the radar let me know. I doubt he'll go back to Cape Wrath.'

'I'm betting he'll bring the fight nearer to home or target something personal.'

'Watch your back, Riley.'

'You too.'

Riley clicked his mobile off. For a moment he listened to the silence in his study. Out the window he saw the night turning to dark ice. In his mind he agreed with Shaw. He had a bad feeling about Brodie and knew that Strang would be back with certain vengeance.

Riley arrived at the restaurant but McAra and Jamesie weren't there. A member of staff pointed along the street to McAra's car. Riley went over and tapped on the window. Jamesie's startled face peered out at him.

'You scared the shite out of me,' Jamesie said through the glass.

McAra unlocked the car and Riley got into the back seat. McAra had set up a laptop computer, mobile phone and other pieces of gadgetry in the front of the car. The computer screen showed a map with a location being traced. McAra's hair was sticking up in wild abandon. It did this when the scientist in him was in the throws of a discovery.

'Jamesie had a note of Strang's phone number,' McAra explained to Riley. 'I made a bogus call to him, blathering on about absolute nonsense, while I plucked the location right out of the air.'

'Is he in Glasgow?' Riley said.

'Yes. Not only is he in the city, he's right over . . . there!' McAra stabbed a finger at the street pinpointed on the screen.

'That's spitting distance from us,' Jamesie said.

'Is he on the move?' Riley said.

'No he's stationery. The address is registered as residential,' McAra said.

'He's home,' Riley said.

McAra nodded. 'Clearly he made it back from Cape Wrath.'

'What about Lucky?' Jamesie said to Riley. The chef's face was etched with concern.

'I'll have a word with Strang,' Riley said, buttoning his warm, dark jacket, ready for the encounter.

McAra shot him a look. 'You're not going in there alone. I'll go with you.'

'Me too,' Jamesie said.

Riley shook his head. 'Phone Valentine and Ferguson. Tell them what's happening.' He got out of the car.

'We'll be watching,' McAra said, leaning out the car window. 'Oh and the poison thing — it was Brodie's computer password. Poison.'

Riley absorbed the details and hurried away.

McAra immediately phoned Valentine.

'We're not letting him go on his own are we?' Jamesie said, watching Riley head up the street.

McAra relayed the information to Valentine who said they were on their way.

As Jamesie opened the car door to go after Riley, the laptop computer bleeped information. 'Get back in the car. Strang's on the move,' McAra said.

'Surely he doesn't know that Riley's coming to get him?' Jamesie said.

'No just bad timing. He's phoning someone. That's all I can pick up.'

McAra closed the laptop, disconnected the tracing gadgets and got ready to drive off. He didn't want to risk phoning Riley. If there was one thing he'd learned it was never to interfere with Riley's plans or phone to compromise him. He intended driving nearer to Strang's location while giving Riley space to do what he was best at.

McAra drove to Strang's home, turned the headlamps off and parked in a darkened area away from any streetlights. The building was part of a two storey complex of businesses and apartments. A doorway led to a close where several routes could be taken by the various occupants.

'Riley could walk right into Strang,' Jamesie said, keeping his voice low and leaning back into the shadows inside the car.

McAra glanced over at him. 'That would be Strang's mistake.'

Riley pressed himself into the darkness of the close. The maze of businesses and apartments were reasonably quiet. Most businesses had shut for the evening and only a few residents' lights shone from the upper windows. Very little light shone down into the back of the close that led on to a concrete garden where rubbish bins were kept. A solitary light bulb protected by a mesh of metal gave off a dim yellow glow.

Riley stepped out of the close into the garden, holding his breath so it wouldn't show in the freezing air and peered out and up towards the rear windows of the apartments. He assessed the situation in seconds and then stepped back into the darkened close.

Footsteps sounded from the stone stairwell. Riley made himself part of the darkness waiting to see who it was. A man emerged from the gloom, lit by a flickering lamp on the wall. It was Strang. He was wearing a long, caramel coloured coat. Any second now Strang would be within striking distance. No clever moves. Riley wasn't taking any chances. An effective take down and restraint was all he needed until Valentine arrived.

Maybe it was instinct, sensing danger lurking in the darkness, the chill that alerts the unwary, but Strang hesitated as if knowing something wasn't right.

Riley held his breath.

Ninety per cent of people would go against their gut instinct. They'd note the warning and then proceed into the danger zone regardless. Strang belonged to the ten per cent who were smart enough to take heed.

Silence.

Strang listened in the half light. No sound, no breath. Nothing was heard. Still he hesitated, his instincts working to full capacity.

Suddenly the sound of a car racing down the street shattered the quiet. The stairwell amplified the noise of the tyres screeching to a halt outside the building. Strang bolted back up the stairs. Riley ran after him. On the turn of the stairs Strang saw Riley and put on a burst of speed but his long coat slowed him up.

Riley kept pace, more determined to catch Strang than ever. He wasn't letting him get away this time.

Car doors slammed and footsteps sounded in the stairwell running fast, more than one man. Voices giving orders to others ricocheted through the building. The footsteps covered all angles. Other cars arrived.

Strang kept running until he reached his front door and forced his key in the lock. Riley was two steps behind and grabbed hold of him as the door slammed open. He rammed Strang's body against the wall but even this failed to stop him pulling a knife on Riley and slicing savagely at his face. Riley evaded the blade, caught Strang's wrist in a vice like grip and twisted the flesh and bones until the knife fell from his grasp.

Strang fought like a beast, his eyes wild with rage and hatred for Riley.

Fast and ruthless, the fight was unforgiving. Both men used close quarter combat techniques. They'd never fought before but Strang had long wanted to pit his ability against that of the SBS hero.

There was no room in the dark narrow hallway of Strang's apartment for grand manoeuvres and the blow by blow struggle was settled with their bare fists. Street lighting lit up the living room and only the overspill of this lit the hall. They fought in the half shadows, punching and blocking each other's moves, neither man backing away from giving it his all.

It crossed Riley's mind in the heat of the fight that one of them might die and it sure as hell wasn't going to be him.

Riley had always been fast. Fast and calm — something that couldn't be learned, you could only be. His speed and hard techniques enabled him to avoid and deflect most of Strang's blows although his jaw had absorbed one hefty punch. Even Riley had to admit that the scientist was strong and skilful. In Riley's world there were two types of successful fighters — the calm and the crazy. Two very hard types to beat. Strang was on the edge of crazy and his rage started working against him. His uncontrolled ferocity made him bite through his bottom lip, drawing blood.

Riley went in for the take down. He overpowered Strang with a strike across his throat to weaken him and then caught him in a strangle hold. In other circumstances he'd have done the world a favour and broken his neck but he had no authority to act outside the law, and neither did he want to. Once the courts saw what Strang was capable of they'd lock the murderer up for a long, long time. Right now Strang was the key to trapping Kier Brodie so he needed him alive. However there was something he wanted to ask the bastard before handing him over to the police.

'What have you done with Lucky?'

There was no reply.

Riley tightened his grip on Strang's throat. 'Don't make me ask twice.'

Strang smiled through a mouthful of blood and then spat his hatred and defiance at Riley.

Valentine, Ferguson and other officers rushed into the apartment. Riley stepped aside. The marks were visible on Strang's neck where Riley's fingers had gripped him but the scientist didn't wince and glared defiantly to the last as he was handcuffed and taken downstairs by the police. Ferguson went with them, leaving Riley to talk to Valentine.

'You were never here,' Valentine said.

Riley looked at him in surprise while wiping Strang's blood from his face. 'I thought the Uncorruptables did everything by the book.'

Valentine kept his voice quiet. 'We can't be bought or blackmailed but it'll be better for everyone if you weren't part of this. I appreciate your help, Riley.

And I'd still like you to work with us on Richard Reece's murder case.'

'I'm working on information. Lucky made notes about Brodie's involvement with Mackenzie. Jamesie gave the notebook to McAra.'

Valentine gave a wry smile.

'The notes mentioned a poison code. Poison was Brodie's password for his computer. I'll see what else I can access with it.'

Stanley Valentine senior made his way up to the apartment. 'You've done enough, Riley. We'll take it from here.' There was a nod of acknowledgement for capturing Strang. It was the nearest he was going to get to a thank you. 'We're taking Strang to the station,' Stanley senior said to his son and then went back downstairs.

'We've no leads on what happened to Lucky,' Valentine said to Riley. 'It was definitely his knife that was lying in the shelter. Forensics found only one type of blood on the walls — it was a match for Lucky's. He obviously put up one hell of a fight.'

'I'm still going to look for him, so if you do get any leads pass them on to me.'

Valentine nodded. 'If it was anyone else I'd say he was as sure as dead but Lucky's a tough wee bastard so you never know.'

The sound of commotion and people shouting was heard from the street.

Riley and Valentine ran downstairs. 'What happened?' Valentine shouted to Ferguson.

'Strang's escaped!'

Further up the street the police car carrying Strang had careered off the road and crashed into a shop window. Smoke poured out of the rear door. A second police car had been following. It sat abandoned in the middle of the road. The driver's door was flung wide open, and a man lay injured in the street. The man was Stanley senior.

Riley and the detectives ran along the street towards the cars. McAra and Jamesie went with them. They'd seen everything that had happened.

A police officer came staggering towards them, his face bleeding from shards of glass. Ferguson grabbed hold of him as he collapsed. 'Strang set off a device,' the officer gasped, choking for breath. 'We didn't have a chance. I think it was in his watch. I couldn't see for the smoke.'

Riley hurried over to the car whose front windscreen had shattered on impact with the shop front. The officer who'd been driving had managed to crawl from the vehicle. Other officers went to help him. The front window of the shop was equally shattered.

The shop was in darkness and no one had been in it at the time.

Ferguson phoned, requesting back up.

Valentine rushed over to his father who was lying on the ground, barely conscious. A small, thin metal spike was sticking out the side of his throat. Blood was seeping from the wound. Valentine knelt down beside him. 'Lie still. You'll be okay. Don't move. The ambulance is on its way.'

In the distance the sirens of the emergency services could be heard.

Valentine glanced over at Riley, his face pale and drawn with hardened shock.

McAra volunteered the details. 'The two cars drove off, then there was a dull thud from Strang's car, it filled up with smoke and veered across the road.'

'What about Strang?' Riley said.

'He got out the back of the car but by this time old boy Stanley's car had screeched to a halt behind him. Stanley tried to tackle him but Strang stabbed him in the neck and ran off.' McAra pointed to an alleyway. 'He got free of the handcuffs, threw his coat off and ran up there.'

Valentine took his jacket off and put it over his father, who was now unconscious and barely breathing, to keep him warm on the icy ground. He looked up at

Riley. 'Get the bastard,' he said, his tone seething with anger.

Riley nodded and hurried towards the alleyway, followed by McAra and Ferguson.

Jamesie picked up Strang's coat where he'd thrown it in the street. A nice coat just lying there. A crowd was gathering in the street and onlookers were being moved back to let the ambulance and police reinforcements through. The area started to be cordoned off. In the melee of sirens, flashing lights and crowd chaos Jamesie disappeared up a close with the coat. No one even noticed.

Chapter Thirteen

Invisible Raiders

Riley ran in the shadows, chasing after a figure, a silhouette moving at a fast rate through the back streets of the city centre. It was not an easy run. There were too many alleys and darkened doorways where a man could hide. The pace was harsh on unfamiliar icy ground. Riley pounded on the ever changing mix of concrete and cobbles, twisting through the narrow lanes and gathering speed on straight stretches, chasing shadows yet again as he had done as an Invisible Raider in the SBS.

McAra wasn't far behind him, taking the racing line on some routes, covering the areas Riley had bypassed, running concurrent like a descant, a counterpoint. They lost Ferguson way back in the amber zone, where the yellow streetlamps ended and the dark side of Glasgow began. Ferguson wasn't a runner. He couldn't keep up and had gone back to where Valentine and the others were raking over Strang's apartment leaving Riley and McAra to chase the shadow. Police cars sounded in the distance searching the area for Strang. Riley had a feeling the police were looking in the wrong vicinity.

Riley skidded to a halt on the frost in a darkened lane. Three routes lay ahead.

Breathing in the icy air he listened. No sound of Strang.

'Have we lost him?' McAra said.

Riley took a moment to think. 'Do you know this area?'

'Absolutely not. Haven't a clue where we are.'

Riley looked up at the buildings, a jagged interlocking web of bricks and slate that obscured the view of their location. Then he saw a distinctive light in the distant skyline on the highest part of a bridge. 'We're near the Clyde,' he said and then ran full pelt in the direction of the river. McAra followed him.

They reached the river minutes later. Not a soul was anywhere to be seen. The river flowed like black liquid glass with the lights of the bridge glistening on the surface. A paved walkway stretched along the edge of the Clyde.

'I don't see anyone,' McAra said, searching up and down the walkway.

Riley leaned over the metal barrier and looked down into the cold black water.

If he'd been cornered he would've jumped into the river and swam underneath the murky surface to avoid being caught. Few would choose such a harsh option especially in freezing conditions and that's why he sensed Strang had taken it. They wouldn't find him tonight.

'Think he went swimming?' McAra said.

Riley nodded. 'One of Strang's biggest mistakes was to stab Stanley senior. The police will hunt him down. He'll have to disappear well below the radar.'

'At least we'll be rid of him.'

'Yes but for how long?'

From the edge of the river below the bridge Strang swam to the surface. His body ached with the pain of the icy water but he stayed submerged up to his neck watching Riley and McAra walk away.

Riley went home after talking to Valentine and Ferguson. Stanley senior had been taken to hospital. The stab wound was serious and a full scale alert had been put out by the police to catch Strang. Riley wasn't getting his hopes up. Anyone who could survive a trip on the rocks at Cape Wrath was going to be a tough adversary even for Valentine.

As he splashed his face with water to wash the blood off, his phone rang.

'Mr Riley?' a voice said. 'Is that you?'

'Who is this?' Riley said.

'It's me, Jamesie.'

'How did you get this number?'

'I eh . . . I got it from Mul McAra,' Jamesie said.

'McAra wouldn't have given you my private number.'

'Well you see . . . he didn't actually give me the number . . . I sort of eh . . . his phone was lying on the table in the restaurant and I eh . . .'

'Just spit out why you're calling, Jamesie.'

'I've found something in Strang's coat. He left it lying in the street tonight and I picked it up. I checked the pockets and you'll never guess what I found.'

'What?'

'A key. And not just any key. It's made with that really shiny gold metal you get at the key cutting shops and it's got a fancy lucky charm fob.'

'And your point?'

'It's Lucky's. All his keys were cut like that.'

'Do you recognise what the key belongs to?' Riley said.

'Definitely. It's the key to his lockup near the old docks. That's where he keeps his hucklebuck stuff, his secret stash of eh . . .'

'Dodgy stolen goods.'

'Correct.'

'Give me the directions.'

'You know the old foundry at the quays. Well that's where the lockups are. Lucky's is number thirteen.'

Riley almost laughed. 'Unlucky for some.'

'It was the only one left to lease.'

'I'll go and check it out,' Riley said.

'I could go with you. I'm thinking maybe he's got Lucky locked up there,' Jamesie said.

'Do me a favour. Stay where you are. I won't need the key. I'll phone you later.'

'Right, okay.'

Riley went to hang up.

'Just one more thing,' Jamesie said. 'About the coat . . . after what Strang did to the police chief I doubt he'll be coming back for it. So can I have the coat?'

'What coat?' Riley said.

Jamesie smiled to himself. 'Cheers, Riley.'

The docks had been dead for years. Gradually the area was having new life breathed into it, being upgraded and developed into an exciting complex of apartments and businesses. The lockups were still steeped in the past, untouched since they were built in a bygone time. Riley drove past the rows of disused lockups until he came to number thirteen. He got out of the car and used a torch from the boot to cast some light on the door which was in complete darkness. No one was about at night and only the distant sound of traffic could be heard.

Riley shone the torch on the door whose wood was dull as black lead. A heavy chain and padlock secured it. Riley didn't need the key. He picked the lock in seconds, unchained the door and opened it slowly and carefully, shining the torch inside. The stench was sickening, like rotting meat and sour drains. The sound of water dripping in the far corner echoed in the silence. He took a step inside. The garage size lockup was damp and cold. He shone the torch around the half empty rails of fashion clothing and then heard a noise to his left. He spun round and saw a figure taking a dive at him, growling like an animal. He sidestepped the attack and the man stumbled and fell to the ground. It was Lucky, barely recognisable. His clothes were stained in blood and his face had been badly beaten. One eye was bloated and he looked like he'd gone twelve rounds in the loser's corner of a boxing ring. Riley recognised the damage inflicted. He'd seen faces like this before. Lucky had been tortured.

'It's me, Riley,' he said, bending down to help Lucky get to his feet.

Lucky staggered and then the realisation dawned on him. 'Riley! Fuck's sake. What kept you?'

'Come on let's get you to the car.' He half carried Lucky outside and drove him straight to the nearest hospital.

Lucky's jaw ached as he spoke. 'That shite Strang. If I ever see him again I'll rip his fuckin' throat out.'

Riley filled him in on the details of what had happened.

'I hope the Clyde choked him but we couldn't be that lucky.'

'What did Strang want from you?' Riley said.

'He'd heard I was digging around in his business with Brodie and Mackenzie, so you can imagine how well that went down.'

'What did you tell him?'

'Fuck all! And then there was the little matter of setting him up at the restaurant. He softened my ribs for that one. I thought he was going to kill me.'

'You're a hard man to kill,' Riley said.

'It'll take a better shite than Strang to put my lights out. I'm starving though.' He rubbed his hands over his face and shuddered. 'And that dirty drainage water tasted like cat's piss.'

'It kept you alive, so don't think about it. Just get your strength back,' Riley said, having been in similar situations where he thought he'd breathed his last but somehow survived against the odds.

'Anger's what kept me alive,' Lucky said. 'Oh for the day I get my hands on that bastard's throat!'

Riley nodded. The fight in Lucky was good. Many a man had survived on nothing more than burning rage.

'How's Barking Bob?' Lucky said.

'Jamesie sorted him out. A neighbour is looking after the dog.'

'Good, good man.' Lucky straightened the blood stained designer suit and stylish winter jacket he was wearing. 'I'll be the best dressed patient in the hospital,' he said, smiling with yet another tooth less than last time. 'Three thousand quid this suit costs. Luckily I had some stuff still hanging up on the rails. I'd have frozen to death in my t-shirt.'

'I'll let Jamesie know you're okay and I'll contact Valentine. Ironically you'll be in the same hospital as his father.'

'Is the old boy going to make it?' Lucky said.

Riley shrugged. 'It's not looking good but Stanley's always been full of surprises.'

'I remember years ago he chased me all the way along Buchanan Street. I thought he was never going to give up. That's of course before I went ninety-nine percent legit.'

'Of course,' Riley said, smiling.

'Got anything to eat?' Lucky said, rummaging in the glove compartment and finding a bar of climber's chocolate.

'They'll be giving you an anaesthetic so you shouldn't eat anything.'

'I've been beaten, tortured, starved and left to rot in a freezing damp hell hole by a psychotic maniac. I've even lost another tooth and I've a definite shortage of those, so I think that sookin' a wee bit of chocolate won't do any harm.'

'You've still got your lucky earring though,' Riley said.

Lucky smiled and then winced when the movement hurt his jaw. 'Thanks for coming to get me. I was hoping you would.'

'It was Jamesie that found the key in Strang's coat pocket and phoned me.'

'And I'll thank him for that — and McAra. We're quite a team eh, Riley? Bet you never thought you'd have a secret four–man team like us.'

'Never in a million years.'

After leaving Lucky at the hospital and having a word with Valentine, Riley phoned Jamesie and told him about his friend.

'That's great! Cheers, Riley,' Jamesie said.

'Don't wear your new coat. The Valentines are in the same hospital as Lucky.'

'No problem.'

Riley clicked the phone off and drove away. The city was strangely silent as if the ice had frozen the life out of it. He deliberately drove past the new casino which was lit up with neon lights. It was time to tackle Kier Brodie. That smug bastard's cage needed rattled from the inside. For all the things that had happened — Reece's brutal murder and Mackenzie and Strang's involvement, everything came right back to him.

There would be little sleep for Riley. He intended ripping apart the files he'd taken from the casino, going over the information piece by piece. Lucky's notes about the poison code could be just the key he needed to access the last remnants of hidden data.

The study provided a welcome calm. Riley worked at his computer by the light of his desk lamp and the glow from the log fire. He discovered something that was very useful — the poison codeword opened up a web of information about Kier Brodie. He'd crossed swords with men like Brodie before but it surprised him how deep the threads of the web penetrated. The computer files he'd acquired from the casino contained a hidden cache showing the flow of money being transferred from the casino into Brodie's pockets. The files showed the casino had nothing to do with it. The casino was simply a steady flow of cash.

He hacked deeper into the files. The intranet comprised of a small, close knit group involving a political factor where men in government exchanged valuable information, similar to a form of insider trading, and received a lucrative flow of wealth in return. In essence, it was all about the money. Money equated to power and it seemed that anyone who got in Brodie's way, like Richard Reece, was eliminated. Reece had initially been part of the intranet but it appeared he'd balked at the level of double dealing required to remain a member. Then he'd made the ultimate mistake of challenging Brodie for his seat in Parliament. At that point he became a threat and a liability.

Using the poison codeword, Riley accessed other names within the intranet clique of politicians and businessmen. He e-mailed the data to Valentine.

Riley wasn't the only one working late. Valentine phoned him immediately after reading the e-mail.

'How's Stanley senior doing?' Riley said.

'It was touch and go but he's stable now. He's a tough old sod. He's well pissed off though, and so am I. Strang's not getting away with this.'

There was a click on the phone line. Both of them dismissed it as a technical fault and kept on talking.

'We found some interesting stuff when we searched Strang's house,' Valentine said. 'Map coordinates to somewhere he refers to as the *Sleeping Warrior*. Does it mean anything to you?'

Riley hadn't heard those words in years. 'He's referring to Arran,' Riley said.

Arran was a large island in the Firth of Clyde off the west coast of Scotland opposite Ayrshire and south of Glasgow. It was known as the Sleeping Warrior. The dark grey profile of the island resembled an ancient warrior, a knight in battle dress, lying on the waterline with his sword by his side and a shield across his chest.

'What's the deal with Arran? Is it another Cape Wrath? A military training area?' Valentine said.

'Not nowadays but it used to be. Arran's where the SBS did some of their original training. My grandfather, Harry, was part of it. That's where it all started.'

'I'll contact the police on the island, see if they know what Strang's up to. We may need your help with this. I'll e-mail the map coordinates to you.'

'What else did you find?'

'Various gadgetry. Forensics is having a field day.'

The e-mail arrived. Riley opened it and read the contents. 'Yes, that's Arran. He could be using it as a secret base to work on his experiments.'

Another click sounded on the phone connection.

This time Riley's senses flicked to red alert. 'Hang up. I'll call you back.'

Valentine got the message and put the phone down. Riley called him moments later.

'I'll make this short. The line's not secure. Someone's listening in. We've got less than one minute before they latch on to our signal again.'

'Okay. Hang up and I'll call you back.'

Riley clicked the phone down and picked it up again when Valentine called.

'Do you think it's Strang who's listening in?' Valentine said.

'Very likely. At least we know he's still in Glasgow. He couldn't pick up the signal if he was on Arran.'

'Would e–mail be more secure?'

'Yes, and I'll send you an alternative phone number for me. It'll take about an hour to get it reactivated.'

They ended the conversation and continued to communicate via e–mail.

Riley calculated the coordinates on the map of Arran and sent this to Valentine. He also discovered that Strang planned to go to Arran at the end of October.

'*If it's okay with you, I'd like to alert Henry about this*,' Riley wrote via e–mail.

Valentine didn't have a problem with this. '*If we can't handle the situation ourselves, we'll call on you and Henry. Whatever happens, I guarantee Strang's not walking away unscathed this time.*'

Riley sensed the hardened determination in Valentine's message. It was guarantee enough.

Part of Riley's past was stored in a large, heavy trunk in the climbing room of his house. He hadn't opened it in a long time preferring to keep the past locked away.

The hinges creaked when he opened it and began rummaging through the contents, searching for his specialist phone. It was an expensive piece of kit he'd used during his time in the Special Forces, incorporating a scrambling device and other capabilities to encrypt his phone conversations without risk of being intercepted.

He found the phone underneath some climbing gear and weapons which were on the cusp of being legal. He laid the phone aside and was about to close the trunk when he saw something that made him hesitate. Tucked down the side he saw an album of photographs that were the partners of the few framed photographs in his study. The difference was that these images had people in them. His father, Alexander, and grandfather, Harry, were in the pictures. A sense of strange loyalty washed over him when he saw them again. Ghosts of the past, frozen in time. Wherever Harry was photographed, there was water. In every snap he was diving into the ocean, paddling a canoe, even standing in the pouring rain smiling beside a submarine during the end of the Second World War. In Harry, Riley could see an image of himself — tall, rugged, dark haired and with grey eyes, though Harry tended to smile more. Riley's looks had skipped a generation and in the pictures of Harry, taken in his prime, the resemblance was obvious.

Some of the sepia photographs had tarnished with age, and ironically, water damage, but nothing could take the shine off all those memories. He looked at a picture of Harry dressed in winter climbing gear standing on top of the highest snow covered mountain on Arran, and in the background was the ubiquitous view of the sea. Harry and Mul McAra's father loved Arran, and even in their twilight years visited it often, reminiscing about their days in the SBS and the training on the island where it all began at the beginning of World War Two.

In complete contrast, Alexander had blonde hair, blue eyes, a tall, lean structure, and was classically handsome. No matter how hot the terrain, he never had more than a pale, golden tan, even in the burnished sun of a scorching desert. He went on magnificent adventures all over the globe in search of historical information and artefacts, often to places where no one had set foot for hundreds of years. Despite a few narrow escapes when he'd vied against the elements, he invariably returned home virtually unscathed and achieved his successes with great aplomb. Alexander suited being the Record Keeper. In most of the pictures he was wearing a white shirt with the sleeves rolled up and clothes in muted tones. That's how Riley always remembered him. Alexander had been a man who had worn his era well but never quite fitted into the new millennium.

And there were pictures of Riley with Nick Deacon, Henry Davenport and another member of the SBS during a climbing trip in America. Apart from Henry, all the others were dead. There was no one left to protect. Nothing more could happen to them. Riley thought about what Catherine had said. There were no faces in his photographs, no people, just miles of desert and harsh landscape images. Born of necessity rather than habit, he'd spent most of his adult life shielding his identity and that of those around him.

He studied a picture of the desert. The desert reminded him of the SBS exercises and assignments he'd tackled in California's Death Valley with Deacon. Both of them had excelled in this unforgiving environment. Alexander had taken Riley to various deserts throughout the world when he was a young boy and he had become accustomed to the heat. As for Deacon, he never flinched whatever the weather . . .

Death Valley was living up to its searing hot reputation. The Californian sun was splitting holes in the ground and the air scorched their skin. Deacon stood on the bonnet of their all-terrain vehicle searching the horizon with a pair of binoculars. He was looking for Henry and the others who were due to rendezvous at the ghost town, an old mining town, now void of any life. The remnants of its bustling history lay broken and rusted in the desert.

'We'll give them another ten minutes and then head for the mountains,' Riley said.

Deacon looked over at the mountainous region in the far distance at the edge of the valley. A rainshadow cast its distinctive dark mark down one side of the slopes where very little rain fell due to the dry climate.

The climbing trip in America was part of a training exercise with US Navy Seals. The American Special Forces team had arranged the reccie but their plans had to be changed when gun runners were sighted near the training area and the Navy Seals were deployed to intercept them. The Brits went with them. What had started out as a training exercise, one the SBS regularly exchanged with the Americans, had escalated into a genuine threat.

Riley and Deacon had taken the open route across the valley, heading for the nearest ghost town with the intention of cutting off the gun runners' escape road south. Henry and the other SBS went with the Navy Seals towards the mountainous region north where it was estimated that the criminals had a hidden route out of the valley. The last Riley had seen of them was when Henry signalled in Morse code to him using a mirror before they disappeared into the sepia darkness of the rainshadowed landscape. The message was short. *Targets sighted. Rendezvous at the shadowline at 1300 hours.*

The line was where the rainshadow split the mountain region in two. Riley estimated Deacon and him could drive there from the ghost town within twenty minutes. They waited for the signal from Henry to confirm the gun runners had been arrested, but as the time wore on and there was no sign of Henry or the Navy Seals, Riley's guts started to warn him that something wasn't right.

A signal finally arrived from Henry indicating that the situation had been dealt with. No Special Forces men had been injured and the gun runners were contained and taken into custody. Riley returned the signal and confirmed they'd rendezvous as planned.

'Ever been to Death Valley before?' Deacon said.

Riley's grey eyes squinted against the bright sunlight that bleached everything the colour of parched bone. 'Once. My father brought me here years ago. I always had the feeling one day I'd be back.'

Deacon jumped down from the vehicle, his boots causing a flurry of dust as he hit the cracked ground. 'I've got the strangest sense that you and I haven't seen the last of Death Valley.'

Riley shivered inwardly, an odd sensation of coldness amid the scorching heat. It wasn't like Deacon to be philosophical, but on the rare occasions when he had, his thoughts had always proved right. However this time he'd been wrong because they'd never gone back to Death Valley together and now there was no chance they ever would. Deacon was dead . . .

Riley put the photographs back in the trunk and locked the past away again. He reactivated his specialist phone ready to counter whatever Strang had planned. It beeped into life as if he'd used it only yesterday. Then he phoned Valentine and gave him the number.

Valentine had been busy. 'I spoke to the police on Arran and they checked out the location you'd calculated from the map. Strang's been using an old holiday cottage as a base. So I'm going to take you up on your offer to involve Henry. See if you can arrange for him to take a Sea King over to Arran tomorrow morning.'

'Do you want to come along?' Riley said.

'No, Ferguson volunteered to go. I'm following a lead on Kier Brodie. We've been keeping a close eye on him and apparently he's upset with his accountant.'

'Really?'

'Yes, someone locked down two of his accounts. Seems they may have hacked into his business dealings and fucked them up.'

'Computers can be a right bastard, can't they?'

'Indeed they can, Riley. Thanks again.'

Chapter Fourteen

Shadow of the Warrior

A grey dawn lingered over the Scottish Parliament building in Edinburgh, taking the edge off the structured skyline. Kier Brodie arrived early and hurried inside. The building smelled of freshly polished wood mixed with the cold October air filtering through the main entrance. In his coat pocket was an envelope, an invitation. He wanted to deliver it personally and strode purposefully down the main corridor, his dark overcoat and briefcase making him look like a lawyer rather than a politician with malice on his mind.

Unknown to him, Shaw watched him approach Catherine's office, suspicious of his intentions. No one was in the corridor as Brodie slipped into the unlocked office. Shaw followed him silently.

Whatever the politician was up to, he'd been barely a minute in Catherine's office before encountering the challenging stature of Shaw when he hurried out.

'Don't worry, Shaw,' Brodie said, smiling tightly. 'I was leaving something for Catherine. I've left it on her desk.'

'Important was it?'

'Yes. Don't worry,' he repeated, 'I'm not making a move on your girlfriend.'

'She's not my girlfriend, as well you know,' Shaw said.

'That's right. Unrequited love — stings, doesn't it?'

Shaw clenched his fists. It was the tone that jarred him more than the comment. 'You know it's against the rules to enter Catherine's office without her authorisation —'

'Everything by the rules, Shaw. Nothing more boring than a man with a badge.' He walked on briskly. 'You need to lighten up. Maybe the women would start taking a shine to you.'

Shaw followed him to the main lobby. 'I'll have to inform Catherine about this.'

Brodie halted and sighed heavily. 'It's just an invitation to a social event in Glasgow tomorrow night. An invitation for two. You're welcome to come along, though I'm betting you won't be the man of her choice. My money's on the Record Keeper.'

A flicker of realisation sparked in Shaw's eyes.

'Oh don't look so surprised, Shaw. You think I don't know about John Riley and Catherine?'

Brodie hurried on again with Shaw in his wake. 'Look, I'm busy. I've a meeting in half an hour, so if you've anything else to say spit it out.'

They stopped in the main lobby.

Shaw's cold blue eyes targeted Brodie, and he spoke in a serious whisper. 'If anything happens to Catherine, and I find out you're responsible, you won't believe how fast I'll come looking for you.'

Brodie forced a smile but he took a step back. Shaw's message had hit home.

The sound of administration staff arriving for work broke the tension. Brodie smiled again, and walked away.

The helicopter picked Riley and Ferguson up from Glasgow airport. Riley made the introductions. Henry shook hands with Ferguson, simultaneously helping the detective climb on board the Sea King.

Ferguson groaned. 'My muscles are killing me,' he said to Riley.

'Been in a fight?' Riley said.

'No, just feels like it.' Ferguson turned to Henry. 'I had to chase a suspect recently and I wasn't as fit as I should've been. I couldn't keep up with Riley and

McAra, not even for a quarter of the distance they ran, so I'm getting in training.'

'You should walk before you run,' Henry said. 'No offence but you're carrying a bit of bulk. Start with brisk walking. It'll build up your stamina.'

Ferguson looked at Riley.

'Henry's right,' Riley said. 'Get up early in the morning and have a half hour walk round the streets. Same again at night. That'll get you fit.'

Ferguson digested the information. 'Thanks, I'll give it a go.' He paused, flexed his biceps and clenched his hands as if lifting weights. 'Do you think I need to get into the weight training?'

'You've got more muscle than your body knows what to do with,' Riley said. 'Concentrate on your stamina and endurance with the walking for two or three months, maybe even swimming, then start with the weights if you're keen, but you'd be better with press ups, chins, and a bit of shadow boxing.'

Ferguson smiled enthusiastically.

'Get outdoors, train in the elements, get some fresh air in your lungs,' Henry said to Ferguson.

'You'll get plenty of that today,' Riley said, sliding the side door of the Sea King shut. Three other members of the SBS were on board preparing for the relatively short trip across the Firth of Clyde to the isle of Arran.

The engines began to roar. 'We're clear for take off,' Pilot one announced.

The powerful vibrations rumbled through the undercarriage of the Sea King. Ferguson's face bore an expression of excitement and trepidation.

'You'll have to wear this,' Henry said, handing Ferguson a bright orange wet suit used in sea rescue missions. 'It's safety regulations for civilian personnel when we're flying over water.'

Ferguson eyed the orange monstrosity.

'Put it on over your clothing,' Henry said.

Ferguson stepped clumsily into the all–in–one suit which reminded him of the brightly coloured boiler suit he'd worn years ago when training as an apprentice ship building engineer before fate pointed him in the direction of the police force.

Riley put a helmet on him, adjusted the comms so Ferguson could communicate with everyone on board and belted him into his seat.

The roar of the engines increased to a crescendo.

'It's going to be noisy. The Sea King's got quite a growl, so speak via your comms,' Riley said.

Ferguson grinned. 'I've never flown in a helicopter before.'

'You'll enjoy it,' Henry said. 'Just one thing. See the lines of yellow tape on the doors and exit panels?'

'Yes,' Ferguson said.

'Whatever you do, don't lean on them, or you'll release the panels and fall out of the Sea King.'

Ferguson's eyes widened and he searched the lines of yellow tape which seemed to be in almost every section of the helicopter.

'Okay?' Henry said, seeking confirmation that the detective understood.

'Okay,' Ferguson said.

Henry and Riley exchanged a nod. 'We're good to go,' Henry said to the pilots via the comms.

The growl of the helicopter erupted and within seconds they were hundreds of feet up in the air and banking around to head south over the Firth of Clyde.

'Jeez–oh!' Ferguson gasped, feeling the rush of power from the Sea King and wishing he hadn't had a fried breakfast.

Catherine saw the silver and white envelope on the desk in her office. It sat on top of a pile of brown envelopes and buff coloured folders that she hoped to plough through during the morning. She tore open the envelope and read the matching invitation. The colour drained from her face when she saw who and what it was from.

A loud knock on the door jarred her senses. She looked up from her desk. It was Shaw.

'Do you know anything about this?' she said.

'Brodie left it for you.'

'Did he tell you what it was?'

'Not exactly. He said it was a social invitation for two in Glasgow tomorrow night.'

She handed him the invitation.

'An invitation to the official grand opening of the new casino in Glasgow?' Shaw said, not disguising his surprise. 'Why would Brodie give you this? I didn't think you were into casinos.'

'I'm not, but I was there the other night, with Riley.'

'Brodie's embroiled in the casino,' he warned her. 'It's not safe there.'

'We were looking for information, and things went further than I'd anticipated.' She gave him a knowing look. 'Riley accessed data from their computer system . . .'

Shaw lips tightened in frustration. 'You got caught snooping around the casino?'

'No, we didn't get caught. We left unchallenged. Brodie didn't even see me, though he did see Riley, but we assumed Brodie hadn't recognised him.'

Shaw read the invitation again. 'Everything you assumed was wrong, or Brodie's been tipped off and seen the security footage.'

'Damn!' Catherine said. 'Brodie's such a devious bastard.'

Footsteps sounded outside in the corridor. Shaw put his hand up to silence Catherine.

Moments later, Brodie popped his head round the door. 'Ah, Catherine. I see you got the invitation. Hope you can make it.'

'It's rather short notice,' she said.

'Nonsense! With our hectic schedules, everything's organised at short notice. Say you'll come to the casino — and bring a friend.'

Catherine garnered a bluff to gauge Brodie's reaction. 'I thought I'd bring John Riley.'

Brodie shot Shaw a look that said — *I told you so*, and then broke into a broad smile. 'Riley's just the man I want to speak to. Perhaps you could introduce us, Catherine.'

Her smile froze. What the hell was Brodie up to?

Brodie continued, 'I think he's known as the Record Keeper, an expert in ancient weapon authentication, among other specialities . . .'

'What do you need Riley to authenticate?' Shaw said.

'Swords . . . and a dagger. If they're the real deal, I'm thinking of adding them to my collection.'

The mention of a dagger sent a chill through Catherine. She thought she'd hid it well, but Brodie picked up on it.

'I don't mean to sound completely heartless,' Brodie said, his tone a fake apology. 'What with poor Reece getting stabbed and all that nasty business.'

Shaw glared at him. 'Whoever murdered Reece is already dead in the water. The culprit just doesn't know it yet.'

Brodie didn't flinch. 'Well, I'm sure the Valentines will nail them. You can always rely on good old fashioned police work. Scottish bobbies have got my vote.'

'But have you got theirs?' Shaw said.

Brodie swallowed any retort he had in mind and reached into his inside jacket pocket. 'This is for you, Shaw.' He handed him an invitation to the casino event. 'It's an invitation for you and a guest. I couldn't have you feeling left out.'

Shaw took the invitation. 'I'll look forward to it.'

'Excellent,' Brodie said, and then focussed on Catherine. 'I hope you and Riley will come along. There will be champagne fountains, entertainment and wall to wall money. I think you'll enjoy it, Catherine. It's going to be a killer of a night.' He smiled coldly and left the office.

Catherine sighed heavily. 'Do you think he heard me calling him a bastard?'

'It doesn't matter. He knows that's what you think of him whether he heard you or not.'

Catherine turned the invitation over in her hand. 'What do you think we should do?'

Shaw slipped his invitation into his pocket. 'Beat Brodie at his own game.'

'His involvement with the casino is legal. There's nothing to stop a man in his position having a vested interest in it as long as he's not doing anything underhand. I've been investigating his association with the casino and there's nothing I can find to incriminate him. He's got the top accountants and advisors in the city.'

'Something's obviously unnerved him or we wouldn't be invited to the casino,' Shaw said.

'Riley set a trap to bait him and get him to make a mistake. Brodie has a web of accounts. Riley made two of his accounts inaccessible and caused a discrepancy that his accountants would pick up on.'

'It worked. Brodie's made his first mistake. Inviting us to the casino shows he's worried that we're getting too close.'

Scotch mist covered Arran in a gauzy drizzle. In winter the rainy mist gave a cold blue tint to the atmosphere and made the Sleeping Warrior's armour hauntingly real. Carved by nature along the twenty mile length of the magnificent granite peaks, the Sleeping Warrior was waiting for them.

'The last time I was on Arran was during a school trip,' Ferguson said. 'We took the ferry. Never seen it from the air before. Where are we landing?'

Riley pointed down towards the isle. 'Between the sword and the shield.'

'The seas look rough. I wouldn't like to be on a ferry in this weather,' Ferguson said.

Riley wondered how Ferguson would like being in an SBS canoe paddling for shore like his grandfather had done many times during the Special Forces early training. Wearing standard trousers and a big, woolly jumper for warmth, and a hat if they were lucky, Harry and the others hadn't ever winced at the challenge. Riley had tried it himself years ago. No mean feat but worth it when he'd reached the coast.

The Sea King banked sharply, lining up for its landing. Ferguson craned to see the varied landscape out the front window. The view of the beaches, lush hill land, mountains, waterfalls and castles came into close focus. Ferguson braced himself for the landing but they touched down on the outskirts of one of the towns without a hitch. Police on Arran had cordoned off the area and were waiting to meet them.

Henry helped Ferguson unravel himself from the orange suit, and once the pilots had given the all clear, Ferguson and the SBS disembarked.

Pilot one received a message for Riley. 'Call Shaw, it's urgent,' he said.

'I will,' Riley said, going over to join Henry and Ferguson who had introduced themselves to the local police force. He activated his phone en route and called Shaw.

'I'm using the old phone number. Have you still got a copy?' Riley said.

'Yes,' Shaw said.

'I'm on Arran with Henry and Ferguson. We're following a lead on Strang. What's happening with you?'

'Brodie's invited Catherine to the grand opening of the new casino in Glasgow tomorrow night. He's grudgingly invited me too. I said I'd be there. Catherine's inviting you to go with her. She told me about your visit there. I think you've rattled a few people.'

'Clearly, but we can use it to our advantage.'

'Definitely,' Shaw said. 'My invitation admits two so if you want anyone else to come along let me know.'

'Okay. I'll contact you when I get back from Arran.'

Ferguson and the SBS were talking to the police outside the holiday cottage Strang used as a base.

'We've hardly disturbed anything, only what was necessary,' the police chief said. He was a sharp eyed, grey haired fox who looked well capable of dealing with their predicament. 'And we've taken photos for evidence and e-mailed them to Valentine in Glasgow. Strang had files and blueprints in a locked cabinet. We left them on the desk for you to see. We'll give you a wee while to look around.'

Ferguson went into the cottage followed by Riley and Henry. It was small, painted white inside and out and furnished with the basics.

'A man of few comforts,' Ferguson said, looking around. 'It's clean, functional and bloody creepy. There's something about Strang that chills my bones.'

Henry nodded. 'I sensed that the first time I saw him at Excalibur. Couldn't put my finger on it. He was pleasant enough. But it was just the way he looked at you, like he knew something that you'd never figure out.'

Riley looked at things from a different angle. Would Strang leave a location like this unguarded? He didn't think so. He searched along the edges of the window frame, the door, the desk where folders containing documents and detailed plans of what looked like architectural drawings were lying.

'What are you looking for?' Ferguson said.

'Hidden security. Bugs, gadgets . . .' Riley said.

'You think he could be watching us?' Ferguson said.

'Strang has invented things that would give you nightmares,' Riley said. 'Keeping an electronic eye on his stuff here wouldn't be difficult for a man like him.'

He paused and felt a wire hidden along the edge of a cupboard. Ferguson and Henry watched him pull the wire free.

'Has he been listening in?' Ferguson said.

Riley followed the wire to its source and ripped it out. 'I doubt he'd keep the connection live in case we traced it to his current location.' He studied the wire. 'Very expensive. Someone's funding him well.'

Henry read over the documents. 'Some of this is written in code, especially the notes he's scribbled beside the blueprints.' He handed them to Riley.

Riley read them briefly. 'We'll take a copy of these with us. It'll take time for me to decipher them completely, but I get the impression it's just notes to remind him to do certain things.' He studied one of the notes. 'Seems he had a deadline at the end of October to meet on this project. He won't be making that deadline now.'

'Valentine says he was probably listening in to your conversation last night and he's aware we know about him on Arran,' Ferguson said.

'Yes, but at least this is one less base he can use,' Riley said. He looked around. 'Collect everything. We can't risk any of this going missing.'

The police chief met them on their way out. 'I've organised something to eat for you.'

'Thanks,' Riley said.

They left the evidence they'd collected in the Sea King. Several police officers guarded it while Riley and the others travelled with the police to the local station. Tea, coffee, sandwiches and hot soup had been laid on for them. The men helped themselves.

'Has Strang done anything we should be worried about?' the police chief said to Ferguson.

'No, he's been using the island as a hideout for his experiments,' Ferguson said.

'Strang knows we've scuppered his plans here. I think this particular book is closed,' Riley said.

The police chief relaxed back in his chair. 'Good, but keep me informed about what happens.'

Ferguson bit into a doorstep of a cheese and pickle sandwich. It was his third. 'Mmm. Valentine and I will keep you in the loop.'

'Ferguson's in training,' Henry said to the police chief.

The police chief's mouth curved into a wily smirk.

'Awe very funny,' Ferguson said.

They took off again in the Sea King, circling over the long shadowed outline of the Sleeping Warrior. The sun had fought its way through the clouds and cast silver glints on the cold, grey sea. Ferguson adjusted his orange suit for the trip back to Glasgow airport and had become accustomed to speaking via the comms.

'Do you miss it?' Ferguson said to Riley.

'What?'

'The Special Forces. The SBS.'

Henry looked at Riley.

'Missing it is a luxury I can never afford,' Riley said.

Henry was silent.

Riley looked out the window. The Sea King soared over the sea. Arran was already out of view. 'All the records I update are someone else's history. But my history's still not complete.'

'Like now,' Ferguson said, trying to understand. 'You're still flying with Henry.'

Riley nodded. 'And there are some people from my past that I'm still waiting to see again.'

'Things from the past left unfinished? ' Ferguson said.

'Something like that,' Riley said.

'I'd miss the police force if I ever had to leave it. And don't ever tell him, but I'd miss bloody Valentine too.'

'Which one?' Riley and Henry said together.

Ferguson laughed.

The men's laughter echoed amid the roar of the Sea King as it powered towards Glasgow, streams of winter sunlight piercing through the small front windows. Another memory for the record.

Riley phoned Shaw with the details of their trip to Arran when he got back to Glasgow.

'Did you tell Ferguson we're taking Brodie up on his invitation?' Shaw said.

'Yes, he's going to inform Valentine. I've said we'll be going in with sound and visuals so we can get some hard evidence on Brodie.'

'I'll be ready,' Shaw said.

'We have to film and tape everything and get these cases cleared up.'

'Brodie could've arranged equipment scanners at the door. We'll need someone on the inside to get us past them,' Shaw said.

'I've got someone in mind. He owes the casino a painting. I'm going to arm it to the teeth with surveillance gear and get him to take it inside.'

'Sounds good.'

'And I've invited Henry to come along with us,' Riley said.

'It should be quite a night,' Shaw said. 'I'm driving down from Edinburgh with Catherine. We'll arrange a time to meet up with you and Henry. It's a dress to impress event so get your glad rags on. Brodie wants to meet you. He wants you to authenticate swords and a dagger for his collection.'

'Do you think Brodie's lying?' Riley said.

'Yes, but not about the weapons. Brodie's only got two methods of play — threats and bribery. I think he knows he can't intimidate you, so be prepared for him making you a very lucrative offer to help him outmanoeuvre the Valentines.'

'He certainly threatened Reece the night he was killed. Ferguson told me Valentine had the security tape you gave him of Reece and Brodie checked by a lip reader. Threats were made. Brodie told Reece he'd better watch his back and shouldn't have walked away from their deal. Reece said if he'd known what he was getting involved in, he'd never have had anything to do with Brodie or his dirty money. Forensics also confirmed a match on the dagger Reece was killed with and the one he took from Brodie's pocket. Marks on the blade are the same, so no surprises there,' Riley said.

'Reece should never have challenged Brodie for his seat in Parliament. That was his biggest mistake.' Shaw said.

'But I don't think Brodie set out to murder Reece. The fight just got out of hand and the night ended bloody. So whatever happens at the casino, we don't let Catherine out of our sight.'

Shaw's tone was cold and determined. 'Brodie's got a lot of back up at the casino but I've a feeling he's playing a game he's just not ready for.'

Chapter Fifteen

It is Rocket Science

Lucky was back in his empire. He sat outside his front door in his favourite chair watching the shopping channels on his televisions. He wore a blanket around him and Barking Bob the scabby dog who had become almost surgically attached to him since he came home from the hospital. Riley walked under the tarpaulin that still kept the rain off Lucky's empire.

'You're looking a lot better,' Riley said.

Lucky smiled. 'Are you talking to me or the dog?'

Riley looked at the dog. 'Bob's looking lighter.'

Jamesie came hurrying out of the house with a soup ladle in his hand. 'The woman who was watching him gave him a wash and shampoo. You'd hardly recognise him.'

Riley smiled. 'Are you talking about Lucky or the dog?'

'It's good to see you, Riley,' Lucky said, extending his hand in welcome.

Riley gave him a firm handshake, a silent emphasis he was pleased the rascal had survived.

'I hear old boy Stanley's home too,' Lucky said. 'I met him in the hospital. He's still raging that Strang stabbed him. Says when he catches him he's going to knit the hairs on his balls into a tea cosy.'

'Do you think you'll nail him soon?' Jamesie asked.

'We're working on it,' Riley said.

'I wouldn't be surprised if Strang disappears off the map again and comes back to have a run at us another time,' Lucky said.

Riley knew this could happen. Strang had vanished before, only to come back stronger the next time.

Lucky pulled the blanket around him. 'I haven't been able to get any heat in my bones since I was in that bloody lockup.'

'The soup should be ready,' Jamesie said. 'Fancy a bowl of hot broth, Riley?'

'Yes, why not. I wanted to talk to you about your art.'

Jamesie spoke to him from the kitchen as he served up three bowls of piping hot soup and crusty bread. 'What about it?'

'McAra mentioned about the paintings you did for the casino. You put one of them up in the restaurant. Where's the other one?' Riley said.

Jamesie came out to the front door where Lucky was sitting. He gave Lucky and Riley a bowl of soup each and put a plate of bread down on a table. 'It's in my house. I'm supposed to take it to the casino. I haven't got round to it yet with everything's that's happened. My boss at the restaurant's decided to keep the other one. Says it gives the place a touch of arty–farty class.'

Lucky sussed Riley's plan. 'Are you going after Brodie at the casino?'

Riley helped himself to the bread. 'Yes. He's invited me and three others to a party tomorrow night.'

'Quite a hoity–toity affair from what I hear,' Lucky said.

Riley nodded. 'Brodie's playing games. I thought we could arm the picture frame with surveillance equipment. The police will be in on it, and I'm taking two men and a woman in with me.'

'Special Forces men?' Lucky said, hardly noticing he was eating his soup for listening to Riley.

Silence from Riley.

'Okay. So they're well capable, eh?' Lucky said.

'Do you want to help?' Riley said to them.

'You need to use my painting to spy on Brodie at the casino?' Jamesie said, giving the soup bone to Barking Bob who jumped down from Lucky's lap to gnaw it.

'Yes. Are you up for it?'

A unanimous agreement came from Lucky and Jamesie.

'I don't have long to set this up. I'll need the painting today,' Riley said.

'No problem,' Jamesie said, bursting with enthusiasm.

'There is one problem,' Riley began. 'We'll be wearing surveillance gear underneath our dinner suits, so if there are any security checks at the doors, we'll need a way to get past them.'

Jamesie smiled brightly. 'That's no problem. My pal, Big Handsome Callum, he works the doors at the casino. We'll breeze through.' Then he added. 'I take it I'll have to deliver the painting myself. It would look suspicious if someone else took it.'

'Exactly. You still up for this?' Riley asked.

'Absolutely. It'll be just like you see in the spy films. Can I wear my posh coat? Strang's coat?'

Riley smiled and nodded. 'Great soup,' he said, helping himself to more bread.

By the time Riley left with Jamesie to get the painting, Lucky was feeling warmer. There was nothing like payback to put some fire in your bones.

Jamesie told Riley all about the painting on the way to his house. They drove there in Riley's car even though it was running distance from Lucky's empire. Set in another cobbled alleyway that time had forgotten, Jamesie's room and kitchen was, by his own description, *the house that didn't exist.*

'You'd never know anyone lived here, would you, Riley?' Jamesie turned the key in the lock of the black painted door that merged with the dark brickwork and cobblestones. He clicked the door open. 'Wait 'till you see this.' He flicked a light on.

Riley heard the buzz of the overhead lighting, and then he could hardly believe what he saw. Jamesie lived in a room and kitchen all right, but this was one big room and big kitchen.

'It used to be a warehouse, but I did a favour for the owner when I worked the nightclubs. He was letting it rot. He wasn't interested in it. I was supposed to live here for a few months, but that was nearly four years ago.' He stood aside to let Riley have a full panoramic view. 'What do you think? I've done a lot to it.' The living room and bedroom area had large rugs for warmth and comfort, and the kitchen was an open plan masterpiece. 'My kitchen's my pride and joy.'

'Very impressive.'

'Cheers. Right, want to see the painting?' He went over to an area where his artwork was hanging up. Blank canvases were stacked in a corner and two large desks were covered with tubes of oil paints and acrylic paints and an assortment of brushes and palette knives. He flicked on a light that illuminated the painting. It was almost as large as the top of one of the desks and had a strong wooden frame painted in bronze to give it a stylish, weathered look. The colours had a nightlife vibrancy. Reds, golds, and fiery orange were offset by a dark sky and shadowy figures merging with the night. Several people were shown in the foreground going into the casino, their faces captured in detail against the glow of the lights that shone from inside the casino.

'It's a wonderful painting, Jamesie.'

Jamesie's chest puffed up with pride. 'It came out just right. I think they'll like it.'

Riley had no doubts. 'Is that Brodie and Strang?' he said, pointing at two familiar faces in the painting. Brodie had a glamorous woman holding on to his arm. Strang was alone, set apart from the crowd, the cold, calculating look in his eyes peering out from the canvas.

'Yes. That's what makes my paintings popular with the bars and clubs. I've always had a brilliant memory for faces. Faces and character. Even when my memory's shite, I still never forget a face. I used to be able to recognise everyone who came through the doors of the nightclubs. It gave a real personal touch to working there. And of course, if anyone did me a wrong, I could pick them out of a crowd a mile off.'

'Who actually commissioned you to do the paintings?'

'Ironically it was Brodie who wanted me to do them. That's why I included him in it. He'd seen my paintings in a posh restaurant and liked my style. I never dealt with him directly, but it was his money that paid for it.'

'What about Strang?'

'He'd been hanging around the casino when I was there to sketch and plan the paintings. He's got a haunted look to him, and with the blonde hair, I thought he'd be an interesting character.'

'What happens now that you're one painting short?'

'Ach, I'll do another one. They take me about a week to sketch and finish, depending on how many shifts I work at the restaurant and whether I fuck up the canvas or not. Oil paints take ages to dry but if I use acrylics they dry in no time. I'll take this painting into the casino and tell them I want to know if they like it before I do the other one.'

'You could make a living out of your art,' Riley said.

Jamesie's eyes had a faraway look. 'Wouldn't that be pure magic.'

'Can you tell the casino that you're bringing the painting in to hang it up in time for the party?'

'No problem.' He showed Riley the back of the painting. 'It's ready to hang. I'll contact Big Handsome Callum and get him to put a couple of mounts in the wall so I can put it up when I take it in. It was supposed to be for the foyer.' He stepped back from his work and viewed it from a short distance. 'I think they'll be pleased to have it hanging up for their party. Don't you?'

Riley agreed, and then he saw another face he recognised. 'Is that Richard Reece?'

'Yes, and see that man standing in the background watching everything. That's Mackenzie. So all four of them are there, plus a few other faces known in the social scene.'

'Did you see Reece at the casino very often?' Riley said.

'I was there a few times to sketch the layout and pick up the atmosphere and Reece was there most times. I already knew Mackenzie. Not personally, but by reputation. And Lucky knew him. Mackenzie was always near Brodie and Reece but they never spoke to him. I got the impression the politicians didn't want the shine taken off their reputations by associating with a forger so they played it cool and pretended not to know him. But I could see what they were doing. I'm not daft.'

'Did you ever see Strang talking to Mackenzie?'

'Yes, but I think Mackenzie was wary of Strang. It was like he was scared of him.'

'Was Mackenzie the nervous type?'

'No, no, Mackenzie was a hard man, that's why it struck me as odd that Strang made him edgy.'

'Any idea why Mackenzie was wary of Strang?'

'Aren't you? I know I am. Okay so I kicked his arse up and down the street but maybe it would've been a different story if he hadn't whacked me on the head.'

He paused then said thoughtfully, 'I'll ask Big Handsome Callum what the deal was with them. He knows everything. He's head of their security and he hears all their secrets.'

'Can you trust him?' Riley said.

'Always have, always will. We watched out for each other during the nightclub security work. Our lives depended on being able to rely on each other. Like Lucky and me. You know what I mean. You can trust your pals, men like McAra.'

Riley understood exactly. It was guarantee enough.

'Where will you put the hidden bugs and cameras?' Jamesie said, lifting the painting down from the wall.

Riley gave him a hand. 'In the frame. The canvas won't be damaged. McAra's going to help me fit the devices.'

'Is McAra going to the casino?'

'No, he'll be monitoring the surveillance information nearby. There will just be three of us to handle any trouble.'

'Four,' Jamesie said, insisting he be included. 'Remember I do martial arts.'

'The four of us. And there's a woman, Catherine. Nothing happens to her. You got it?' Riley said.

'I'll keep an eye on her.'

Riley took the painting to McAra's house. He decoded the security keypad and let himself in.

McAra's red hair had a wild and woolly look to it. 'What are you wearing to the casino?' he said as soon as he saw Riley.

'Shaw says it's a glad rags event, so I'll wear a white shirt, tie and dinner jacket. Why?'

'I've discovered a quirk that could be very useful,' he said excitedly. 'I'd been trying to photograph my latest rocket science work. I won't go into it,' he mumbled. 'Everything's got to be pictured, proved, logged.' He paused and took a deep breath. 'However, I can't take a photo of my experiment because of these.' He held up a thin wire with a tiny LED light on the end of it. The light shone with a white brilliance. 'I can't even capture it on the video camera.'

Riley put the painting down. Jamesie had wrapped it in plastic to protect it.

'Oh, you've got the painting. Great,' McAra said. 'But just let me show you this.' He held up an ordinary white vest. A wire dangled out the bottom of it on one side. A small battery was attached to the end of the wire. 'It got me thinking you see . . . remember how you and Shaw were all over the news. That's what gave me the idea. The television camera crew filmed you, but various others had taken pictures with their mobile phones.'

Riley sighed. How could he forget?

'Well, what if I could invent something that would prevent you being photographed . . .' Without giving Riley a chance to reply, McAra thrust a digital camera at him and flicked a switch that was attached to the vest's battery. 'Take a photo of the vest.'

Riley held the camera up, focussed on the vest and then realised that a white light was shining into the camera lens. The look on his face signalled the reaction McAra had been hoping for.

'I've woven infra–red LEDs into the vest. About two hundred of them.'

Riley examined the vest. 'Are they switched on?'

'Yes, full power. You can't see them though, can you?'

'No,' Riley said.

'That's because they're infra–red. They're invisible to the naked eye, but CCTV and digital cameras see it as white light. With these extra bright lights it's like shining a torch in the lens, only twenty times more powerful with the number of LEDs I've got hidden in the vest.'

Riley tried again to focus on the vest but all he could see through the lens was a dazzling white light that would stop any clear photo being taken.

McAra ran his hand through his wild hair in an attempt to tame the front of it, but as always, when he was in the throws of an exciting experiment, it took on an extra static life of its own. 'Wear this vest under your shirt. Keep your dinner jacket open, and it should help deflect CCTV and mobile phone cameras from detecting you clearly. You'll be a white blur from the waist up.'

Riley put the camera down and examined the vest. 'So it's not ultraviolet?'

'No. While the human eye can't see ultraviolet, we still see some purple light, so if I used ultraviolet LEDs, you'd have a purplish glow from your vest which would no doubt draw attention to you.'

Riley grinned. This would work. 'You're a genius.'

McAra smiled with a gap-toothed grin. 'If you look at a remote control for a television for instance, you can't see it working. But point the remote at a digital camera and voila — whoever is taking the picture will see a little white light distorting the image.'

Riley stripped his jacket and top off and put the vest on. He slipped the battery, which was connected to a wire from the bottom edge of the vest, into his trouser pocket. He smiled to himself. Worn with a shirt, no one would ever know he was wearing it.

'The only camera that could take your photo would be an old fashioned film camera, but no one uses those anymore. You're likely to be snapped by a mobile phone or digital camera. CCTV works the same way, so they're all screwed. I have of course, altered the voltage and added a few elements to ensure nothing gets past it,' he said, giving a wink. As with all things McAra invented, it was the quirky touches, the elements of genius that made them work.

'How long will the power last?' Riley said, studying the small, lightweight battery.

'LEDs are low power consumption. I've rigged them up to a video camera battery. It'll last a few hours. There's a switch you can turn on once you get to the casino.'

Riley took the vest off. 'How long did it take you to make this?'

'About two hours. I wove the thin LED wire through the material. If I'd to make another one, it wouldn't take me long now I know what I'm doing.'

'Could you make another two?' Riley said.

'Yes, if I had another vest. I only bought a pack of two.' McAra looked at him thoughtfully. 'Why do you want three?'

'For me, Shaw and Henry. We're going to need every edge we can get.'

Riley sat the painting up in his study at home. McAra had done a great job of arming it with the latest surveillance equipment. Pinhole covert cameras, tracker devices and miniature transmitters to pick up conversations were attached magnetically and hidden in the frame. It was ready to go.

The faces stared out at him. Reece, Mackenzie, Brodie and Strang. Two dead and two still breathing, for now. Brodie was hiding behind a political shield, living on a reputation he'd long since destroyed and sealed his fate the night he stabbed his rival to death. And Strang — a bitter waste of scientific talent. Riley studied the faces, their characters etched in colourful paint, jaws and cheekbones carved by the cutting edge of a palette knife, eyes watchful of everything and each other. Jamesie's painting saw more than he probably realised. He'd painted not so much what he saw, but *how* he saw it. If ever a picture told a story . . .

Riley viewed Strang, this time in more depth. A figure alone, eyes cold and calculating. Earlier, at first glance, he'd thought Strang was peering out of the canvas, but now he realised he wasn't. He was staring with a killer's look at someone. And that someone was Mackenzie. The forger had no distinguishing features. Brown hair, brown eyes, of average build, and forgettable, the ideal template for someone in his line of work. But the look on his face showed the underlying relationship between him and Strang. Fear was etched into his profile with every mark of the artist's palette knife. And the man who was causing the fear was Strang.

Moments later, the phone rang. It was Catherine.

'Are there any nasty surprises I should know about before we meet up tonight?' she said.

'Stay sharp and stay close to me and Shaw. Henry will be there too. He's a naval officer at Excalibur —'

'Shaw explained about him — and about Jamesie and the painting. It's an excellent idea. We should call Brodie's bluff and go to the casino.' She paused and he sensed the nervousness in her breathing.

'You don't have to go, Catherine.'

'Yes I do. I just don't want you or Shaw or anyone else getting hurt trying to protect me.'

'Do you trust me?'

'Of course.'

'Then trust that I'll do everything I can to prevent that from happening.'

'I will.'

'And one more thing,' Riley said. 'What are you wearing tonight?'

'A black evening dress, why?'

'Have you got something that's dazzling? Something that'll sparkle in the light.'

She thought for a moment. 'I suppose so. I've got a dress that I've never worn. Never had the right occasion. It's hanging at the back of my wardrobe.'

'Wear it. I'll explain why later.'

'Okay, Riley. See you tonight.'

Deciphering some of the information they'd gathered from Strang's house took up the remainder of Riley's day. Valentine e-mailed the data back and forth to him.

Later, McAra arrived with the three vests. He put them down on Riley's desk. 'Are those the notes belonging to Strang you were telling me about?'

'Strang has written a lot of coded messages,' Riley said.

McAra glanced over the notes that were lying on the desk. He leaned closer to read them.

'They're some sort of mathematical equations. I haven't figured them out yet,' Riley said.

'Scientific equations,' McAra said, sounding concerned. 'These are standard equations for dark matter. Because we don't know exactly what dark matter and dark energy are we use mathematical formulas to work around the various theories.' He flicked through the rest of Strang's notes. 'Map coordinates,' he said, stabbing a finger at the groups of numbers at the bottom of the page.

Riley went over to one of the large world maps framed on the wall. 'Read out the coordinates.'

McAra gave him the details.

Riley found the location — an area in America's west coast. 'Death Valley!'

McAra walked over to the map. 'Judging by the level of his equations, Strang's not in a position to cause any major damage yet, but give him time and he could become a serious threat on a grand scale.'

'The last time I was in Death Valley was with Deacon. He said he'd a feeling we'd be back there again one day.'

'Deacon's dead,' McAra said, more for his own realisation than reminding Riley of something he was never likely to forget.

'I know . . .' Riley said thoughtfully, unable to shake off the feeling that fate would someday take him back to the desert one last time.

Chapter Sixteen

Special Forces

After McAra left, Riley went through to the diving pool to clear his thoughts in his little piece of paradise. The party wasn't for another two hours, so he changed out of his clothes into swimming trunks and climbed up on to the highest springboard. He took a deep breath and dived in, his body cutting through the blue water, down into the depths, feeling it wash away the strife of the day. When he surfaced, a flashing light on the wall signalled he had visitors on his property. He climbed out quickly and ran to see who it was on the security monitor. Two men approached his front door and he went through to let them in.

Valentine and Ferguson hardly blinked when they saw Riley standing there, soaking wet and dripping water on to the floor of the hallway. 'I wanted to talk to you about tonight,' Valentine said. 'There could be trouble.'

Riley showed them in. 'What kind of trouble?' They followed him through to the diving pool. Riley grabbed a towel and gave his torso a rough dry.

Valentine took a document from inside his coat pocket and handed it to Riley. 'I got a warrant to search Brodie's accountant's office earlier today while you two were in Arran. I found this.'

Riley opened the document and started reading the list of names and monies.

'It's a copy of payments made by Brodie in the past few months,' Valentine said. He pointed to one particular name on the list. 'Look who was on the payroll.'

'Mackenzie.'

'Exactly,' Valentine said, taking the document back and putting it away in his pocket again. 'Brodie's accountant fucked up. Payments made to Mackenzie were never supposed to be logged into Brodie's accounts. Payments for let's say, just for the sake of argument, forgeries of historical documents — maps, letters, perhaps even scrolls. Anything that Brodie could sell as authentic, as supposedly part of his private collection of artefacts, and pocket the money.'

'Or recycle the money to fund his political career,' Ferguson said, going over to the pool and looking into the water. He crouched down and put his hand in to feel the temperature.

Valentine stood talking to Riley. 'Brodie's worth quite a bit, but he's a tight fisted bastard. The fakes, the forgeries, were a constant top up of free cash. A very lucrative way to finance his ambitions in government.'

'What about Richard Reece? What was his involvement?' Riley said.

'Reece was small time compared to Brodie but he was being tempted into the web and getting way in over his depth,' Valentine said. 'Then when he wanted to back out, and at the same time rip Brodie's seat in Parliament out from under his nose, well . . . things got messy and ended in the fight that night up in Edinburgh.'

'Can you arrest Brodie on the evidence from the accounts?' Riley said.

'Unfortunately it won't be enough to convict him of murder. It would be forgery and fraud at the most, and with a good lawyer Brodie could walk away from this. Mackenzie had wiped all trace of their dealings. Even you couldn't find anything on Mackenzie's computer that we could use as hard evidence. And even with the hit list we'd be spitting into the wind.'

'What do you need to convict him?' Riley said.

'Brodie's rattled. You did a great job sticking a spanner into the works of his accounts. We need him rattled again. Kick up a stink at the casino, see what floats to the surface and we'll take it from there.'

Riley agreed, and then they both looked at Ferguson who was gazing longingly into the water.

'Any good at diving, Ferguson?' Riley said, with a slight smirk and nod to Valentine.

'Rubbish. Got any tips?' Ferguson said.

Riley and Valentine were waiting for him to ask. Ferguson didn't disappoint them. 'Can I have a go?'

Riley smiled. 'Yes.'

'I don't have any swimming trunks with me, but my boxers are clean on this morning. Is that okay?'

Riley was trying not to laugh.

Valentine shook his head and smiled.

Ferguson stripped off to his boxers quickly and put his clothes on a chair.

'What about you, Stan?' Ferguson said. 'Didn't you used to dive every weekend?'

'When I was young. I haven't dived in about fifteen years,' Valentine said. 'I used to be a member of a diving club. Then I began police cadet training and went straight into the force. After that I didn't have the time.'

'Have a go, Stan,' Ferguson urged him.

Valentine looked at Riley to gauge his reaction.

'On you go, Stanley,' Riley said, thinking he'd say no.

Taking them both by surprise, Valentine took his clothes off, leaving only his dark blue boxer shorts on.

Neither of them said, but the detective had a better physique than they'd thought, perhaps honed from years of diving training in his youth. He had a trim body with lean muscles and Riley saw the harsh look of his father, Stanley senior, in him, and the potential to be quite handy in a scrap.

'Where do we start?' Ferguson said.

Riley kept the towel around his shoulders and instructed from the side of the pool. 'Climb up on to the board. Get your balance, take a breath, exhale and go for it. Try to keep your body straight on entry, fingers pointed, chin tucked in.'

Ferguson climbed up the ladder, and tottered on to the springboard. He turned and looked down at Riley.

'Don't look at me. Look at the water.'

Ferguson stood for a moment at the edge of the board and they could see he was trying to do what Riley had instructed. After a deep breath he attempted a flying dive and plunged into the pool causing a thunderous splash. Moments later he bobbed to the surface smiling as if he'd scored a winner.

'Not bad,' Riley said. 'Have another go, and this time keep your posture strong. Focus on where you want to dive, clear the board, get some height in the dive and then straighten up.'

While Riley explained this to Ferguson, Valentine climbed up and stood on the edge of the springboard. Riley and Ferguson became silent. Valentine put his arms out to the side, raised them up and then powered off the board. He somersaulted once before plunging vertically into the water with hardly any splash.

Riley and Ferguson gave him a round of applause, and for the next half hour the three of them practised diving, and left aside any thoughts of the impending trouble of the night.

'What's this for?' Ferguson said, as they were leaving. A small mirror was hanging on the inside of the front door.

'It's for signalling,' Riley said. 'I always keep one handy and put it in my pocket when I go out.' Riley opened the door, letting the cold night into the hallway and sending a shiver through Valentine and Ferguson who were still mildly damp from their diving challenge. Riley wore warm training gear but the temperature felt like ice against his wet hair.

Valentine stepped outside. Ferguson angled the mirror trying to get it to catch the light from the doorway. 'What's an easy signal?'

'Two flashes in succession can be seen over a long distance. It's the easiest signal in the world.'

'What does it mean?' Ferguson said. Valentine turned around to listen.

'Stand still, don't move. Help is on its way.'

Ferguson flashed the mirror twice and then followed Valentine to the car.

'Good luck tonight, Riley. We'll be around if you need back up,' Valentine said.

Riley went to close the front door but Valentine added, 'Can I ask what you're involvement with Catherine is? Is it becoming personal?'

'No.'

'She's a very attractive woman. You're both single.'

'I'll be honest with you, I do find her attractive, but I won't let anything cloud the investigation. I made that mistake once before and I'm still paying for it.'

'What about Shaw? We know how he feels about her,' Valentine said.

'I don't think the feeling is mutual, though I can't be certain.'

'Women can change their minds on the flip of a coin.'

'You sound like you're speaking from experience,' Riley said.

'The police can be like the forces. I was engaged a few years ago but the job got in the way. Ferguson was married and that didn't last. We're all a poor, bloody advert for finding a woman who'll put up with us and the job.'

'But we live in hope,' Ferguson said.

'Some days,' Valentine said, and then they got into the car and drove off.

Riley closed the door and went through to the study. He stood near the fire enjoying the warmth. Henry would be here soon. Sparks from the fire crackled in the silence and the light glinted off the swords on the wall above the mantelpiece. He took one down and automatically adjusted his grip. The firelight flickered off the metal cross guard. What type of swords and dagger did Brodie want him to authenticate? And would he have them with him at the casino tonight?

He put the sword back and looked at the three vests lying on the desk. It was time to put his glad rags on.

Henry looked dapper in a traditional black dinner suit with white shirt and dark tie. He stood near the window in Riley's study drinking a cup of tea. Even with no hint that he belonged to the forces he had an air about him, an immaculate manner bred from years as a naval officer that signalled he was a military man. Underneath his shirt he wore the vest with comfort and had tucked the transmitter into his trouser pocket. No one would ever guess. McAra had given each vest a number. Riley was one, Shaw two and Henry three. The rocket scientist had rigged the vest to a mechanism in his car, along with several other hi–tech devices in the vehicle, to monitor them while they were inside the casino.

'Here's McAra,' Henry said, seeing the car pull up in the driveway. 'I suppose he's got the car armed with enough gadgets to launch a small spacecraft.'

'Just about,' Riley said, adjusting the knot on his grey silk tie as he went to open the front door. Riley's suit was a modern classic in almost black, worn with a white shirt. Vest number one was completely hidden underneath it.

McAra breezed in, casually dressed for warmth and the likelihood of a long night's surveillance in his car. He had a digital camera in his hands. 'Switch your vest on so I can test that it's working,' he said to Riley.

Riley flicked on the small transmitter in his pocket.

'Brilliant,' McAra said blinking from being slightly dazzled by the effect when he'd looked through the camera at very close range.

They went through to the study.

'Evening, Henry,' McAra said, still seeing a few stars. 'How's the vest?'

Henry switched the transmitter on. 'Sheer genius.'

McAra held the camera at arms length this time. 'It's working a treat. You can turn them off now. Save the battery power.'

Henry gave McAra a business-size card and a mobile phone. 'Dial this number within ten minutes of us being inside the casino. The lads at Excalibur have kitted me out with various gizmos that'll pick up conversations within a short radius of the devices. You'll be able to hear what's going on.'

'Is it a silent connection?' McAra said.

'Yes, one way only with no clicks or sounds on the initial connection. Ninety-nine per cent of background noise is omitted so you'll have no distortion on the conversations.' Henry indicated a socket outlet on the mobile phone. 'You can plug the phone in to any standard recording equipment if you want to make a copy of what's said.'

'Very nifty,' McAra said, putting the phone and number in his pocket. 'Two of the buttons on Riley's jacket are miniature cameras. Have a guess which ones.'

Henry looked at the buttons. 'I can't tell which ones are the cameras.'

McAra rubbed his hands together. 'Neither will anyone else.'

Riley checked the time on his wristwatch, which could do a lot more than just tell the time. 'We'd better get going. I told Jamesie we'd pick him up and drop him off near the casino.' He lifted the painting which was bubble wrapped within an inch of its life. 'I'll put the painting in the boot of your car,' he said to McAra, who had kitted out the vehicle with the necessary receivers and transmitters — and a flask of tea and sandwiches.

Jamesie was waiting for them in the street. He wore Strang's coat and had attempted to gel his usual nondescript mousy hair into an artistic quiff. As with his chef's hat, it did him no favours, but the expensive coat made him look like the type of man he hoped to be.

'Have you got the painting?' Jamesie said to Riley through the car window as they pulled up beside him.

McAra kept the engine running while Riley got out of the passenger seat and showed Jamesie the painting in the boot.

'Unwrap it carefully once you get inside the casino. I've marked where to tear the plastic so it won't dislodge the devices. Start at the top and work your way down. Everything's well hidden in the frame,' Riley said.

'I'll sort it myself. I won't let anyone touch the painting except me and Big Handsome Callum,' Jamesie said.

'Let's go.' Riley said firmly.

'Nice suit,' Jamesie remarked, giving a thumbs up to what he was wearing.

'Nice coat,' Riley said with a knowing wink.

'Strang's a lot bigger than me but I think I get away with it 'cos expensive coats are usually looser. I think it does a lot for me.'

'It does, Jamesie. You'll do fine tonight.' Riley opened the rear door of the car. 'You're in the back with Henry.'

Jamesie and Riley got into the car and McAra drove off.

'Are you a secret squirrel too?' Jamesie said to Henry by way of introduction.

Henry smiled and shook hands with the chef.

Jamesie relaxed back in the seat. The less they said, the better they were. Henry was undoubtedly another Riley. It was going to be quite a night.

Shaw and Catherine were waiting in Shaw's car at a pre–arranged street out of view of the casino so that Riley could give him vest number two. He kept the lights off and only the glow of a streetlamp lit the darkened interior of the car.

'Pull up beside the driver's side,' Riley said to McAra. He opened the window and they spoke without leaving either of the vehicles. Riley handed Shaw the vest. 'You know how it works?'

'Yes,' Shaw said. 'I'll be two minutes behind you.'

Riley looked over at Catherine. He couldn't see what she was wearing but whatever it was glittered and sparkled like fireflies in the dark.

Riley gave McAra a nod and they drove off to park opposite the casino.

'Are they the other two who are going in with you?' Jamesie said.

'Yes. Catherine works as a government investigator in Edinburgh,' Riley said.

When Riley gave no details of the man, Jamesie got the message. It really was going to be quite a night.

Shaw got changed into his vest in the front seat of the car. He took his black dinner jacket and white shirt off. Catherine noticed the scars like silvery strands of a web etched on his strong forearms. Light from the streetlamp shone through the window, emphasising the marks. He sensed she'd seen them and self consciously hurried to put his shirt on to hide the scars of war.

'I'm glad you're here tonight,' she said, suddenly feeling the urge to be kind to him.

He smiled at her, something he didn't do very often. Strangely, she'd become accustomed to his serious attitude to everything. Knowing now about his background in the Special Forces, she could see the SAS man in him. Riley was different. He had an extra layer of guile that shielded his capabilities. Perhaps other SBS men were like that too or maybe it was only Riley.

She pulled her velvet wrap around her shoulders. 'Do Riley and you have a plan worked out?' she said, feeling nervous about what Brodie had planned for them.

He adjusted his dark blue silk tie, clipped a tie pin on that beeped a signal and then became quiet, hid wires from a miniature device on the inside pocket of his jacket and put his jacket on. 'We're going to rattle his cage, see what tumbles out, secure information and then leave.'

'Is that what the wires are for?' she said, motioning at the device that resembled a wafer thin pocket calculator.

'Yes.' He put the car into gear and drove off. 'Take a look in the glove compartment.'

She opened it, thinking it would be yet another piece of surveillance wizardry belonging to the former SAS man. And it was, but not quite what she expected.

'You don't have to wear it if you don't want to,' Shaw said.

In the distance the bright lights of the casino lit up the car, causing the diamond–like bracelet to dazzle in her hands. She slipped the bracelet on and held her hand at arms length to admire it. Three rows of zircons sparkled on her wrist. 'It's lovely,' she said.

'If we get separated in the casino, I'll be able to find you,' Shaw said.

She laughed nervously. 'It's a piece of gadgetry?'

'It emits a signal so I'll know where you are. It's got a range of five hundred metres.' He sounded almost deflated. Had she thought it was a genuine bracelet? Was she disappointed that it was part of the surveillance equipment?

'Thank you, Shaw,' she said sincerely. 'I appreciate you looking out for me. And the bracelet really is beautiful.'

The muscles in his jaw clenched as he suppressed a smile. How could he tell her how worried he was about her safety without unnerving her? The invitation from Brodie was the equivalent of a veiled threat or warning that he knew she'd been to the casino with Riley, and Brodie wasn't a man to have his livelihood curtailed by the likes of her.

Jamesie held the painting as if his life depended on it. They'd dropped him off at a shadowed side street. Wearing his coat unbuttoned to emphasise the sway of the material, he made his way to the front of the casino carrying the painting with him.

From McAra's car, parked in the street opposite the casino, Riley watched Jamesie give a nod to Big Handsome Callum and go inside.

'Remember to unbutton your jackets before you go in and switch on the transmitters in the vests,' McAra said, making adjustments to the recording equipment in the car and giving Riley an in-ear transceiver that functioned as a transmitter and receiver so they could communicate.

'Will do,' Riley said, keeping a sharp eye on what was happening outside the casino. Tonight's special event doubled as an official grand opening for the new casino which had been running for a handful of weeks. People milled about the front steps and glass door entrance, and arrived in expensive cars. Photo journalists stood nearby and the flashes from their cameras gave a movie premier look to the night. Guests varied from city bigwigs and political types to business and media hotshots. Riley didn't recognise anyone, but that didn't mean that they weren't well known. His world fell outside the celebrity circuit, though he wondered how the photo journalists would react when they saw the glare from the vests. Nothing was ever simple.

Shaw's car pulled up behind McAra's. The men got out of the cars. The night was dry but bitterly cold with a layer of sparkling frost over the entire street vying against the lights of the casino for dazzling brightness.

Shaw left Catherine inside the warmth of his car while the men discussed their tactics. She watched them through the windscreen, thinking they were probably the three most able men invited to the event tonight. She'd never met Henry, but Shaw had explained who he was, and judging by the description, there was no mistaking the navy officer. Three Special Forces men and one of the top rocket scientists in the country were planning a daring rendezvous with trouble against a powerful and murderous politician in one of the most glamorous settings in Glasgow. And she was right in the middle of it. How quickly her life had changed from the night Reece was killed. She looked at the bracelet on her wrist. Did she really belong here? Call it female intuition, or the cold shiver of fate warning her to beware, but she had a bad feeling about the evening. A very bad feeling.

Riley walked towards her and opened the car door. 'Ready?' he said, offering her his hand to help her step out.

'Ready,' she said, knowing it was too late to turn back now.

She took the velvet wrap off her shoulders and cast it into the back seat. Riley had asked her to dress for maximum dazzle so there was no point covering it up. The dress had been designed by her father years ago for a special collection of his fashion business. She'd never worn it before and never thought she would.

Riley couldn't hide his reaction when he saw her step out into full view. She lit up the night.

Shaw, Henry and McAra stopped talking.

Catherine wore a full length dress that looked like liquid silver. The fabric and style skimmed her figure, cut low on the back, displaying the curve of her body from her shoulders to her waist. Barely there straps glittered with hundreds of diamante gemstones and the only jewellery she wore was the sparkling bracelet given to her by Shaw and diamond earrings. Her hair was loose and full.

'Henry, this is Catherine,' Riley said, introducing them.

'It's a pleasure to finally meet you,' Henry said, shaking hands with her.

'You too, Henry.'

McAra handed her a makeup compact. 'Put this in your handbag. It's got a tracker in it and that way I'll know where all four of you are. I've hidden the tracker behind the mirror.'

Catherine put the compact in her silver evening bag, and they got ready to go.

McAra got into the car, locked the doors and watched them disappear into the bustling activity across the street. Riley, Shaw and Henry unbuttoned their jackets and McAra's gadgets showed three signals clearly. The miniature cameras on Riley's jacket clicked into action, and McAra intended linking up to Henry's special mobile phone within the next ten minutes as planned.

'Take hold of my arm and stay close to me until we're inside,' Riley said to Catherine.

She linked her arm through his and kept pace as they made their way through the press and other guests. Henry and Shaw followed closely, ensuring the foursome wouldn't be split up by the crowd.

Riley found himself calculating how many security staff worked the doors, checked for an alternative exit and assessed the calibre of those around him within seconds. A force of habit, it always kicked in when he needed it.

Two photo journalists exchanged a surprised look and checked their cameras for malfunctions. Henry gave them a friendly smile and hurried on.

Riley kept a lookout for Big Handsome Callum. By all accounts his name wouldn't have contravened the trade descriptions act. Jamesie assured him the head of security was six feet four, build like a brick house and was a fine looking lad with reddish blonde hair. Only one man fitted the mould. He was keeping an eye on everyone going in and glancing at his watch.

'Come on, Jamesie, get us through security,' Riley muttered.

Jamesie was inside the foyer fixing the painting up on to the wall.

With seconds to spare before they reached the doors, Jamesie gave the nod to Big Handsome Callum that this was Riley and co.

'Good evening,' Big Handsome Callum said, waving them unchallenged through the doorway.

Riley gave him a thankful nod and in they went. Jamesie played his part well. He stood on top of an ornate table hanging the painting up and pretended he didn't know any of the four.

Catherine's sparkling dress got the blame for the security monitor at the entrance reacting to the dazzling fabric and causing nothing but a shiny bright image on the screen. The Special Forces men had been a blur of white light on the monitor, their identities obscured by the glare.

Riley gave Catherine a look of assurance. They were in safely without alerting suspicion.

To the uninformed, they looked like a couple, but it was a Cinderella arrangement. He had to give her back at the end of the night.

Chapter Seventeen

Viva Glas Vegas!

The casino was the colour of new money, all shiny and bright. Crystal chandeliers hung in the main areas, and overhead spotlights lit the gambling tables, most of which were already busy with guests trying their hand at everything from blackjack to roulette. Few were seasoned gamblers, and the atmosphere was more of a party mood filled with light hearted laughter and gasps of excitement. No serious money was exchanging hands. But the night was young.

Brodie was talking to a group of the casino's major shareholders, the money men backing the venture. He broke away from them when he saw Catherine and came over to meet Riley and the others.

'Catherine, you look wonderful,' Brodie said. Before she had a chance to introduce him, he introduced himself. 'Kier Brodie,' he said to Riley. 'You must be the Record Keeper. I'm so glad you could come along tonight. What do you think of the casino? Isn't it superb?'

'Just like a piece of Las Vegas in Glasgow,' Riley said, wishing he could be less polite to the murdering bastard, but he'd bide his time. This wasn't the moment to throttle the truth out of the lying scumbag.

'Ever been to Vegas?' Brodie said to Riley, eyeing him up to see if he could fathom whether the ex–forces man was as good as his reputation claimed.

'Once, a few years back,' Riley said with a quiet smile. If only he could have told him it was during a mission to contain and capture drug dealers who thought they had found a niche in the globe that was safe from the Special Forces. The SBS were teamed with American Navy Seals. Suffice to say, luck wasn't on the side of the dealers during that particular mission.

'Then you'll be sure to try your hand at the tables,' Brodie said.

Riley smiled and gave no such assurance.

Brodie turned to Shaw. 'How about you, Shaw? Are you a gambling man? Or are you just here to keep an eye on Catherine?' He said it with a smile but it was a snide dig in the ribs to Shaw as Catherine was obviously there with Riley.

Riley was sure that a part of hell had frozen over with the look Shaw gave him. Even Brodie took a step back, smiling jovially but keeping out of punching distance all the same.

'This is Henry,' Catherine said to Brodie.

They shook hands. 'And what business would you be in, Henry?' Brodie said.

'Boats, mainly,' Henry said, smiling.

And SBS canoes, minehunters and submarines, Riley thought.

One of the party organisers came over and whispered an urgent message to Brodie.

'You'll have to excuse me,' Brodie said to them. 'I commissioned a painting for the casino and it's ready for the grand opening. They want me to unveil it.' He then added, 'Perhaps you'd like to join me. It's over here. Help yourself to a glass of bubbly from the champagne fountain.'

A few of the organisers were talking to Jamesie, who was still standing on the table, adjusting the painting on the wall. One of them handed him up a large piece of dark gold material. Jamesie seemed to be arguing with them, not causing a scene, but trying to avoid covering up the painting. The casino had decided to take advantage of the painting being available and had insisted it be unveiled as part of the official grand opening.

Jamesie had no choice but to cover the artwork, effectively cutting out the view for the hidden cameras. Standing on the table he glanced at Riley.

'No visuals from the painting,' McAra said in Riley's earpiece.

'Give it five minutes,' Riley said quietly, his surveillance microphones relaying the message to McAra.

'Stay close,' Riley said to Catherine as they went over to stand beside the fountain. Shaw and Henry went with them. Catherine put her handbag down beside the fountain and helped herself to a glass of champagne. She offered to fill glasses for the others but all three of them politely refused. None of them were hardened drinkers anyway, but they'd never risk a social drink when they needed their senses sharp.

Riley was concerned about Brodie making the link with him to Jamesie. Had Strang divulged the incident at the restaurant? He took a long look at Brodie. No sign of him being any the wiser. Brodie had a rough idea what was going on, but not all the dots had been joined. Jamesie's connection to them had slipped through the loop. One less problem to deal with.

'Can I have your attention for a moment?' Brodie said, used to claiming a crowd's undivided attention. Guests gathered round. Jamesie jumped down from the table and stood listening to the politician. 'It gives me great pleasure to unveil this artwork which has been painted specially for the casino. The artist is standing beside me.'

Press photographers got their cameras focussed to take pictures of the painting as Brodie uncovered it.

'I haven't seen the painting,' Brodie said, 'but I'm told that I'm in it, so let's see.' He took hold of the covering and pulled it free to reveal Jamesie's work of art. Press cameras flashed, snapping Jamesie in the scene, and guests gave an enthusiastic round of applause.

Brodie looked up at the painting. 'Oh you have put me in it. Well done, well done!'

A journalist said to Jamesie, 'What was your inspiration for the painting?'

'They paid me,' Jamesie said.

'Right,' Brodie said, curtailing further inappropriate gems from the mouth of the chef. He smiled at everyone and stretched out his arms. 'Enjoy your evening everyone.'

'Is that Richard Reece?' a female journalist said to Jamesie, pointing at the painting. 'The politician who was murdered in Edinburgh?'

'Yes,' Jamesie said, delighted people recognised the faces. 'And that's Mackenzie. He was —'

Brodie put his arm around Jamesie's shoulder and swept him aside. 'Brilliant painting. Here, have a flutter at the tables.' He put a handful of chips into Jamesie's palm.

'Cheers, Mr Brodie. I was just thinking it's strange how Richard Reece and Mackenzie are in my painting and now they're both gonners.'

'Ach don't you bother about it. That's in the past. I'm thinking we'll get you to do another couple of paintings for us.'

'I'm working on your other one, but I wanted to see if you liked this one first.'

'It's fantastic, so finish the next painting and there'll be a bonus in it for you.'

'Cheers,' Jamesie said again.

Brodie left him and headed over to Riley. Jamesie turned to the painting and gave it a wink. He hadn't been as stupid as Brodie gave him credit for.

Riley was talking to Catherine and Shaw.

'I was wondering if I can have ten minutes of your time to cast your eye over some antique weapons,' Brodie said to Riley. 'That's if I can pry you away from the intriguingly beautiful Catherine.'

'Why not,' Riley said. 'Do you have them on the premises?'

'They're in what I like to call the *dark side* of the casino, behind the scenes so to speak. Where all the real drama takes place.'

Brodie led the way through the hub of the casino to a doorway near the back. Riley looked over his shoulder before stepping inside. Shaw was watching where they'd gone, and kept Catherine safely beside him.

Riley stepped into the dark side and Brodie closed the door behind them.

Unless he was mistaken, Shaw had caught Brodie giving a sly nod to a very attractive woman, a hostess for the casino, as he went past her with Riley. His instincts proved right when the walking temptation in deep violet satin came sashaying over to him, unperturbed that he was with Catherine.

'Hello,' she said to Shaw. 'I'm Veronica Blonde.' Unlike Big Handsome Callum, her name didn't tie in with her appearance. Stunningly attractive, the hostess had long, glossy dark hair and a pale complexion.

'Is that your real name?' Shaw said. No hint of interest in his voice.

'Near enough,' she said. 'I liked the name Veronica.'

Catherine decided to give them a few minutes to chat, though Shaw wasn't keen on this idea.

'Can you tell me where the ladies room is?' Catherine said to Veronica.

'Over there.' Veronica pointed to a sign in the distance.

'Thanks.' Catherine went to walk away but Shaw grabbed her hand.

'Don't wander off,' he said, giving her a worried look. 'You know what I mean.'

'I'll be right back,' she said, and then edged her way through the crowd to the ladies room.

Veronica Blonde's tone changed as soon as Catherine left. 'You're causing a problem for security tonight,' she said, confiding earnestly. 'You're all lit up and it's causing the CCTV cameras to go haywire. They can't get a picture of you.'

Shaw searched her face for the type of game she was playing.

'Don't look at me like that,' she whispered. 'I'm doing you a favour.'

'Brodie said I was to distract you, but Big Handsome Callum said I should warn you. I'm taking a bloody risk. Brodie's men would nail me to the wall if they found out.'

Shaw listened but kept a constant lookout for Catherine. 'Is there another exit out of the ladies room?'

'No.' She hesitated and then said, 'No, wait a minute. There's an exit through the ladies cloakroom but no one uses that door.'

Shaw planned to give Catherine another few minutes before he went to look for her. His eyes searched around for Henry who was scoping the gambling tables. He gave Henry a nod of acknowledgment, keeping in constant contact. Jamesie hadn't succumbed to the gambling tables. Instead he was queuing to cash in the free chips.

'Big Handsome Callum says you guys are okay. You're Jamesie's pals,' Veronica said through a faux smile, trying to make it look like she was flirting with Shaw in case Brodie's men were watching her.

'Do you work for Brodie?' Shaw said.

'No. I work for the casino. Brodie acts like he owns it, but he doesn't. He's got a share in it, nothing more. Big Handsome Callum works for the casino, not for Brodie. Brodie's got his own men, like bodyguards or well paid hoodlums to do his dirty work for him.'

She sounded genuine and nervous of what Brodie would do if he caught her telling tales. Shaw gave her his full attention for a moment.

'I'm going to make it look as if I've given you the brush off, okay?'

'Okay.'

'It'll seem like you tried to distract me but I just wasn't interested.'

She stepped closer and put one hand on his chest and smiled up at him. 'Make it look convincing.'

She really was beautiful, but his interests lay elsewhere. 'I'm going to push your hand away in a moment and step back. It'll be clear I want nothing to do with you. If they're watching, and they probably are, tell them there was no getting through to me.'

'I'll tell them you're a cold hearted customer — but I'll be lying.'

'Ready?' he said, feeling strangely sorry for her.

She smiled and moved in even closer, pressing her body against him.

Shaw pushed her away, politely but plainly.

Veronica tossed her hair over her shoulders and turned away.

'Veronica,' Shaw said.

She looked back at him.

'You can do better than this,' he said.

'I'm trying to,' she said and then walked away.

Instinct suddenly hit him. Where was Catherine? He caught Henry's attention. Henry came over. 'Catherine went to the ladies. She hasn't come back,' Shaw said.

'I was watching. She didn't come out,' Henry said. He used the hidden transmitting device from the mobile phone he'd rigged up to talk to McAra. The phone device was in his jacket pocket and he looked as if he was chatting to Shaw rather than secretly communicating with McAra. 'Catherine's missing. Can you locate her?'

McAra checked the compact's location. 'According to this, Catherine should be standing right next to you.'

Henry saw her handbag beside the fountain where she'd left it. He picked it up. 'She hasn't got the compact with her,' he said to McAra.

Shaw sighed in exasperation and muttered. 'She's always leaving her bag in the office and running off without it.' Then he checked the tracker in her bracelet. 'She's in another part of the building,' he said, cursing to himself.

Henry had surreptitiously studied the layout of the casino from the fire regulations on the wall near the stairs while scoping the gambling tables. 'Narrow the area,' he said calmly to Shaw.

'Nine o'clock. Ground floor level.'

'The kitchens,' Henry said. 'Go on two?'

'Yes, I'll go first.' Without hesitation, Shaw edged through the revelry to the kitchen doorway.

Henry followed two seconds behind. He'd just reached the doorway when Jamesie came running up to him, pretending to bump into him.

'Where's Riley?' Jamesie said.

'With Brodie.' Henry's words were clipped. He was in a hurry.

'We need to get out of here. We don't need to stay anyway,' Jamesie said.

'Explain.'

'We're here for information on Brodie. Something to nail him on. Right?'

'Yes.'

'Well we've got all the information we need,' Jamesie said.

'Where did you get it?'

'Big Handsome Callum. He knows *everything*.'

'Catherine's missing,' Henry said, planning to deal with Jamesie's contact later.

'I'll see what I can do,' Jamesie said.

Henry hurried to the kitchens. 'McAra?' he said via the phone.

'Have you found her?' McAra said.

'No. Keep checking the visuals. Shaw and I are going into the kitchen. He's got a tracker on her.'

The trouble had already started. Shaw had demanded the keys to the storerooms, several of them, which were locked. The kitchen porters refused to unlock the rooms where Shaw had tracked Catherine. He wasn't going to ask them twice. As Henry hurried in, Shaw grabbed a fire hatchet from the wall, ripping it off with his bare hands, and began tearing into the doors, hacking the locks to pieces and kicking the storeroom doors open.

Henry helped him. The kitchen staff were a rough looking crew but no one wanted to stand between Shaw and his rage, or Henry, as they effectively decimated the storeroom. In one of the rooms Shaw found Catherine's bracelet. Had it been torn from her wrist during a struggle? Or had whoever took her known it contained a tracking device and left it there to deliberately muddy the trail?

Shaw grabbed one of the kitchen porters in a vice like grip. 'Where's the woman? Where is she? Where did they take her?'

One of the other porters went to press a security alarm on the wall. Still keeping a tight grip on the man, Shaw threw the hatchet with a force that split the alarm into pieces and embedded itself in the wall. He turned his focus on the first man. 'Where is she?'

'Through the back, near the loading bay,' the man stammered.

Shaw threw him aside.

Henry checked the layout as they ran through the maze of corridors that became ever darker. There had indeed been a dark side to the casino. They were in it. They paused to check their location. Shaw was seething at himself for letting Catherine out of his sight.

'If anything happens to her . . .' he said to Henry.

Henry silenced him with a look. They had to stay calm. Fierce, determined, but calm.

Shaw took a deep breath and focussed on the layout. 'Where would they be taking her? This route leads right back to the main area of the casino.'

Then it dawned on Henry. 'We're being baited.'

'Or kept busy while they deal with Riley?'

Either option wasn't good.

'I've lost the signal to McAra,' Henry said.

Voices sounded further along the concrete corridor. Henry reached up and unscrewed the light bulb overhead, adding another layer of shadows to the already dimly lit corridor.

They pressed themselves into the shadows, switched their vests off, and pulled their dark jackets shut to cover their white shirts. Within seconds they had vanished.

Three of Brodie's man went right past them. Not a breath, not a movement from Henry or Shaw gave away their position.

Brodie had spent fifteen minutes showing Riley around the small collection of antique weapons in a VIP room kitted out like a hotel suite except it had no windows. Riley was impressed by the pieces, but not by Brodie.

'These are only a few of the weapons I've collected over the years,' Brodie said, strutting around the plush carpeted room, sure that he'd have Riley in his pocket by the end of their meeting.

'You're wasting your time,' Riley said finally.

Brodie blinked and smiled. 'Oh come on now, every man has his price. What will it cost to have you work for me?'

'It's what it would cost me to work for you,' Riley said.

Brodie's smile never faded. 'Ah, we're talking about integrity eh? Okay, what if I were to triple my initial offer? How does that sound?'

'Empty,' Riley said, his voice echoing off the walls with a resonating finality that left Brodie in no doubt that he really was wasting his breath.

Brodie smirked and sat down on the edge of the antique desk. 'The Valentines are a pair of cheapskate police who'll never appreciate your worth.' He leaned forward and confided. 'And between you and me, this case the Valentines have got you involved in, it's never going to be solved. It's going to end up in a drab manilla folder marked — *we haven't got a clue.*' He paused and continued breezily, 'But if you won't work for me, perhaps you'd like to come and see my full collection of weapons, Knights shields, some unique pieces, at my home in Edinburgh. I'm throwing a big party there at the weekend — a real Scottish ceilidh. I have one around this time every year. I'd be delighted if you'd come along.'

Riley hesitated. He hated to admit it, but the manilla folder was a distinct possibility. Men like Brodie sometimes got away with bloody murder. If ever there was a case for keeping an enemy close . . .

'Come on, Riley. Bring Catherine with you, and Shaw and Henry. Bring the lot of them. Hell! Invite the ruddy Valentines. Kilts and Highland dress are compulsory of course. Though I doubt we'll get that mangy old boy Stanley in the tartan.' Brodie paused and laughed. 'Can you imagine those knobbly knees in a kilt?'

The atmosphere was strangely lighter. Like two enemies with a common aim of dark satire before going into battle against each other. Unwritten rules that men like Brodie knew and men like Riley wished they didn't.

Riley nodded.

Brodie slapped his hands against the front of his thighs and stood up from the desk. 'I'll have the invitations dropped off to you tomorrow.'

Riley picked up the antique dagger from Brodie's desk and then put it back down beside the two swords he'd dated at around the fifteen century. Then he noticed something happening, an incident caught on the small security monitor on the desk. Brodie hadn't noticed.

'I really should get back to Catherine,' Riley said.

'Yes, of course. I'm sure we'll have time to chat again at the ceilidh.'

Riley walked towards the door. Brodie went to show him how to get back from the dark side of the casino. 'That's all right,' Riley said. 'I know where I'm going. See you again.' He left, and closed the door to the VIP room behind him.

Catherine was agitated. She made her own way back to the main area of the casino, looking for Riley, Shaw and Henry. The only one she saw was Jamesie, who'd seen her first. He came scurrying over.

'Pretend we're talking about my painting,' Jamesie said.

'Where's Shaw and Henry?'

'They're away searching for you,' Jamesie whispered anxiously.

She sighed heavily. 'I heard two men talking about Brodie. I went through a side door near the ladies cloakroom and got lost. The men thought I was a threat to security and tried to lock me in a storeroom until Brodie confirmed who I was.' She held up her wrist. 'I struggled and got away from them but I lost the bracelet Shaw gave me. It had a bugging device in it. And I've left my bag down somewhere.'

'Did the men hurt you?'

'No, I suppose I looked suspicious. They were only doing their job.'

'I think it was a set up.'

Catherine frowned at him.

'I think they did it on purpose. I've seen things like that before. They deliberately let you hear their conversation, then lure you away.'

'That's ridiculous,' Catherine said.

'Is it?'

Catherine looked around the casino and then back at the painting. 'Where did Shaw and Henry go exactly? And where's Riley?'

'Riley's still with Brodie as far as I know. The others went through to the kitchen. I haven't seen them since.'

Her face drained of colour. 'What should we do?'

'I'm hoping McAra's doing something. He's watching us.' Jamesie mouthed up at the painting. 'Where's Riley?' Then he said to Catherine, 'I'm going to tell Big Handsome Callum what's happening. Stay here so we know where you are.'

Jamesie scurried off, leaving Catherine alone in the busy foyer.

The concrete structure of the dark side of the casino cut all communication with McAra. The painting was the only clear signal. If Riley didn't contact him within the next ten minutes, he'd phone Valentine — either one of them.

'Ah, there you are, Catherine,' Brodie said, taking her by surprise. 'Had any luck at the tables yet?'

'Where's Riley?' she said.

'I thought he'd be with you. He's agreed to come to the ceilidh I'm having up in Edinburgh and I'm hoping you'll come along too.'

Reading lies on the faces of politicians was a skill she'd acquired the harsh way. She realised Jamesie was right. She'd been set up.

Two of Brodie's men approached him. The men confided something to him. 'Sort it out,' Brodie said. The men hurried off.

Then she saw Big Handsome Callum run through the crowded foyer, flanked by other members of the casino's security.

Jamesie ran over to Catherine and Brodie.

'What's going on?' Brodie said, sounding as if he already knew.

'A fight's kicked off through the back,' Jamesie said, giving Catherine an anxious stare. 'And one of the men has climbed outside the building.'

For a moment Brodie turned to explain what was going on to one of the guests.

Catherine took her chance to whisper to Jamesie. 'Is it Riley who's climbing?'

'No,' Jamesie said quietly. 'It's definitely not him.'

Chapter Eighteen

The Dark Side

Henry clung to the side of the building by his fingertips. The freezing cold wind bit into his hands like razor cuts. He gritted his teeth and edged his way along the narrow ledge high above the sheer drop of the street below. To his right, he saw the neon sign of the casino emblazoned across the front of the building and was careful not to touch any power cables running along the brickwork to prevent being fried into oblivion.

The wind gusted around him, blowing through his open jacket. He dug his fingertips into the rough, cold stone, held on tight and looked up. One more floor and he'd reach the roof of the casino. He could do it.

People poured in and out of the casino, cars picking them up and dropping them off; their voices distant. Not one of them saw him climbing, the determination in him not giving in.

The top ledge was in sight but he'd need to make a grab for it, strong and sure. The wind became stronger now as the building was higher than those on either side, whose structures had shielded him from the full force of the gusts. He took a deep breath and reached for the ledge, stretching until the muscles in his shoulders burned like fire. One final wrench and he hauled himself on to the flat top roof.

The lights of the city glistened all around him, and for a second he felt someone watching him, but he brushed the sense aside, and tried to figure out the layout of the building. Where the hell was the stairwell vent leading down to the first floor? Then he saw it, a few feet away. He ran to it, forced the hatch door open and slid down the outer edge of the metal stairs. He landed in a carpeted corridor exactly where he needed to be. Now all he had to do was run.

Meanwhile, Shaw fought for his life against a number of them. He'd vanished earlier into the shadows with Henry, keeping out of sight of Brodie's men. The next time they hadn't been so fortunate. He'd been forced to fight back to back with Henry but they'd become separated when one of Brodie's men slammed a fire door shut between them. Shaw was on his own now, vastly outnumbered, fighting like a tiger. He knew Henry would find a way to get back into the fray but time was running out.

Riley heard the flick of a knife in the darkness. He pretended otherwise.

The loading bay at the back of the casino was steeped in faded light that merged with the dark and caused a sense of disorientation. Where the concrete bay joined the street was a vague web of shadows.

The man had seen him and was lying in wait, but what you see and what you think you see are two different things. Riley stepped into a streak of light and then stepped into the shadows and seemed to disappear.

Silence.

The knifeman waited and then came looking for Riley. This was his first mistake.

Riley threw a forceful punch into the man's chest, the blow so fast it hardly registered until the pain hit him.

The first strike was a warning.

The knifeman didn't heed it. This was his second mistake. He repeatedly jabbed the knife at Riley, stabbing wildly, but Riley moved out of range of the blade each time, and then finished the encounter with a knife-hand strike to his attacker's throat.

The man crumbled to the ground, gasping for breath.

Riley hurried on, across the loading bay which bore the scent of an icy October evening. The knifeman had been alone but he knew others would be on their way. He kept close to the shadows and spoke to McAra in short, sharp bursts. 'McAra? I'm at the rear of the building. Can you hear me?'

'Yes, but I've lost contact with Henry and Shaw.'

'I saw them on the security monitor. They're in trouble. I'm going to get them.'

'They were looking for Catherine. She went missing but she's back in the foyer with Brodie — and Jamesie.'

'Is she hurt?'

'No.'

Riley heard footsteps running in his direction.

'Should I call Valentine?' McAra said.

'Hold on that, for now.' He ceased communication and pressed his back against a rigid shutter and felt a long metal bar jammed across it. He wrenched the bar free and held it firmly with both hands.

The crackling sound of a stun gun electrified the air.

Despite being armed with the electrical weapon that could shoot a debilitating number of volts through Riley's body on contact, his attacker had made himself a clear target. He stepped forward into the path of Riley who hit him across the knuckles with the metal bar. The man dropped the stun gun and writhed on the ground in pain. His knuckles had been broken.

Riley raised the bar up, and the man winced thinking he was going to be hit across the face, but Riley brought the bar down on the stun gun smashing it to pieces. Then he ran through a doorway leading into the building, slammed the door shut behind him and jammed the metal bar across the lock, effectively shutting both injured attackers outside in the cold.

He heard voices raging further inside and ran the full length of a dimly lit, damp corridor, homing in on the noise — running towards a vicious sounding fight.

'McAra?' Riley said, but the signal was blocked. He was too deep in the dark side of the casino to be heard.

No weapons, no communication and no back up. It was just like old times.

The skin on Shaw's knuckles felt raw from punching one too many hard jaws. Two of Brodie's men had broken noses, the central bone curved where the bone had cracked. Whether they'd broken them before or after their fist fight with Shaw was anybody's guess. It was when the knives came out that the fight stepped up a level.

Shaw dropped the first knifeman with a thunderous punch to the jaw. The man's anger outweighed his pain and he came at Shaw again.

Henry kicked the door open and entered the fray, felling the knifeman to the ground with a body blow. Two dirty fighters wrestled Henry to the ground. In the fury that followed Henry ripped one of their mouths into a wider smile and smashed his heel into the other's cheekbone. Grappling was Henry's forte. He looked like a gentleman but looks can be deceiving.

Henry got up and stood strong with Shaw.

A few of Brodie's men stepped back — right into the jaws of Riley.

It was now three of them against an unknown number.

Riley grabbed the nearest man in a neck lock and used him as a bodyweight to send another two flying.

Wielding an open razor, a man lunged at Riley, swiping the blade near his face. Riley countered the attack with a punch to the assailant's face, crunching his jaw into dislocation, disarming him of the razor and following through with a powerful right hook that felled him unconscious.

'Catherine's missing,' Shaw shouted.

'She's safe, unharmed,' Riley said, grinding his fist into the face of someone who hadn't learned to give up, and then bodily lifting the next man and throwing him against the wall. 'I'll clear the other doorway, and then we're out of here.'

Henry and Shaw nodded. They were hardened fighters, but Riley had a rare talent that could never be taught. He'd always been able to forge through an onslaught of attack, using speed, power, technique — and something else. Something that was special to Riley. A force that took some beating.

Riley fought through several of them to the doorway. Fights, real fights were messy. For a man who'd seen more than his share of brutal action, he found no rush of adrenalin in a bare fists battle. He was a clear headed fighter, a calculated adversary some would say. Maybe it was a curse, but he'd always thought of it as the edge that had saved his life many times.

By the time Riley had secured the doorway there were more men lying on the ground than standing up. It was the signal to go.

Riley led the way, running through the empty corridors, followed by Shaw and Henry, finding the quickest route back to the brighter side of the casino.

'Men ahead,' Riley said, stopping suddenly, hearing them approach. 'However, it's the only way forward.'

Brodie's men barred the only way back. None of them were dead, so it was likely that a few still had some fight in them and would go another round if Riley and the others turned back. They chose to go forward, alert to whatever was coming at them next.

A tall, broad shouldered man stopped a short distance ahead of them. It was Big Handsome Callum. 'What happened to you lot?' he said. He was backed by six of the casino's official security men.

'We ran into a disagreement,' Riley said. Before he could explain further, Brodie appeared on the scene and stood beside Big Handsome Callum.

Brodie spoke in a low tone just out of earshot of Riley. 'Everything is okay, Callum. My men are handling this. Go back to where you were.'

'This is my turf, Brodie. I'm head of the casino's security,' Big Handsome Callum said.

Brodie fixed him with a steely eyed stare. 'Not tonight you aren't.'

With those words, Brodie sealed his fate with Big Handsome Callum who cursed the situation and went away, taking the other security men with him. Brodie had a lot of pull with the backers of the casino and he wanted to keep his job, but information was a powerful weapon and Callum had plenty of that.

Brodie smiled and walked up to Riley. 'My apologies, Riley. I certainly didn't want any trouble between you and my men.'

Riley stared hard into the eyes of Brodie. 'Say that again.'

Brodie took a cautious step back, but ever the politician, he was still smiling. 'What?' he said, shrugging his shoulders and holding his arms out at his side, palms up.

Riley kept his tone dark and level. 'I just wanted to look you straight in the face to see how bad you're lying.'

Brodie rocked back on his heels. He laughed but he was nervous. 'I promise you that my men will be severely reprimanded for their over zealous behaviour. It's inexcusable. Again, my apologies to you and your friends.'

It was obvious to Riley that it was an excuse, not an apology.

'Get out of there. We've got all the information we need on Brodie,' McAra's voice whispered urgently in Riley's earpiece. The connection was patchy but Riley understood.

Shaw went to have a go at Brodie but Riley deflected it. 'Apology accepted,' he said to Brodie.

Shaw swallowed his rage, realising Riley had another plan.

Brodie could hardly believe his luck. He took Riley's hand and shook it firmly. 'That's very magnanimous of you.' He shook Henry's hand and then seeing Shaw's red raw knuckles, slapped him on the shoulder, and led them out of the corridor towards the main area of the casino. They passed a few of Brodie's bruised and beaten men. 'The dentists in Glasgow are going to be busy,' Brodie said jokingly to Riley. 'Not with any of you three I may add.'

Henry smiled. Shaw didn't.

Riley chose his words carefully. 'You've got quite a number of men guarding your corner. I never realised politics was such a dangerous business.'

'I guard my corner fiercely Riley, as do you. We each look out for our own. Strange loyalty — isn't that what they call it. And with over two hundred VIPs in the casino tonight I thought I should step up the security. I may of course have over egged the pudding.'

Catherine saw them enter the foyer. She hurried over. 'Are you okay?'

'Yes,' Riley said, giving her a look that said they'd explain everything later.

She understood.

One of Brodie's main men came up to him. He had a deep scar across his cheekbone, a remnant from a past fight, though he'd collected a few other cuts from his encounter earlier with Riley. The scar tightened as he spoke. 'The guests got wind of the fight. Maybe you want to explain to them what happened.'

Brodie gave him a nod and gathered people's attention in the foyer.

'There's been a wee skirmish through the back. But it's settled. We're all friends now. It was just a silly misunderstanding. Security thought robbers were in to steal your money, but if anything, it proves that while you're here in this casino, you and your cash are a hundred per cent in safe hands.'

The hands of one of Brodie's men looked the worse for wear. He held his fingers, supporting them cannily because every knuckle was shattered and his digits dangled like putty.

'He'll not be giving us a tune on the old piano then, eh?' Jamesie whispered to Henry who tried not to smile.

Henry had straightened his tie and looked almost as immaculate as when he'd first come in. Shaw's hands were raw and he'd a graze across his cheekbone where a fist had connected, but apart from that he was fine. Riley's face bore no evidence of what he'd been through, and even though the muscles across his back throbbed where he'd been hit, no one would ever have known the strife he'd endured yet again.

'Shall we go?' Riley said, offering Catherine his arm. She linked her arm through his.

Brodie took hold of Riley's hand and smiled jovially. 'For luck,' he said, forcing several high value chips into it. 'It means you'll always come back to the casino. And I do hope you'll come to the ceilidh.'

'I wouldn't miss it,' Riley said.

As Brodie waved them off, Riley pressed the chips into Jamesie's hand, and winked.

'Thanks, Riley,' Jamesie said, and hurried off to cash them in.

Big Handsome Callum bid the four of them goodnight as they approached the front entrance.

'Thanks for your help,' Riley said to him.

'We'll speak soon. I've got a lot to tell you,' Big Handsome Callum said quietly. He turned to Henry. 'You're some climber. No offence, but you don't look it, not dressed like that,' he said, indicating Henry's dapper suit.

'Thank you,' Henry said, smiling at the compliment.

As they left the warmth of the casino, Riley reminded Shaw and Henry to switch on their vests. 'The press are still hanging around the front entrance.'

People were busy outside.

No one saw the man on the roof. A shadow in the distance, he assembled the long range rifle with calm precision and lined up the shot.

Riley and the others walked out of the casino. Henry, Riley and Catherine were at the forefront. Shaw was three steps behind them, watching their backs. McAra was in the car listening and recording everything the surveillance devices picked up.

Henry buttoned his jacket against the cold night air.

'Did you win tonight?' a smiling, well dressed man said as he headed into the casino. A social comment from one stranger to another.

'Oh yes,' Henry said, smiling, the smile reaching up to his eyes, saying more than his answer implied.

And then it happened.

The force of the shot striking his chest sent Henry flying back. He hit the ground hard.

In that second, Riley heard the silent rage inside him explode, and he ran to help Henry who was lying motionless. Catherine stood like a statue, shocked by what had just happened. What had happened? Riley looked up at a roof across the street from the casino. Movement. A glimpse of a man, with a long range weapon, disappearing into the shadows of the skyline. It was Strang.

Shaw pulled Catherine back, shielding her with his body.

A gawping crowd gathered quickly. Others ran screaming for cover.

Riley shouted to Big Handsome Callum who rushed out of the casino. 'Keep the crowd back.'

Callum's strong arms forced the onlookers aside.

McAra's voice sounded in Riley's earpiece.

Riley whispered to Shaw. 'Help me get Henry to the car.'

Catherine was standing, almost motionless, her face drained of all colour. 'Come on, Catherine,' Riley said.

She looked at him blankly.

'Now!' he said, jolting her senses.

She hurried behind Riley and Shaw as they carried Henry across the street to McAra's car.

Cameras flashed eagerly as the press tried to capture the incident without success. The bright glare from the vests ruined any attempt they made, and caused further confusion to the situation. One of the journalists put his camera down and looked at Riley and Shaw in the flesh, without the lens of a camera between them. He thought their faces looked familiar. Were they the same two men who'd saved the drunken fairy? He wasn't sure.

Riley and Shaw put Henry in the back seat of the car.

'Vest three. I've still got a heartbeat,' McAra said, staring wide eyed at Riley and then at the slumped body of Henry.

Riley ripped open Henry's jacket. No blood on the white shirt. No bullet wound. Henry moaned and tried to sit up.

'Get Catherine into your car,' Riley said to Shaw, who acted immediately.

Riley examined Henry's chest, and then it dawned on him. The jacket! It was a Henry special! 'You're wearing bloody body armour,' Riley said.

'Did it work?' Henry said, groaning as if he'd been hit in the guts by a sledgehammer.

'The bullet didn't penetrate. You're winded and bruised from the impact.' He looked at the jacket. 'What the hell were you wearing?'

'It's a new type of fabric the navy's working on. The science lads at Excalibur thought I should wear it just it case. I added a couple of thin strips of lightweight armour to the inside panels but nothing on the chest, so the fabric seems to have worked by itself. The science buffs will be pleased.'

McAra leaned over the back seat to examine the jacket. 'Very lightweight. Feels just like a good quality designer jacket. What's it made of?'

'Fibreglass and manmade viscose, polyester and some sort of secret ingredient that makes it extra resilient. The material's woven to create a shield against attacks.'

'Amazing stuff,' McAra said.

Shaw came over and saw Henry was all right. 'Catherine's in a bit of a state. I think I should get her home to Edinburgh.'

'Follow us back to my house first,' Riley said. 'It'll lessen the shock when she actually sees Henry's okay.'

Shaw agreed.

Jamesie stood beside Big Handsome Callum at the front of the casino. McAra's car drove past, followed by Shaw's car. Riley caught Jamesie's attention. He gave Jamesie a surreptitious thumbs up.

Jamesie got the message. Henry was all right.

The two cars pulled into Riley's driveway. Henry was out of the car first, stretching his bones, trying to shake off the effects of the impact. He'd been hit by bullets before when wearing full body armour, the kind that weighs a hundred odd pounds. He knew what it felt like to take a pounding. A couple of painkillers and a cup of tea would do the trick.

They drank tea and coffee in the study by the warmth of the fire. Shaw had cleaned the wounds on his hands and face, and a sense of calm settled in as they realised they'd all made it back safely. The night had been a success.

'Ironic, isn't it,' McAra said. 'You're armed to the teeth with the latest technology and it all comes down to bloody fisticuffs.'

They laughed. Henry held his ribs which hurt like hell when he laughed.

'What are you going to do about Strang?' Catherine said.

'Taking a shot at Henry, he's got the military and the police after him now,' Riley said.

'The press saw everything. They'll have it as front page news tomorrow,' Catherine said.

'But they won't have photographs,' McAra said, pleased the vest had worked.

Catherine opened her handbag and took out the compact. 'I suppose I should give you this back,' she said to McAra.

'Hold on to it,' he said. 'It's only active when connected to the tracker receiver. If you ever get lost again,' he said light heartedly, 'we'll know where to find it.'

'And Catherine will be nowhere near it,' Shaw said, smiling.

They laughed again.

Henry saw a car approaching the house seconds before Riley's security system flashed a warning on the study wall. 'We've got company. It looks like Ferguson.'

'I left a message on Valentine's phone about Callum having the information we need on Brodie,' Riley said, thinking this was the reason for the visit. He went to let Ferguson in.

'Valentine's in trouble,' Ferguson said. 'We need your help. They're going to kill him. Old Stanley's there now. It's not looking good.'

Riley grabbed his jacket. 'Where is he and who's going to kill him?'

'We think they're Brodie's men. It's payback for getting a warrant to search through Brodie's accounts.'

Henry, Shaw and McAra offered to go with them.

'Take Catherine home. She's seen enough tonight,' Riley said quietly to Shaw.

Shaw understood and hurried Catherine out to his car.

Riley went with Ferguson while Henry and McAra followed in McAra's car.

The night wasn't over yet.

Chapter Nineteen

The Uncorruptables

Valentine had tried to fight them. He'd almost given as good as he got. Almost. But he'd been outnumbered three to one. Brodie's men had softened his ribs and trailed him on to the balcony of an abandoned four storey building overlooking the river Clyde. And it wasn't to see the view.

Riley saw the bridge in the distance, lit up in the night. Police cars and emergency vehicles cordoned it off from both sides. The bridge was the nearest they could get to the building on the edge of the river. Ferguson drove at speed with an emergency light flashing on the roof of the car. McAra's car followed.

'The first I knew about it was when the police spy in the sky helicopter radioed in that they'd seen Valentine bundled into a car near the station,' Ferguson said.

'What the hell are they playing at?' Riley said.

'We think they planned to rough him up a bit, threaten him to back off from Brodie, but the chopper chased them and they dragged him into the building. Now we've got a stand off. They're threatening to kill him if we don't cut them loose.'

'Who've you got covering the exits?'

'All exits are covered and we've got police marksmen on the roofs opposite and on the bridge. Marksmen have injured two of Brodie's men, but they've disappeared into the building. They could be long gone. The third's got a knife at Valentine's throat. He's the problem. Sounds like a real, hardened nutter.'

'Who's negotiating the deal?' Riley said.

Ferguson hesitated. 'Stanley senior. He's taking a hard line tactic. It's working but I don't think he can push it any further.'

'Can a marksman take the man out?'

'It's too dodgy. A long, long shot at night at this range. And the knifeman's too close to Valentine. We need to get him to move back so they can get a crack at him.'

They approached the bridge. Police officers waved Ferguson's car through, and McAra's.

The formidable, silver-haired figure of Stanley senior stood on the bridge holding a megaphone. He wore a woollen scarf around his neck to cover the plaster where he'd been on the wrong end of the metal spike.

He seemed pleased to see Riley which was a first, though the initial words out his mouth to Riley were less than welcoming. 'About fuckin' time. You know how these scumbags operate. Suggestions fast.' He thrust a pair of night sight binoculars at Riley.

Riley focussed in on the scene. The knifeman had already drawn blood from Valentine's face. The pressure of the blade in a nervous, angry hand had sliced the skin near the detective's cheekbone. It wasn't looking optimistic. He'd seen men like this before, pressured and pushed to the edge.

'What have you offered him?' Riley said.

'I've told him we'll let him go if he drops the knife,' Stanley said.

'His response?'

'He doesn't trust us.'

As they spoke, the knifeman shouted at the police in a voice that didn't need a megaphone. They heard the knifeman loud and clear. 'I want all you bastards off the fuckin' bridge pronto.' His voice increased in aggressive volume as he added, 'Or I'll kill him!'

Henry and McAra approached. Henry looked at Riley. A silent decision was made.

Riley turned to Stanley senior. 'Tell your marksman to take him out.'

Stanley had resigned himself to this. He waved the marksman over. Brief words were spoken between him and the marksman, who lined up the shot.

A hush descended over everyone present on the bridge. Ferguson's guts wrenched as he stared up at Valentine.

The marksman hesitated and then realigned the shot. He hesitated again. 'I can't get a clean view. Valentine keeps moving. He's struggling. I can't risk taking it.'

Stanley senior nodded and the marksman stood down.

Valentine had decided to fight and risk being slashed by the knife. The situation was escalating out of control. Stanley senior acknowledged that the marksman didn't seem confident to take the responsibility. Maybe the marksman knew his limits, and if so, his decision was professional. But that wouldn't save Valentine.

Henry stood next to Stanley senior. 'Riley can make that type of shot,' he said.

Stanley senior glanced at Riley, the look of a father trying to save his son rather than a chief of police.

Riley was as sure as he needed to be. The silent exchange between him and old Stanley said it all.

Stanley senior motioned to the marksman to hand over his rifle, which he did immediately. Stanley senior gave it to Riley. They were going to ask if Riley knew how to use this particular rifle but Riley had already clicked it into action, adjusting the weapon to suit his needs.

Everyone stood back a pace. Riley closed one eye and peered through the sights. Fuck! Valentine was having a real go, struggling to fight his attacker, but he was losing and only one of them had a knife. Then he remembered. He reached into his jacket pocket and brought out the small mirror that had hung inside his front door. Another old habit he'd yet to break. The last thing he'd done before leaving tonight was to slip it into his pocket. Now he had to hope that Valentine was as sharp as he believed him to be. He handed the mirror quickly to Henry. 'Give Valentine two flashes.'

Henry took the mirror. He knew exactly what the signal was, though he wondered how Valentine would know. This wasn't the time to discuss it. Riley wouldn't have asked if he didn't think it was feasible that Valentine would get the message.

Riley looked for a split second at Stanley senior, who gave him a slow blink, the equivalent of a nod to do it, just do it. The attacker was going to kill Valentine anyway. It was worth a try.

Henry saw Riley line up the shot. He flashed the mirror twice, strong, bright and clear, using a police car headlamp to provide the light he needed to create the signal.

Valentine saw the double flash. He remembered what Riley had said to Ferguson. *Stand still, don't move. Help is on its way.* He stopped struggling and stood strong and motionless. The man held the knife at Valentine's throat ready to strike.

The shot was going to be close. Riley didn't hesitate. There wasn't time. Technique, ability, experience and instinct all came into play as he pulled the trigger. The sound of the bullet piercing the night air became another memory Riley would never forget. Neither would anyone else who was there on the bridge that night. The sound was instant yet seemed to last a full three seconds, as if time had slowed down at that one brief moment when fate could have gone either way.

The shot hit its target, straight into the skull of the knifeman. He never knew what hit him. He dropped lifeless to the ground, but his bulky bodyweight thrust Valentine forward, pushing the detective over the edge of the low balcony into the river. The fall would have killed most men. The balcony was at least another storey higher than the bridge level.

Stanley senior gasped and others held their breath as Valentine plunged towards the water. Only an experienced diver could have righted their position and entered the dark water so straight and strong. He disappeared below the surface. No one knew whether to cheer or not. Had he made it?

Riley and Henry cast their jackets off and dived in after him.

'Get some light on to the water,' McAra shouted.

The police used everything they had to illuminate under the bridge, and the emergency services dashed off yet again to both sides of the Clyde to help with the rescue.

Stanley senior picked up the rifle where Riley had left it and handed it back to the marksman. As chief of police, he'd deal with the flack and red tape if necessary.

The brightness from the lights wasn't effective enough, so McAra showed them how to reflect one light off the other to increase the power five fold. Now they could see the three figures swimming in the freezing water.

Three figures. Stanley senior sighed with relief.

They climbed out of the water on to the embankment, reaching it just before the emergency services arrived.

Valentine spat the river water out and pushed his soaking wet hair back from his face. 'That was fucking close, Riley,' he said, smiling.

'You'll never know.'

'Was it Brodie's men?' Henry said.

'Yes, but we'll have a hell of a job proving it. Brodie's always one step ahead of the game. He'll have a fireproof alibi,' Valentine said. 'But we're not backing off. Scare tactics don't sit well with me and the old man.'

Riley smiled. 'We'd expect nothing less from the Uncorruptables.'

Valentine's feet squelched as he stepped up the embankment, and the blood began to seep again from the cut on his face, having been washed away by the water. He gave a wry grin. 'Being awkward bastards sometimes has its merits.'

'You're making a habit of this,' McAra said to Riley, handing him, and Henry, a blanket for warmth when they got back up to the bridge. Valentine was taken away to the hospital though he seemed to have survived with only minor cuts and bruises.

The police gave Riley and Henry a cheering welcome. Stanley senior shook their hands. Nothing more was said from the old codger. He'd a pile of bloody paperwork to tackle.

As Riley was leaving Stanley senior called to him amid the crowd of police and rescue workers.

'Have you got any family in Glasgow?'

'I've no family left. They're all gone,' Riley said.

Stanley senior nodded and went to walk away. Then he paused and said, 'My wife makes a traditional

Sunday lunch with all the trimmings. When this whole case is finished. One o'clock. Don't be late.' He walked on. 'And bring that dithery scientist with you.'

'What about Henry and Shaw and Jamesie?' Riley said, jokingly.

Stanley senior didn't even turn around. 'Don't push it,' he said and walked away.

'You're in the newspaper headlines again,' McAra said, turning up at Riley's house first thing in the morning with fresh rolls and milk for the tea. He put two of the Scottish tabloids down on Riley's desk. Both papers had pictures of the previous night's shooting in front of the casino, though the three men's identity was obscured by the bright glow from the vests.

Riley read the gist of the story. 'One man shot, others glowing in the dark. Two of the men were the heroes who saved the drunken fairy recently from the Clyde.' He'd read enough.

'At least the tabloids don't know who you are,' McAra said, going through to the kitchen to switch the kettle on and butter the rolls.

Riley relaxed back in his chair. He'd got to bed late and been up early, though he wasn't tired, just eager to close down Brodie and Strang.

'I got quite a bit of useful information last night from the cameras on your shirt buttons, though the sound isn't clear,' McAra said from the kitchen. 'The solid concrete wasted our other efforts, but if it's true Big Handsome Callum is going to spill the beans on Brodie then it was still worthwhile.'

'Jamesie's bringing Callum round here later this morning.' He checked the time on his watch. 'In about an hour.'

'I thought the Valentines would question him down at the police station.'

'No, Callum's got a phobia about being arrested, so he's agreed to talk to the police here. Apparently Callum's got a history with the Valentines from years ago, so Ferguson's doing the interview. I said I'd record it.'

McAra came through with the tea and rolls as Ferguson arrived at the house. Riley let him in.

'I know I'm early, but just as a one off, I wondered if I could have a wee shot of your climbing wall to see if my fitness has improved,' Ferguson said.

'Help yourself,' Riley said. 'We're having our breakfast, but you know where it is.'

They could see the hesitation on Ferguson's face at the mention of breakfast. They tried not to laugh.

'I'll put a roll aside for you,' McAra said.

'That would be great,' Ferguson said, heading off to challenge the wall. 'And Valentine's fine by the way.'

Big Handsome Callum looked like he was alone when he walked from his car to Riley's front door. Riley watched him on the security monitor and wondered where Jamesie was. Then he saw him, hidden behind the big, bulky stature of the nightclub security man. Jamesie wore Strang's coat and an expression that reminded Riley of a child anticipating a great day out. It was going to be a long morning.

Jamesie couldn't take his eyes of the world maps and historical artefacts in Riley's study. 'You see things like this in films, but you don't think they really exist. I could get lost here for a week.'

'You should see his diving pool and climbing wall,' Ferguson said.

'What's a climbing wall?' Jamesie said.

'A wall you climb up. You use it to keep fit,' Ferguson said. 'I've had a go. It's brilliant.'

Riley could see the cogs working in Jamesie's head. 'How do you climb up it?'

'Can I show him?' Ferguson said. 'It'll only take a minute.'

Riley nodded, and they hurried off.

'I'll be running off now,' McAra said, leaving Riley and Big Handsome Callum in the study. And he meant it in the literal sense as he ran back to his house.

'Is everyone here fitness crazy?' Big Handsome Callum said, smiling.

'It's just one of those mornings,' Riley said. The security monitor on his desk alerted him to another visitor on his property.

'Very nifty,' the security man observed.

Riley studied the figure approaching. Whoever it was parked their car in the driveway and walked confidently up to the house. The man looked like a well dressed thug.

Big Handsome Callum glared at the monitor. 'What the bloody hell's he doing here?'

'You know him?'

'He's one of Brodie's men. I can't be seen here.'

'I'll get rid of him. I think he's dropping off invitations to a ceilidh. That's all.'

Big Handsome Callum appeared edgy for the first time since he'd arrived. 'If Brodie found out that I was here —'

Riley raised his hands to assure him that everything was fine. 'Stay put.'

'Are you Riley?' the man said in a voice that sounded hollow.

'Yes.'

He reached into the inside pocket of his coat and took out a fancy envelope edged with tartan print. 'From Brodie.'

Riley took the envelope. They exchanged a curt nod and then the man left.

Riley went back to the study. Ferguson and Jamesie were there now.

'Invitations to dance with the devil,' Riley said, reading the invitations, before switching on the recording equipment.

Ferguson gave his full name, 'Detective Anthony Ferguson.' And the interview began.

'Remember, I'm not going on the official record with this,' Big Handsome Callum reminded the detective.

'We understand. You just give us the information and we'll take it from there. The Valentines have given their word.'

Despite his differences with the Uncorruptables, Big Handsome Callum knew the Valentines' word was reliable. And on the outside chance that it wasn't, it was worth the risk to sell out Brodie. 'The man has become a fuckin' monster. So has Strang.'

'What do you mean?' Ferguson said.

'Brodie's so full of his own importance, especially because he's this bigwig politician. He's loaded with money from various sources.' He paused. 'I hear that Valentine turned over his accounts and that's why Brodie's men nearly killed him last night. I hope Valentine had his gloves on 'cos those accounts are burning hot.'

'What about Strang?' Riley said.

'That one's a fuckin' killer. He bumped off a few of his science rivals and stole their research work. And Mackenzie helped him. Brodie supplied the back up, financial and otherwise.'

'Mackenzie was found dead at his computer,' Ferguson said.

'He made a mistake, or so I heard. I hear everything that goes on through being head of security at the casino. Brodie likes to talk big when he's in safe company. Likes to show off his money and who he's got in his back pockets.'

'What mistake did Mackenzie make?' Riley said.

'Mackenzie was making a name for himself as a top forger. Then Brodie wanted him to make fake documents, ancient maps, stuff like that so they could sell them for a small fortune. Mackenzie made a scroll. Brodie was going to get you to authenticate it. If it fooled you, then they'd easily fool buyers.'

Jamesie jumped in on the conversation. 'Tell them about Mackenzie hacking into Riley's computer and nearly giving the game away.'

Callum explained. 'That's why Strang bumped Mackenzie off. He doesn't like loose ends. And Mackenzie became one. He tried to hack into your computer but your security system nearly traced him back. Do you remember anyone hacking into your computer, probably a wee while before Richard Reece was killed?'

Riley did remember. Not many people got that far. The hacker was a knowledgeable one. 'Yes, but they didn't manage it.'

'Well, Strang went crazy when he found out Mackenzie risked everything by alerting you. Mackenzie wanted to hack into your stuff to steal information to help with the forgeries. That was all.'

'Why did Mackenzie's computer say he didn't exist?' Riley said.

'He was just that type. Never used his own name. And didn't leave any traces. Everything had to be silent and sneaky.'

Jamesie jumped in again. 'But it turned out that Strang was a better hacker than Mackenzie. He left stuff on Mackenzie's computer for Riley to find. He put Riley's name on a hit list.'

'Why?' Ferguson said.

'Because Strang hated Riley,' Callum said. 'It was reason enough. The grudge went back a long time. It was his chance for revenge.'

It had always been about revenge, Riley thought.

'Who killed Reece?' Ferguson said.

'Brodie. It wasn't planned to end in a stabbing. Brodie's always got daggers and shite like that on him. Gives him a thrill. Anyway, they were political rivals and

Brodie thought he could put the pressure on Reece to back off, and he probably could have, but fights don't always go according to plan.' Anticipating their next question, Big Handsome Callum continued, 'He hung the scroll around Reece's neck 'cos he was trying to muddy the scene. Maybe even throw suspicion on Riley.'

'The scroll had a message for Riley. Why was that?' Ferguson said.

'It was Mackenzie's joke. Brodie and Strang thought it was funny. If Riley could read it, then they'd failed with the forgery.'

'Who attacked Catherine that night?' Riley said.

'Strang. Brodie wanted him to frighten her because she was poking her nose too close into his business.'

All the necessary details were recorded, and then Ferguson took the evidence back to the police station.

'I hope that helps you get a conviction,' Callum said to Riley.

'I'm sure it will,' Riley said, though as Callum and Jamesie left, he knew the hunter's game wasn't over yet.

Lucky's empire had expanded. Another tarpaulin had been added, stretched across the walls and tied with ropes. The rain was battering down on the sturdy material, creating a strangely cosy outdoor haven.

Lucky was feeling especially fortunate. He'd come into a small windfall of hard cash. Nothing too grand, but enough to make his afternoon brighter despite the weather.

Barking Bob sat on his remnant of creamy coloured carpet that wasn't as good a match for his fur since he'd been shampooed. He saw Riley approach before Lucky did. He didn't bark or get up from his warm rug but his tail wagged, just once. Bob's welcomes were getting friendlier.

'Riley!' Lucky said. 'You got my message?' He'd left a message on Riley's phone.

Riley admired the new tarpaulin. 'Expanding are you?'

'I've been busy. Folk are snapping up a new range of fashions I acquired for the autumn. Metallics and retro chic are in this season.' He paused. 'And thanks for the casino money. That was very nice of you.'

'What money?'

'The gambling chips you gave to Jamesie. He cashed them in and shared them with me. We always share our luck. Brings us new luck. He's not daft. Other punters would've gambled it away, but not Jamesie.'

'You're welcome. You've been a great help to me.'

'Have we? We were wondering about that. For a man who tries to fight for the underdog, you're always up to your arse in . . . what's that word you use . . .?'

'Strife.'
'That's it, strife. That's why I phoned. I've got something for you. It'll maybe help you catch Strang. Hold on a minute.' He hurried into his house and came back with an address, written on a scrap of paper. He handed it to Riley.
Riley read the address. 'Edinburgh?'
'Strang's staying there. That's where he's holed up. Probably registered under a false name. It's a rental property right in the centre of the city. Jamesie mentioned you were invited to Brodie's ceilidh in Edinburgh tomorrow night, so I thought as you'd be up there anyway, you'd like to chap his door.'

Chapter Twenty

By Strength and Guile

The lights of Edinburgh castle could be seen towering above the city in the distance, cutting through the fog. Edinburgh certainly was the City of Spires, evident from the sharp skyline visible by the castle's light.

There was no mistaking where the ceilidh was. Pipers in full Highland dress stood playing the bagpipes at the entrance to Brodie's castle–like mansion in the heart of the city. Top of the range cars lined the stone gravel driveway, giving an indication of the calibre of the guests. As Riley drove up with Henry, he took in the full extent of Brodie's house. It was exactly like its owner. A mansion dressed as a castle, trying to be larger than it really was, and with illusions of grandeur.

Shaw's car pulled up behind him. Catherine drove up moments later. They'd all arranged to meet and go into the party together. Riley and Shaw wore tartan kilts and sporrans. Riley wore Black Isle tartan, a black and white weave mixed to create a shadow grey tartan. A

Scottish dagger, a Skean Dhu, was tucked into one of his knee length black wool socks, worn with brogues. Less traditional was his trusty hunting knife hidden in the other sock. Polished silver belt buckles and a white shirt, waistcoat and cropped black jacket with silver buttons completed the outfit that he hadn't worn for quite a while.

Shaw was of similar attire, only his kilt was of a dark blue–green tartan, and he was minus the hunting knife. Knowing Shaw, he'd have some form of weaponry and surveillance gear on his person.

Henry wore his full naval uniform as was quite acceptable for a naval captain. Catherine had a long, red tartan skirt, cream blouse and ladies tartan sash held in place with a silver Celtic brooch inset with a large amethyst gemstone.

'What happened with Strang?' Shaw said to Riley.

'His house was in darkness. He was out. But we know where to find him now.'

Riley handed their invitation to the doorman.

'Welcome. All the guests are in the banqueting hall. Drinks and food are available, and the main event is starting soon.'

Henry smiled. It certainly was.

They made their way down the tall corridor that echoed with the sound of jovial Scottish music coming from the main hall. The corridor was lined with some of

Brodie's collection, pieces of 14th and 15th century knight's weaponry and shields, and a full suit of armour at the entrance to the hall.

'Brodie obviously likes to show off his interest and warn people at the same time,' Riley said, referring to a particularly brutal double edged sword above the lintel.

Riley dated artefacts and weaponry, but his interest was in their history, unlike Brodie whose personality could be seen lined on the walls of his egotistical home.

They walked into the main hall which was alive with music and around three hundred guests. The ceiling was almost two storeys high. Wood panelling lined the walls and was decorated with swords and shields, and paintings of Scottish battles from days gone by. Groups of people danced in fast moving circles to the lively music, while others stood in front of the baronial log fire, warming themselves with a glass of whisky.

Brodie saw them and came striding over, the swagger of his kilt adding to his over confidence. His eyes betrayed his surprise at seeing Henry still breathing and none the worse for having been shot by Strang outside the casino. He quickly covered his reaction with a big smile. 'I'm delighted to see you all. The main entertainment is just starting.' He exaggerated glancing past them. 'Are the Stanley Valentines not coming?'

Riley's presence bore down on Brodie. 'Not tonight.'

'Ach well, never mind.'

Catherine couldn't keep her thoughts to herself. 'If you read the newspapers yesterday you'll have seen the incident where Valentine, the younger one, ended up in the Clyde after being nearly killed by mindless thugs.'

'Yes I did. Awful business. But I thought Valentine would bounce back from his ordeal and come up to Edinburgh for a jig. He's the type of man who won't let go of something once he's got the bit between his teeth. Rather like his father, gritty to the last.' He turned to Riley. 'Wasn't your father an adventurous laddie in his day, Riley? I'm sure I heard somewhere that he was handy with a sword. Are you into a wee bit of swordsmanship yourself?'

Riley swallowed his anger. 'Yes. Are you?'

Brodie rocked backwards and laughed. 'I think I've just been challenged to a sword fight. Well, okay, you're on! But I have to warn you, I'm very handy at it, so I hope you're a good loser.'

The entertainment began in the main hall. Singers and Highland dancers started with a traditional rousing song.

'If you'll excuse us,' Brodie said, nodding and smiling to everyone as he led Riley to another room in the house. The walls were filled with antique weapons. Riley studied them as he walked past.

'Have you had a chance to reconsider my offer to come and work for me?' Brodie said.

'I'm not interested.'

'Aren't you fed up jumping in that bloody Clyde rescuing people? You'd save everyone a pile of trouble if you'd reconsider. The Valentines can't handle the situation on their own. That's why you're inveigled and entangled up in their mess. Step aside. Forget about any so-called hit lists and authenticating scrolls that aren't worth the fake parchment they're written on. We both know how things stand. Just step aside and it'll all go away.'

Riley shook his head.

Brodie sighed and smiled tightly. 'Take your weapon of choice. Any one you like. I'll match you. I've used them all.'

Riley stood where he was.

'Oh come on, we're just play fighting. It's all a game. Men like you and me know that. It's what makes us different from those that scurry down the safe route every day of their bland little lives.'

Riley stepped closer. 'Are you any good at politics, or are you only in it for the power trip?'

Brodie grinned and lifted a lightweight sword from the wall, whipping it through the air, testing its efficiency. 'I think you already know the answer to that.'

'Indeed I do,' Riley said, selecting a sword of similar calibre. 'You're the same as Strang — a sheer waste of potential for what you could've been.'

'I'm nothing like him,' Brodie snapped. He took a deep breath and regained his sweeter composure. 'I'm what some men would call, fiercely ambitious. If that makes me a monster, so be it.'

'No, it makes you a loser. Strang's the monster.'

The insult bounced off Brodie's pride without making a dent. 'I've been in the political arena too long to rise to the bait.'

Riley thought his way around Brodie's confidence. Then as he held the sword in his hand it dawned on him. His expression changed to one that focussed on the ornate hilt of the sword.

'What do you think of it?' Brodie said proudly, not expecting the response that was heading his way.

Riley placed the sword back on the wall, and searched for another one.

'Can you not find anything to suit you?'

Riley walked over to him, smiling wryly. 'Where's the real stuff?' he whispered.

'This is it,' Brodie said, his arms outstretched.

'Then you've been robbed.'

For the first time, Riley saw Brodie's confidence take a severe hammering. A dent had been made.

'What are you talking about?' Brodie said.

'That's what you get when you deal with forgers.'

'Mackenzie didn't have anything to do with the weaponry,' Brodie said, his face becoming flushed with rage.

'No, he just made scrolls that even the Valentines knew were fakes.'

Brodie rushed over and grabbed a weapon from the display. 'This is a genuine, 14th century short sword.' He handed it at Riley.

Riley studied it. 'Yes, it is. But that one there, and those over on that wall, are fakes.'

Brodie paused for a moment. 'You're lying, aren't you? You're winding me up.'

'No,' Riley lied.

'Some of these can't be fakes. They cost me a small bloody fortune.'

'They're not even well made,' Riley said, bluffing. 'Look at the poor workmanship of the hilt on that one. It's obviously a fake.' He pointed to a larger sword. 'And the Claymore over there — the cutting part of the blade is all wrong,' he said, laughing.

Brodie's blood felt like fire in his veins, annoyed by Riley's laughter at his precious artefacts.

'Who authenticated this stuff for you?' Riley said, a note of distain in his tone.

'I did . . . but I got others to value their real worth.' He sounded flustered.

'There's nothing real about any of them.' Riley laughed again.

A few guests with drinks in their hands wandered through. 'Mind if we watch the sword fight?' one of the men said.

'Yes!' Brodie roared at them.

The guests left them alone, muttering among themselves.

Brodie railed on the Record Keeper. 'Choose your weapon this time, Riley. And choose it well.'

Riley pulled a sword from the wall. A mid range weapon of adaptable ability.

Brodie wrenched a lightweight sword from the display and turned to use it without giving his opponent a chance to get ready, all etiquette cast aside.

Riley blocked the attack with such force he sent Brodie reeling, but he managed to stay on his feet and lunged at Riley again.

For several moments their swords clashed, attacking, blocking, again and again. Riley had to admit that the politician was a fair adversary, skilled in swordsmanship, but Brodie had been right earlier. Riley's father had been a renowned swordsman, a skill he'd passed on to him, though he was nowhere near as adept as Alexander.

Brodie's face was bursting red with the effort he put into beating Riley. A couple of times Riley could've impaled Brodie with his sword but killing him wasn't an option. He needed him alive to confess to the murder of Richard Reece and the monetary backing he'd given Strang. He'd agreed with the Valentines he'd do this. And he planned to do it right. The trail of blood and bruises leading from this murder investigation was already unacceptable. There were other ways to trap a rat.

Taking the opportunity, Riley punched Brodie on the jaw, knocking him to the ground. His sword clattered on the polished wooden floor. The fight was over.

Brodie raised himself up and staggered to his feet. The punch was a warning not to pick up the weapon again. Brodie thought about it, and then left it lying on the floor. But he smiled suddenly when someone, a figure higher up on the next floor, looked down over the railing.

Gut instinct told Riley who it was. The man was dressed in all black casuals, like a well dressed burglar, certainly not dressed for the ceilidh. Without any hesitation he went after Strang, dropping the sword so he could climb up the wooden beams, the quickest route to the second floor, and chased him to the open roof of the mansion. Up on the makeshift battlements, the air was heavy with the fog of a smoky October night.

'You're finished. Give yourself up,' Riley said.

'I'm far from finished, Riley,' Strang raged.

Riley steeled himself for the fight. It was never going to end well.

Downstairs at the ceilidh, Brodie entertained his guests but one of them noticed blood on his arm from a gash.

'Oh it's fine. I nicked myself on one of my own swords. It caught on my sleeve when I was walking past. I'll stick a wee plaster on it and be right back.'

Catherine danced a reel with Henry while Shaw stood watching from the sidelines. Shaw was never going to be the man for her. Neither was Henry.

'Are you not dancing, Shaw?' Brodie said in passing.

'Where's Riley?'

'Oh is he not with you?' Brodie said, smirking.

'You'd better think fast,' Shaw warned him. 'Or I'll really liven up this party.'

'We've always been at odds you and me, haven't we, Shaw? But I'm not being awkward with you tonight. I don't know what Riley's doing right now.'

Shaw alerted Henry, and they started an immediate sweep of the building, leaving Catherine in full view of some of the main guests, her only assurance that Brodie wouldn't harm her in front of the crowd.

Riley and Strang stood on either side of the roof, facing each other. If ever there was to be a true test of their skills it was now. Alone to do battle, this was one fight Riley wasn't going easy on. No quarter given.

'It still never needed to end like this,' Strang said.

'You wasted your talents,' Riley chided him.

'My talents never got a chance! It's all right for you, Riley. You got to be what you wanted — one of the SBS. That's what I wanted but the navy never gave me a chance. The SBS needed men who were fit and intelligent.' His voice increased in anger. 'Well I'm fit, and I'm intelligent, more intelligent than any of you, but I got shunned by the forces!'

'You're a bloody murderer,' Riley roared.

Strang stretched his arms wide and welcomed the fight. 'So kill me!'

Rarely had Riley been given a more tempting offer.

The air burned with their anger.

The first exchange was so quick neither of them had a chance to defend themselves and both suffered body blows. They both went to the ground, and visions of literally ripping each other's throats out with their bare hands jolted Riley's senses. He fought to get back up on his feet and so did Strang.

They clashed again, fists flailing. Riley's defence was stronger but Strang's obsession gave him a strength that was hard to beat. One punch hit Riley in the ribs, but he countered with a debilitating kick almost sending Strang tumbling over the battlements around the roof.

Strang got back into the fight and again they went to the ground, using combat techniques of grappling and gouging. Riley's knees were ripped raw on the rough rooftop. The pain barely registered. Strang snarled, the rage getting the better of him, while Riley's clear thinking was winning through.

Strang saw the Skean Dhu in Riley's sock, drew it quickly and tried to stab him. The point of the blade would've done damage but the cutting edge wasn't as sharp as it needed to be to penetrate Riley's jacket where Strang tried to slash him.

The confidence in Strang increased now that he had a weapon, a knife, but it wasn't the only knife. Riley withdrew the hunting knife and without hesitation plunged it into Strang's shoulder, burying it deep, feeling the blade slice through the shoulder bone.

The roar that Strang let out echoed in the night but no one heard above the loud revelry of the ceilidh. No one but Riley.

Somehow Strang found the grit to fight on with the hunting knife sticking out of his shoulder. As if determined to give it everything he had, Strang lunged at Riley with the Skean Dhu. Riley blocked the attack, and backed against the battlements which couldn't hold the bodyweight of two men. The old stonework crumbled and one man fell. The other clung precariously over the edge, his ribs feeling as if they were being ripped apart from the strain.

Shaw and Henry ran across the roof and grabbed hold of Riley.

'Strang fell,' he said.

Henry and Shaw looked down from the battlements and saw a figure disappearing into the foggy night. Only his blonde hair was clearly visible.

'Something's sticking out his shoulder,' Shaw said.

'My hunting knife,' Riley said, breathing deeply to ease his ribs.

Brodie came up behind them on to the roof. 'Did Strang get away?' he said.

Shaw iced him with a look. Brodie knew fine well he was gone.

'Ah well, never mind,' Brodie said. 'He'll disappear again. He won't be back for a while. That's his style, isn't it? But when he does, you can all stand by.'

'You're not getting away,' Riley said.

Brodie smiled. 'Oh I think I am. Enjoy the rest of your evening.'

Jamesie put the finishing touches to the sketches he'd done for the new painting for the casino. He sat it up on a homemade easel in his house and stepped back to gauge the perspective. Not bad he thought.

He checked the time. Riley had asked to talk to him.

Riley arrived moments later and went over to study Jamesie's latest work of art.

'Did you enjoy yourself at the ceilidh last night?' Jamesie said.

'That's what I wanted to talk to you about. Strang's done a runner. He's disappeared off the map.'

Jamesie took in everything Riley told him.

'And we can't nail Brodie, even with Big Handsome Callum's evidence, without substantial proof.'

'So Brodie's going to get away with murder?'

'Not if you want to help us get a confession out of him. On tape, on the record. If we can get him to admit that he stabbed Reece, we'll give the tape to the Valentines, and they'll arrest him.'

'What do you want me to do?' Jamesie said.

'Bring your new artwork. We're going to the casino. Brodie's in there today.'

Jamesie held his latest sketch up in the foyer of the casino in front of his original framed painting.

'When this one is done, I'm going to call it the lone gambler,' Jamesie said to Brodie, who was very interested in Jamesie's idea for a painting based on him. 'Could you stand near the big painting so I can visualise it in my head. My memory's a bugger these days.'

'Of course,' Brodie said, clearly believing his own hype. He stood right where Jamesie needed him to be.

'You'll be an absolute babe magnet,' Jamesie said, dishing out the flattery. 'The women love power, don't they?'

Brodie smiled, pleased with himself, and then asked casually. 'What do you know about John Riley, the Record Keeper?'

Jamesie pretended he had to give his mind a chance to think. 'My memory's not so good since I got stilettoed. Riley . . .? Lucky knows him. He turns up about once a year, like a bad penny, and tries to strong arm information out of Lucky. No chance. He got a cheap suit off him though. Nae class.'

Brodie was delighted to hear Riley taken down a peg. He put his arm around Jamesie's shoulder. 'How would you like to do a wee job for me?'

'Sure thing, Mr Brodie.'

'I'd like you and Lucky to find out anything you can about Riley. He's been a bloody thorn in my side for too long. I want him out.'

Jamesie winked. 'Got ya! Lucky says he pokes his nose in where it's not wanted. Acts the big shot.' He looked at the painting. 'He was trying to muck rake about what happened to Reece and Mackenzie and causing all sorts of trouble. Lucky said he was trying to implicate you in the politician's murder.'

'Seeing as how you're working for me now,' Brodie said, confident he had Jamesie in his pocket. 'There's a few things you should know . . .'

'Have you got it?' Riley said to McAra.

'Every word, clear as day. And on film.'

The Valentines were waiting for the signal to go in and arrest Brodie. Riley took great pleasure in making the call.

Stanley senior was the first in. Riley and McAra watched from McAra's car across the street. The painting had come in handy.

'Framed by the painting,' McAra quipped. 'No pun intended.'

They saw Valentine, Ferguson, Stanley senior and other officers accompanying Brodie from the casino. He was going down this time.

Catherine arrived at Riley's house a few days later. She'd made a decision. She was quitting her job in parliament and taking off, maybe to see her parents in Spain. No firm plans.

Riley was clearing his desk ready for the next measure of strife. A photograph of Deacon lay on the desk. Catherine picked it up.

'Striking looking man.' she said, her voice full of admiration. 'One of your sort?'

'He used to be. Deacon's dead.'

She sighed and put the photograph back down. 'A lot of the good ones are.'

She didn't stay long, and as she was leaving, he went to bid her goodbye.

'Don't say goodbye,' Catherine said. 'We don't know what the future holds. I'll let myself out.' She walked away. 'Oh and Riley, don't let the bad guys get you.'

'Don't let them get you first,' he said.

Jamesie had a gift for Riley. He'd brought it to Riley's house. He was excited as he unwrapped the painting and handed it to him.

'When I was here in your house the other day with Big Handsome Callum, I couldn't help but notice how you've no people in your photos. No one. Just pictures of landscapes. Lucky says it's because you're a secret forces bloke. Everything's kept quiet. So I thought you'd like a painting.'

Riley was speechless for a moment, then he said, 'It's brilliant.'

'I put you, Shaw, Henry, McAra, the Valentines and Ferguson in it,' Jamesie said, pointing to each of the figures in the Glasgow street scene. 'And there's Lucky with Barking Bob and me in the background. I didn't make us as big. And I didn't put Catherine in it. I didn't think she belonged with you. I know you'll think I'm daft, but there's something about her. Shaw fancies her but she can't even see him. I don't think she's part of your life.'

Riley nodded. Never a truer word.

Jamesie had captured McAra's wild red hair perfectly. Everyone was easily recognisable. Riley had his long greatcoat on, Shaw and the others were smartly dressed. And he hadn't included Catherine. Riley wouldn't have minded if he had, but he didn't really mind that he hadn't.

'I thought it would be appropriate to have a memory where we're all together at our best,' Jamesie said.

'I couldn't ask for a better gift.' He hung it up on the wall of his study right away, and they both admired it.

'You've got a strange life, Riley. I know a lot of blokes would like to be a secret sort like you, but no offence, I'd rather be like me — happy. Your life's never settled, is it?'

Riley shook his head. 'They say it's never really over for men like me.'

'Are they right?'

Riley nodded. 'Maybe one day things will be different, but for now the past isn't over yet.'

CPSIA information can be obtained
at www.ICGtesting.com
Printed in the USA
BVHW030340021118
531868BV00002B/192/P